Across All Boundaries

Suspense & Romance You Can Fall For

L. J. Vant

All Around Publishing, Inc.

Across All Boundaries
Copyright ©2020 by L. J. Vant

First Publication Date: March 2021

Cover art by Zequeatta Jaques
All art and logo copyright © 2020 by All Around Publishing, Inc.

ISBN:978-1-7344314-0-7

Printed in the U.S.A.

Publisher
All Around Publishing, Inc.
www.allaroundpublishinginc.com

Across All Boundaries

L. J. Vant

Chapter One

As the sun rises this day—a day not too far in the past nor or a day too far in the future—a life-changing day it is.

Pixie unfurled her body, rolled onto her back, and stretched her legs out to their fullest extent. Reaching out, she stopped the *musical notes* that sounded from her phone, her morning alarm. The air-conditioning unit along the wall beside her bed gusted cold air as she burrowed back under the bedcovers. She glanced around at the cheap hotel room that wouldn't rate a five-star on its best day, but she decided it wasn't bad. She squinted and looked at the sleeping man in the bed next to hers.

She yawned wide.

Sleep seemed short. However, it was time to get the day started. She and her traveling companion TJ had stopped late in the night the evening before, or rather early that morning—one a.m. to be exact—in Oklahoma City. They had been on the road for four days together, carpooling from New York City to here. They hadn't been in any hurry as they'd traveled, taking their time, sightseeing, and snapping pictures of the countryside that they passed. This morning they planned to meet up with her friend, Lynn.

Giving another drowsy yawn before slipping out from under the bedcovers, Pixie tiptoed to the hotel bathroom.

Humming, she turned on the bathtub taps.

Glancing toward the large mirror behind her as she straightened, she stuck her tongue out at herself. She always felt that she looked somewhat like an elf. Not pretty. Not pretty, at all. She wasn't as tall as she wished and her nose was a little too pointed. Her mother always rolled her eyes when Pixie complained that she must agree with her that she resembled one of those Christmas Elf dolls to saddle her from birth with the name Pixie.

Scooping out her morning toiletry items from the brightly colored makeup bag abandoned on the countertop the night before, Pixie glanced back into the room to the man still snoozing. Reaching out her hand, she clicked the bathroom door shut. She would let TJ sleep a while longer before she roused him. He had been crabby the night before and frankly, she was a bit tired of his attitude.

Stepping into the tub of steaming bath water, Pixie sat down. The hot water eased her sore muscles, and with a sigh of pleasure, she lay back, a towel rolled and propped behind her head. Traveling seemed to make her legs ache. Too much sitting, she guessed.

"Damn it," Pixie murmured a grimace given as she rose to stretch across air space for the forgotten razor left on top of the bathroom counter. No hair stubble allowed on her legs. Water dripped onto the floor. Grasping the handle of the razor, Pixie straightened and then sat back down. She looked forward to seeing Lynn that day— the goal of this trip she and TJ took together. She and Lynn had been childhood friends since the first grade, and she had missed her outrageous personality these past few months. Pixie and TJ had only been friends for the past two years.

They hadn't begun as friends.

In fact, the first time they'd met she'd thought TJ was gay. Not that it had bothered Pixie one-way or the other if he was, although, he hadn't been too happy with her misconception. Their mutual-friend Lynn had laughed that day gurgled with it in fact over Pixie's blurted question and TJ's stuttering response and rising red flush after she'd introduced them. Pixie guessed she was too outspoken. Sometimes it was best to keep one's mouth shut. A trait she hadn't learned in her nineteen years of life. Not since she'd begun to talk, her mother told her.

Listening, Pixie heard TJ moving about.

"Son-of-a-bitch," he stated from the other room. TJ liked everything in order and in its place. She'd left her suitcase open and lying on the floor in front of the television set. He had probably stumbled over it.

The television set came on and the newscast could be heard talking about the possibility of storms that day.

"Hurry the hell up, Pixie," TJ hollered.

Rising from the water, Pixie grabbed the close by white hotel towel. Drying off, she stepped from the bathtub to pull on her wrap.

"The bath's all yours," she drawled as she strolled from the bathroom. Steam rolled from behind her into the chilled room to where TJ sat.

"Dammit, Pixie, don't you know how to put anything up? I stubbed my toe on your stupid suitcase." TJ jumped up from the side of the bed where he sat. Apparently, he'd been doctoring his big toe, ever the victim.

Pixie rolled her eyes. "Poor baby, you want me to kiss your toe for you?"

TJ scowled, his irritation obvious. "I don't know if I can stand another seven days with you. You're mouthy and messy, two traits that annoy the hell out of me. If Lynn wasn't such a good friend, I would've never agreed to travel with you."

"Well, I never!" Pixie placed her hands on her hips and frowned heavy, copying TJ's facial expression. She tried not to laugh but it bubbled forth anyway.

TJ stomped into the bathroom. He popped his head back out through its doorway and his gaze met hers.

"You're spoiled, Pixie. That's what your damn problem is."

"Oh, please. Not that crap again."

TJ's head disappeared and the bathroom door slammed shut.

Laughing, Pixie plopped down onto the edge of the bed she'd risen from earlier and picked up her phone. She tapped out Lynn's number. It was ten a.m. Lynn would've been up for ages. The girl seemed to need no sleep.

"Hey you, he's at it again," Pixie drawled when Lynn answered.

Lynn's laughter echoed through the phone. "You don't say. Where are you two?"

"We're on the west side of Oklahoma City just off the I-40 interstate. We got in early this morning."

"I've some bad news. I won't be free until later this evening."

"Shoot," Pixie responded as she rubbed the towel that she held against her wet hair.

Lynn laughed. "Shoot is the problem. I'm in a scene today and if everything goes as it did yesterday it won't be a good day."

As a struggling actor, Lynn was happy at the offered bit part in the film shot in Oklahoma. She was from New York City, same as Pixie, and their families lived next door to each other in a gated community.

"What is there to do around here until you're free?" Pixie looked at her fingertips as she spoke. Her manicure looked excellent. She wouldn't have to touch it up.

"You can shop."

"Yuck. No thanks."

"Don't need anything?"

"A new sidekick, the one I've got is getting on my last nerve. And you know me, I can always shop, but not with *that* complainer!"

Lynn laughed again before she stated, "Some of us on the movie set just visited a little town further west from where we're shooting. They have a place called Red Rock Canyon Adventure Park. You and TJ go there. You'll like it. You can hike. You both enjoy that."

"How far is it from where we're at?"

"About forty-five minutes or so I think. A quaint town called Hinton not too far off I-40. Go straight through the town and you'll come to the park. It'll be on the left side of the road."

"Do they have any Indian activities to see at this Adventure Park?"

Lynn laughed. "I doubt it. They're all here it seems. Today, I get captured. Got to go! I hear my name shouted. I'll call you!"

Pixie smiled as she laid her phone aside on top of the crumpled bedcovers. Hiking sounded fun, and TJ would enjoy the activity. It was something they had in common.

"It is going to be a hot one today folks with severe weather possible. We will keep you advised," the weatherman stated as Pixie switched off the television set.

Chapter Two

"Sorry I got pissed earlier," TJ stated in the quietness of the speeding car.

Pixie looked across the seat from where she sat as a passenger to meet TJ's dark brown returning gaze.

"No problem. I'm messy and mouthy just as you said."

"And spoiled. Rich and spoiled, I should say."

"Please, TJ, let's not do that same old song and dance today. I'm tired of it."

TJ reached out and ruffled Pixie's short, cropped hair. "You get away with everything because you're too cute, that's your problem."

He waved a hand in mock surrender at her instant frown.

"Okay...okay...let's forget our disagreement and just enjoy the day and explore this park that you mentioned until Lynn calls," he exclaimed.

Pixie smiled and TJ grinned back, his anger of that morning she knew was gone. TJ was a tall, slender built man, six years older than she was and from a different background. He didn't know his father. His mother struggled with daily living and wrestled with staying off the booze and drugs. He'd had to raise himself as a child. He worked odd jobs as a teen and put himself through college as an adult. Pixie's parents paid for her college expenses. Actually they shelled out for everything—even the car that TJ drove that morning.

"Hey, we passed the Calumet turnoff where Lynn said they were shooting." TJ glanced in the direction to where Pixie pointed her finger before she dropped her hand back to her lap. It was just past noon and the heat outside the car shimmered across the landscape.

Pixie gave a grimace.

Poor Lynn, she must be miserable in the day's heat.

Looking out the window again, Pixie idly watched the passing scenery. Black clouds loomed to the southwest, and she frowned when she noticed them. Hadn't the reporter said something about possible severe weather? It was tornado season in Oklahoma, wasn't it?

"We might better listen to the weather," Pixie stated as she leaned forward and adjusted the channel of the car radio searching for any local news broadcast. TJ didn't respond as he continued to look ahead. Abruptly, he swerved the vehicle to the side of the road causing Pixie to grab hold of the car's dashboard.

He stomped on the brakes and slammed the vehicle into park.

"Look at that!" he shouted.

Glancing up to where he stared, Pixie drew in a sharp breath. A giant, swirling monster was before them. Wind whipped and dirt flew up and the car began to shake.

"Hunker down and hang on!" TJ yelled.

Pixie didn't move. She couldn't. Her eyes glued to the thing before them. *Weren't they supposed to get out of the car?* The swirling black mass seemed alive—a dark, breathing thing that sent frissons of fear spiraling down her spine. It moved with precision menace, as cars on the opposite side of the interstate it picked up and slammed down. Some it slung out of its way as if mere toys. The thing paused and hovered, as if it searched, hunting for its next victim.

People scrambled from vehicles yanked to the same side of the highway as TJ had done with hers.

The spinning beast barreled down on the running men, women, and children, and Pixie screamed. The creature shrieked in response and turned as if hearing her cry. The vehicle she and TJ hid in quivered. Air seemed in short supply, and Pixie struggled to breathe. Yanking her down onto the seat of the car, TJ sprawled over her, trying to body hug her.

Squeezing her eyes shut, Pixie cried out in prayer, "God, God save us!"

Normally, Pixie wasn't the praying type, at that moment however, she prayed, prayed for the Almighty to reach down and rescue them. She begged His All-Supreme Power to intervene. The car tilted and Pixie's nausea rose as it began to rotate. The air pressure built forcing her ears to pop in response. A mixture scent of wet soil and grasses assaulted her nostrils. The noise outside the car rose to a fever pitch. Pixie continued crying out her prayer as she tightened her fingers around TJ's, holding tight. She pressed her face against the seat of the car. Her eyes tightly closed. The twisting metal of the car squalled and the monster bellowed in response.

The monster's roar and the slapping of debris against the car rose in volume with Pixie's scream.

Chapter Three

Two Feathers jumped back in startled surprise when the clear blue sky dropped something at his feet. In shock, he stared at the body of a woman and woman she was, although her short, cropped hair confused him. He looked at his three companions. They stared at the woman at his feet also, their eyes wide.

A second body landed directly beside that of the woman's.

All four men vaulted, running backward. Two Feathers, the first to stop, stepped forward toward the prone and lifeless bodies. His companions followed. None spoke. They only stared in fascination.

"You think they're dead?" he inquired.

"Dead? Crow ask where they come from," Crow responded. Rock and Too Little nodded their heads in agreement with Crow's assertion.

Two Feathers glanced up into the clear blue sky. The two seemed thrown from the heavens, as if the Master of Life had found disfavor with them. Both were pale-colored as if having come from the light. Two Feathers glanced at the nearby trees. He knew the bodies hadn't fallen from them.

"Master of Life throw them down."

At Rock's declaration, Two Feathers looked at him. Could it be? He had just thought the same himself. The Master of Life brought the day and the night. He made the animals and the plants. He made man and woman. Two Feathers guessed; The Master of Life could actually throw people from the heavens if He wanted.

The woman groaned, and Two Feathers and his companions

inched closer. The female was average built and her breasts a mere handful. Two Feathers drew his gaze from their naked exposure. It was odd the things the woman wore that drew his attention. He had never seen such possessions. On the bottoms of her feet were flat leather pieces with leather straps attached to their sides, each going up over the top of her arches, holding the leather bottoms in place. Covering her womanly area was a contraption that seemed kept together magically. It had no ties that he could see. That only piece of clothing rode low on her hips and ended way before it should, her legs left bare. Curiously, bunched up around her waist was a strip of material.

Squatting, Two Feathers pulled on the strange piece. It gave in to his tug.

Shiny armlets encircled the woman's wrists and shiny stones lay atop her fingers. Clasped in her hand was a bag. Two Feathers reached down to touch it and recognized the feel of leather.

The bag had gleaming items hanging from it that caught the sun's rays and reflected them back to him. The woman's fingernails and toenails were a bright red. Two Feathers took one of her hands to study her fingernails, painted the tips it seemed, from what he didn't know? When he rubbed the ball of his thumb over one nail, the paint remained.

At the groan from the man lying beside the woman, Two Feathers glanced toward him. Setting the woman's hand down on the ground, he pivoted to scan closer the man by her side. The man also wore strange clothing, and his hair a hue not before seen on a person, the color of grass in winter. He had a long, jagged gash across his left jaw. A scar would form as that wound healed.

Two Feathers looked toward the woman again. She seemed such an oddity that he couldn't keep his gaze from her. She didn't have any visible injuries that he could see although she didn't move. Reaching out, he grasped strands of short, black hair.

Rubbing his fingers together, the strands felt silky to the touch. *Why short? Punishment for whatever wrong she'd done?* he wondered in bemusement.

All of a sudden, the woman's eyes opened to meet his and then widened to the extreme with fear. She arched backward and screamed a shrill scream. The sound pierced his eardrums.

Chapter Four

Oh please, please, don't let me be in hell! Please, God. Please.
Pixie couldn't catch any air. Her heart lodged high in her throat. She watched the creature beside her rise and back away, his gaze fixed on her. His head was clean-shaven of hair except for a thick, black strip left down the center. It was cut short and standing straight up, yet left long in the back, she noted when the creature swiveled to look toward his three companions behind him.

Woven deep into that thick hair, and close to the back of his head, were two large, black feathers, almost invisible, blending in with the color of his hair. A large tattooed feather spanned down each of his shoulders to his elbows. Pixie's gaze went to the man's companions. They seemed the same as him—his companions— creatures of the underworld although no large tattoos sported on their arms.

"Pixie?"

At the raspy, raw issue of her name, Pixie sucked in much needed air. Breathing again, she quickly rolled toward the sound, her back given to the devil and his cohorts. *A mirage surely*, she thought, and her racing heartbeat slowed. TJ lay beside her and he reached out toward her. Pixie touched his shoulder and groaned with pain at her movement as she did so. With his face saturated in blood, TJ's gaze met hers.

"TJ...oh, TJ," Pixie breathed in sympathy scanning his face.

"Are you okay, Pixie?"

"Better than you, I think. Oh, TJ, your face, your poor face."

"The tornado must've slung us to where Lynn's shooting her movie. I saw Indians in costume, didn't I?"

Pixie glanced back over her shoulder. The men were in full movie attire, she realized, TJ's comment making sense. The one who'd scared the hell out of her scrutinized her still. His three companions glanced between her and TJ, all silent, none offering their help. Pixie looked past their naked shoulders to scan the land mass behind them. There was no camera crew about. No other actors, and no equipment, nothing apart from the four men before her, and they seemed to be in a state of disbelief and shock.

With a frightened thought, Pixie turned back toward TJ. "I don't see Lynn or any others, only those four men. Oh, TJ, do you think all were swept away except for those four?"

Before TJ could reply, Pixie raised her gaze back to the man who she'd woke to. "Did the tornado arc through here and take everyone and everything except you four?"

The man looked to his companions, and his expression reflected confusion. They shrugged at him. He glanced back at Pixie and spoke. It was a guttural, choppy sound.

"Oh please," Pixie murmured exasperation rising, the thought of Lynn's safety a concern.

"What did he say?" TJ asked.

"Who knows?"

"I must be in shock. I thought he spoke his native language."

"He did. I guess," Pixie responded. She looked back at the man.

"Look, I can see you're in distress. Pull out of it. You are not acting now. Do you know my friend Lynn? She's an extra in the movie."

The man and his companions glanced at each other again, their expressions bewildered. The one who'd been squatted beside her let his gaze slide down over her torso. Pixie looked to where that black gaze traveled and she gasped. With a quick embarrassed movement, she pulled her white summer top upward from where it lay bunched around her waist at the top of her jean shorts. Putting her arms through the straps of the bra lined stretchy top, Pixie gave a quick upward jerk of the material.

"Don't just stand there and ogle! Call for help," she snapped. The man didn't move. *Damn pervert.*

Looking back at TJ intent on expressing her disgust, Pixie with surprise noted her purse on the ground between them. Plunging her hand inside the newly purchased handbag, she searched for and found her cell phone. She would call Lynn. The face of the phone was cracked, Pixie noted, as she skimmed her fingers over the phone. She frowned. Would it work?

"Oh, Lynn, please be safe," she murmured.

The call didn't go through. *Damn, damn, damn.* Pixie shook the phone and then moved her hand around in the air and watched the instrument as she did so. Not one lousy signal bar reflected.

"Pixie?" TJ rasped from beside her.

Stopping her agitated movement to let her arm drop back to her side, Pixie turned. The men who hovered over her and TJ inched closer as if in a trance. It unnerved. *The tornado must've done a mental number on them for sure*, Pixie thought in passing bewilderment at their odd behavior.

"What's wrong with my face?" TJ questioned. His gaze clung and Pixie gave a wince of sympathy. She'd be direct. It'd be kinder. He was fastidious about his looks, never a hair out of place.

"You've got a large gash across your left jaw and you're going to need stiches. You'll have a scar when it heals. I'm sorry, TJ, I know it must hurt. It looks wicked and you'll hate that scar."

"I can't feel my legs, Pixie."

Pixie felt her eyes widen.

"Use your schooling and check me out," TJ demanded.

Rising to her knees, Pixie leaned in close and she groaned as her bruised body shrieked in pain.

"I've just started my first year of nursing. What would I know?" she argued.

"Just check me out, Pixie. Please."

"Make a fist then," she ordered. Pixie let her hand rest on top of TJ's shoulder as he did as instructed.

"Now the other one."

He fisted his left palm.

"Can you move your feet?"

Pixie noted the slight movement of TJ's feet. He groaned at the attempt and sweat popped out on his forehead. Pixie frowned. Movement obviously pained him, and he had to work at movement.

"I really can't tell anything, TJ. However, it's a good sign that you can move your feet no matter how minor. Don't try to move any more, okay? It's best to just lie still until we can get you the proper help."

Standing, Pixie raised her gaze to those of the four men who hovered. They looked from her to TJ and then upward toward the sky. Pixie glanced toward the heavens also copying their actions.

The sky was clear, with no hint of the tornado that had slung her and TJ to this place. How she and TJ managed to get free from the interior of her car, she didn't understand, nor did she see her car anywhere. The last she knew and felt was the metal of the vehicle twisting around them and its wails of protest in response.

"Did all of you get caught up in the tornado, same as us?"

The men looked at each other and then back at her. None replied. They just stared.

The four were a puzzle as was the absence of any movie equipment or any other actors. The bold one, the one who she'd woke up to, met her gaze directly and Pixie stepped toward him.

"Where's the rest of the film crew? Do you know a woman named Lynn?"

****

Two Feathers, stared at the woman's mouth, he couldn't help it. He didn't understand a word she issued. He could tell that she was getting annoyed as she glanced from him to the bleeding man stretched out on the ground. Her companion must have been hurt more than he appeared. He lay stiff and unmoving.

He had questioned the woman earlier if they'd been cast from the heavens. Disfavor found with the Master of Life? When her face twisted in confusion, Two Feathers knew she hadn't understood what he'd asked.

He pointed to the sky.

The woman stopped speaking to watch him.

Motioning with his hands, Two Feathers made as if he tossed someone down. Crow, Rock, and Too Little watched his actions from where they stood beside him.

The woman whirled to the man on the ground and spoke to him, her agitation evident.

"Woman not understand what Two Feathers ask," Crow stated.

"Man can't seem to move," Too Little observed.

Sprinting away, the woman left her companion. She darted here and there. Searching it seemed, frenzied and unsettled.

"Woman senseless," Rock drawled in his gravelly voice. "Maybe both are and why thrown from heavens. It is bad omen we stay here."

"What think woman search for?" Crow asked. He gave a sharp laugh as he watched the woman's erratic actions.

Two Feathers frowned.

Crow was a best friend since childhood, and yet it grated that he found amusement in the woman's distress.

She disappeared.

They waited and watched. Before long, she came back into sight, running as if in a panic. She slid to a stop directly in front of Two Feathers. Gesturing back to where she'd been, her movements animated, she yelled up at him, and the words she issued a jumbled, gasping mess. It seemed she wanted him to go see something over the horizon.

Two Feathers looked toward the direction to where the woman pointed. She nodded; her motion vigorous.

He began to walk to where she indicated. His companions stayed rooted in place, and scrutinized the strange acting woman. She waved her arm in the air again, and chattered non-stop. Two Feathers wondered if she were begging the Master of Life to return her and her companion back to the light. What did she hold? It was a thing he'd never before seen, small and black. Not a weapon, he was sure of that.

As if in defeat, the woman let her arm drop back to her side.

Turning his head and with a slow trot given, Two Feathers abruptly stopped his forward motion upon noting the bison herd spread out over the landscape.

Was that what the woman had wanted him to see?

Had the animals scared the woman? He and his companions hadn't tried to kill a calf when they found the herd that day. Its meat wasted with just the four of them and they didn't want the herd scattered.

Two Feathers returned to the woman's side.

She looked at him and he shrugged. He didn't know what it was that she wanted from him.

****

With disgust, Pixie whirled from the man in costume.

Wiping at her eyes and then drawing in a deep breath, she held back her desire to howl her despair.

"What's going on, Pixie?"

Returning to TJ's side, Pixie squatted beside him. "My cell phone isn't working and those men are freakin' bizarre."

Leaning forward, Pixie frowned down at TJ.

"When I left your side to see if I could find help, you must've heard me scream. There's a whole herd of buffalo out there and that actor just shrugged it off as if it were no big deal. There's no fence between us and that herd!"

TJ frowned and then gave a wince of pain at his facial movement. "Maybe we landed in the middle of the buffalo's pasture?"

"Let's just hope those beasts don't decide to wander our way. We've nowhere to go if they do." Pixie shuddered and glanced back over her shoulder. Her gaze met the dark-eyed stare of the two-feathered man.

He watched TJ and her as if fascinated, as if they were a type of species never before seen. He looked up into the sky again and Pixie's gaze followed his. Why did he and his companions keep doing that? Were they watching to see if the tornado returned?

Pixie looked back at TJ. "I don't know what to do, TJ. You need medical care and those actors are addlebrained from what they went through. There's no help coming from their direction and I can't leave you here by yourself to get help, not in the condition that you're in."

Wiping away her tears that erupted, Pixie winced at the shot of pain across her wrist at her action. Drawing in a deep breath, she looked around at the landscape again. It puzzled her. There was no evidence anywhere that a tornado had come through where she and TJ landed—no debris, nothing. With a frown, Pixie sat down completely beside TJ, and she scrutinized the strange men. They talked low amongst themselves, they and their costumes, so authentic looking that they impressed her. Their outfits looked aged, worn, even handcrafted. For a low budget film, a lot had gone into those costumes.

****

"Crow say leave them," Crow replied, no apparent thought

given to Two Feathers' question.

Rock shot Two Feathers a quick glance.

Two Feathers could tell that he agreed with Crow but was indecisive about going against the Chief's son, the one next in line to lead their people.

Too Little quickly agreed to help after his question as to whether they should give the two their assistance. Too Little watched the couple with interest and ignored Crow's continued argument to leave the two behind to fend for themselves.

"If Master of Life found disfavor with them, why should we give help?" Crow persisted.

Two Feathers had wondered the exact thought. Yet, what if this was a test? Were they not to show compassion could they face punishment themselves? He'd had enough heartache in his twenty-five summers to last him a lifetime. He wanted no more sorrow. The image of his son rose and Two Feathers' insides twisted. Turning toward Rock, Two Feathers forced his hand.

"If Rock say no, we leave strange couple behind."

With one last glance in Crow's direction, Rock replied, "We give assistance."

Crow spun away, anger in his stance.

"Look!"

At Too Little's startled bark, Two Feathers and the others glanced to where his finger jabbed. The woman dusted dirt from her legs. Two Feathers didn't see anything that should've caused Too Little's sudden excitement.

Glancing up, the woman's gaze widened, and her action faltered.

Two Feathers then noticed what had caught Too Little's attention. He went to the woman's side and bending, reached for her leg. She scurried backward. Snaring her right ankle within his hand, Two Feathers halted her escape attempt. She slapped at his fingers and he tightened his grip. He studied the mark on her leg above her ankle. After a moment, he lifted his gaze to hers.

Releasing his fingers from around her ankle, he backed away. The woman was marked his.

****

"Now what?" TJ asked, his lips barely moving. He slanted his gaze to catch at Pixie's.

Glancing down at the tattoo above her ankle that seemed to fascinate the strange men, Pixie shook her head. She had only had the tattoo for a year. "I don't know, one of the actors grabbed hold of my leg and scrutinized my tattoo as if it were important."

She and Lynn had been in Las Vegas for a weekend, and impulsively, they decided to get tattoos following a night of gambling and drinking. Lynn had chosen a four-leaf clover to be located above her right ankle, and Pixie for some reason drawn to a small black feather above hers. The design that now held the men's interest.

It was a delicate thing, nothing outrageous. Although her mother exploded upon seeing it when she'd returned home the following Monday, her parents had been unaware of where she'd gone. It was then they had demanded that she decide what she wanted to do with her life or her allowance would be cut off.

Pixie looked back up.

The four men were making themselves comfortable as if to settle in for the night. Two of them, the short one and the one with the gravelly voice, listened while the one with the black feathers in his hair spoke to them. When he finished, they nodded and strode away. She noticed the hand-honed bows and arrows they had strapped across their backs. *Finally, and about time you go get help*, Pixie thought, relief rising at the two men's departure.

Smiling down at TJ, Pixie reached out to pat the top of his hand. "It seems that the actors have decided to seek help after all. How are you feeling?"

"My back tingles now. I couldn't feel anything until about a half an hour ago. That's a good sign right?"

"It's better than to have no sensation I'd say."

"That's what I thought when it started hurting," TJ responded. "I'll take the pain." He gave a slight smile.

"Can you believe that I clung to my purse through that tornado?"

"You wanted to have your phone afterward, I'm sure," TJ drawled.

Pixie laughed then sobered. "I wish it worked. I'm worried about Lynn."

"Me too."

With another pat to the top of TJ's hand, Pixie glanced up to find that the remaining two actors watched them. The two-feathered man seemed to have a look of possession in his eyes as he flicked his dark gaze down to her hand that covered TJ's. Pixie shivered and drew the appendage back to her side. The man turned away. Satisfied it seemed.

The actors talked amongst themselves as time passed. They worked to start a fire.

Pixie gave a smirk. *Do they really think to impress with the use of the primitive stones they hold to start a fire?* They slapped together their individual stones. Strike one. Strike two. Strike one. Strike two.

They squatted beside flames started and began to blow gently on them. The flickers flared large, and took hold of the surrounding kindling.

Pixie's eyebrows rose. *Well okay*, she thought, and she was impressed. The two men stood as the sun lowered with no sign of their companions' return. They talked quiet ignoring her and TJ.

I hope help shows up soon, Pixie thought as she looked down at TJ. He worried her. He seemed to doze on and off unaware of his surroundings. She remained still, and quietly watched the actors, not wanting to disturb his rest.

After several minutes passed and with increasing discomfort, Pixie couldn't hold out a minute longer. She needed to empty her bladder, an embarrassing situation by far; however, she couldn't stand it any longer.

Standing, Pixie started toward two large bushes several yards away from the campsite. The actor who'd grabbed her leg rose to his feet as if to follow and Pixie abruptly halted.

"Don't you even think it, mister!"

The man halted and Pixie sprinted on behind the thickets. Impatiently, she made a motion with her hand for the actor to turn around. It surprised her that he actually did.

Walking to sit back down beside TJ, Pixie snagged her hand sanitizer from the depths of her purse. The actors watched her actions, as if never before having seen such a thing, and they chattered amongst themselves as she squirted the bottle's liquid onto her palms and then rubbed her hands together.

Pixie shook her head. The sudden desire to stick her tongue out at them rose. She scolded herself. The poor things were addled-brained from the trauma they'd all experienced. She really should sympathize. She gave the one who wore the feathers in his hair a huge smile.

His eyebrow rose.

Pixie quickly lowered her gaze. What was she thinking? The man might take her gesture as a come-on.

The reddish tinted sun slid completely from view and with its departure copious stars blinked. Pixie stared at the overhead display, the glittering presentation making her mouth drop open in awe.

Abruptly the two actors stood, causing her to jump to her feet too. Pixie's heartbeat slowed when the two men who had departed earlier strolled back into the camp toward the light of the fire. With anticipation, Pixie took several steps toward them but then halted.

The men each held a rabbit in their hands. Lifelessly, the

animals dangled, their heads swinging close to the ground.

Pixie felt revulsion rise.

In that instant, she knew, the four men weren't actors. They were crazy people who thought that they lived in a time-gone-by age, and she and TJ had the misfortune of landing within their midst. Taking short, quick, backward steps, Pixie dropped back down beside TJ. She reached for his hand and she cautioned, "TJ…"

"Hmm…."

"TJ…wake up…these men aren't actors," Pixie's voice seized with thoughts of things to come. She had watched enough movies dealing with crazies that her mind spun.

TJ struggled to open his eyes.

Oh please, don't let him have concussion, Pixie prayed, her gaze fixing upon the bizarre scene unfolding before her. Under the light of the stars and the flame of the fire, the men made short work of the skinning and gutting of the animals they'd killed. They washed them and then skewered the bodies of the poor things onto sticks—broken from the surrounding bushes—and then angled them across the low-burning fire.

The meat began to sizzle and pop as it cooked and despite herself, Pixie's mouth began to water. She couldn't remember the last time she ate.

The men talked amongst themselves as if what they did were an everyday thing.

The one with the feathers in his hair hadn't seemed crazy, just scary looking same as the others. He had to be crazy though. They all had to be. Why else would they be dressed in primitive costumes, speaking their native language, and planning to eat a kill as if wild men? The two-feathered man turned the cooking meat for a third time, and as he did so, he glanced toward her. Lowering his gaze, he reached with lean fingers to tear off a piece of cooked flesh from one of the animals. He stuffed the sizzling piece into his mouth.

His gaze rose to hers again and he stood, holding a second piece of meat.

Pixie stiffened as she watched him. She jumped to her feet when he took a step forward toward her.

What was he doing?

He motioned to the cooked meat he held in his hand and he offered it to her. The words he said sounded harsh and made no sense.

"No. No!" Pixie shrieked when he took another step toward her. She waved for him to stay put.

He seemed so much taller than earlier, broader in the shoulders, crueler looking.

He halted and gave her a frown.

One of his companions behind him snorted, and Pixie glanced the man's way. He was the same one who earlier that day had seemed to argue with the one who wore the feathers. His look held disdain. His gaze direct and insulting as it moved down over her breasts and legs. Instant dislike rose in Pixie and it seemed that the feeling was mutual. The man brought his gaze back up to meet hers again. He crammed the meat that he held into his mouth and chewed. His mouth slanted in scorn toward her as he watched her. No offer to share given from him. His features were broad and not as refined as the other one. What did these men have in store for her and TJ? Pixie collapsed to the ground when the one standing, with a shrug of shoulders at her refusal of his offered meal, turned back to his companions. He squatted down within their midst as he said something to them. They all gave a nod.

"Crazy. Every damn one," Pixie breathed. Inching closer to TJ, she kept vigil.

Upon finishing their meal, the men stretched out on the hard ground, and before long, Pixie realized that all four slept with no attention or thought given to her or TJ.

Pixie fought to keep her eyes open as her own sleep lured with the passing of the night. The one with the feathers in his hair, he frightened her; yet, he seemed forthcoming enough. The two men who'd carried the dead rabbits into the camp seemed not to give her a thought. There was something about the other one, the one who'd refused to offer his meal, that she didn't care for. Something about him that she couldn't put her finger on. He exuded an underlying maliciousness it seemed.

"What?" Pixie asked, when for a third time, she felt her shoulder nudged. In irritation, she shrugged that same shoulder. She ached all over. Couldn't her mother leave her alone? Snapping her eyes open, Pixie stared at TJ who stared at whoever stood behind her. The sun was up.

Swiftly, turning her head, Pixie groaned. Her neck was stiff. She had slept after all. The feathered wearing Indian loomed and it alarmed her, his closeness.

He made a sharp gesture with his hand. Pixie didn't understand his words. She understood though that he wanted her to move from where she lay. She looked back at TJ.

"Do what he wants," TJ implored, his words subdued.

Reluctantly taking her arm from around TJ's waist, Pixie tried to rise to her feet, she stumbled. Lean fingers gripped her upper arm and she gave a grimace of pain before snatching her arm from within the man's hold. He scowled, insulted it seemed.

Had she really thought this one approachable? He didn't appear so this morning. He seemed downright nasty.

TJ attempted to rise.

"No, TJ, don't move," Pixie ordered fully standing.

"I can do this, Pixie. I even..."

The man beside Pixie leaned forward to grasp hold of TJ's upper arms, ready to pull him into an upright position.

"No! Don't you dare move him!" Pixie shouted and smacked his hands away. "Jeez, you could cause paralysis without a doctor's okay."

In a split second, Pixie, stunned found herself gazing upward at the two-feathered Indian. He now stood over her, his fists planted at his hips, anger vibrating in his stance.

She was in the grass on her backside.

He said something to his companions, his voice low, and rumbling. Pixie didn't move. She couldn't, she was petrified, frozen. The one who'd snorted so deliberate the evening before strolled forward. Bending at the waist, he pulled her to her feet to force her several paces away from TJ. Dropping his hands from her, he turned and walked away.

Pixie cried out with concern when TJ, jerked upward to his feet, stumbled sideways before being caught, and held upright.

The two-feathered Indian looked toward her. He threw up his hand signaling for her to stay put when she took a step forward.

"I am fine, Pixie," TJ rasped.

He continued as he looked toward her, "I tried to tell you, I can feel my legs. I moved them during the night and even stood for a moment. My back still hurts like the dickens though. Are you okay? Did he hurt you?"

"I'm okay. Oh, TJ, you have to be careful. You don't want to cause permanent injury to yourself."

The Indian holding tight to TJ's arm glanced between them, his expression stunned. *What's his problem? Didn't he think TJ would ask me if I'm okay?* Pixie glanced away from the man's bare chest and barely covered loin area. All four of the men seemed comfortable in their state of undress. The strips of pounded out animal hide that concealed their fronts and backsides held in place only by thin bands of leather which rode low around their hips. Moccasins protected their feet. Pixie recognized the authority that emanated from the one who clasped TJ's arm. He was in charge of the group. He glanced between her and TJ again as if waiting in anticipation for them to speak. He made a motion for her to come toward him. Taking a small step forward at the sharp directive, Pixie then hesitated, and halted. Why did he want her by TJ's side now, when earlier, he'd ordered her to be taken away?

He was deranged, a mad man.

He watched her, his look expectant. Pixie didn't move any closer, too scared to do as he wanted. When she remained motionless, the man released his hold of TJ to let his hands drop back to his sides. Stepping backward, he put distance between himself and TJ, as if willing Pixie to come forward and giving her the space to do so. Pixie persisted where she was.

TJ spread his legs to brace himself. Pixie could tell that he was in pain. She looked at the Indian again.

"What do you want from us? Please, tell me. He needs medical attention can't you tell?"

****

Puzzled, Two Feathers stared. He turned to his companions. "Do you understand what woman say?"

Crow, Too Little, and Rock all gave a shake of their heads.

"Does Two Feathers?" Crow asked.

"Two Feathers understand man earlier. Two Feathers not understand either now," Two Feathers replied.

Too Little always on the skittish side took several steps backward.

"They control what peoples understand," he babbled.

"Don't be a woman," Crow snapped.

Too Little bristled. "At least Too Little have woman!"

Two Feathers stepped between the two men. Blows of fists would fly if he didn't intervene. He gestured toward the strange man and strange woman as he addressed Too Little.

"Too Little have nothing to fear. Look at expressions. Man and woman confused as we are. They've no powers. They are as us. The little Two Feathers understand man couldn't move was why man lie so still on ground, woman protective."

"Woman belong to man," Crow drawled.

Two Feathers' gaze collided with the woman's and he frowned. Crow must have realized his sentiment felt about the woman and thought to tease. He hadn't cared to see her curled so intimately against her companion upon his awakening and noticing her position. It was why he'd ordered her and her man to part from each other. The couple thrown from the heavens watched him and Crow, their expressions fearful.

He had planned to give the woman assistance in standing when waking her. His companions observing her dismissive action toward him had embarrassed him. Moreover, when she struck his hands away from the injured man, his anger had spiked. Any and all who wore the black feather was his, wife or slave, and none disobeyed an order or tried to hit out at him. There would be no further emotional attachment allowed between the man and the woman.

"Woman no longer belong to man, woman now Two Feathers'."

Crow laughed in amusement at Two Feathers' assertion.

****

Pixie drew her gaze from the Indians. She had believed the short one and the broad faced one, the one who'd made it obvious that he didn't care for her, were to fight. Now that same man laughed. His calculating gaze on her at whatever the tallest one said to him.

"We've got to get away from these men, TJ. There is something seriously wrong here."

TJ nodded at her low words. "If they'll let us leave," he replied in the same manner.

"What'll we do if they don't?"

"I don't have a clue," TJ responded. Sweat had broken out over his upper lip and his complexion pasty.

With sympathy, Pixie took hold of his arm. She could tell he was in terrible pain.

The Indian who'd forced TJ to his feet stiffened. He didn't move, however, or come forward. He just watched.

Wrapping an arm around TJ's waist, Pixie looked up in inquiry. "Do you need help to lie back down?"

TJ's eyes swiveled toward the man who scrutinized them still and he gave a shake of his head. "No. Help me to move around."

"I'm scared we'll cause permanent injury if I do that."

"I think," TJ responded and he nodded his head toward the man who'd jerked him to his feet, "that he might have something to say about my lying back down. I believe he wants me to move around."

"The hell with what that weirdo wants." Pixie turned to glare. The recipient of her look stiffened and flung back his shoulders.

"No, Pixie, don't do that. Be civil," TJ rasped.

The four men who held them captive, and at the same time didn't, chatted amongst themselves as the day continued. It seemed they waited, but for what, Pixie didn't know. They didn't bother her or TJ again as she and he worked on his mobility, walking in circles, stopping often so he could rest.

She cleaned the gash on TJ's face using her hand sanitizer and then grabbed the Band Aids she'd found in her purse to gently put them over the cut. As she pulled the jagged edges of the wound together, she noticed the men had gathered to watch her work.

The men chattered and gestured, their words choppy and spoken in guttural tones, sometimes their words pronounced through their noses.

Pixie ignored them.

The men caught rabbits as the day wore on, and each skinned and cooked them, they as well flushed out from their ground shelter, two medium-sized brown birds. Pixie was so hungry that she accepted the meal when offered this time. TJ followed suit and eagerly tore the steaming meat from the bones of the animals.

The meat was tasty Pixie had to admit or maybe she was so starved anything would've tasted good.

The water offered after their meal, she swallowed with gratitude, closing her mind and eyes to the appearance of the container that held the thirst quenching liquid.

****

Another night closed in on their small group.

The soft light from the billions of stars lessened the darkness left behind when the sun made its ritual exit. *A beautiful night it would have been, if the circumstances were different*, Pixie thought, scooting in as close beside TJ as she could. She tensed when the two-feathered man rose to his feet and proceeded to walk toward them, his eyes upon her.

Pixie hunched inward, leaning against TJ.

"TJ?"

"Stay calm," TJ appealed. He limped upward to step in front of Pixie, blocking the man from her. The Indian made a motion indicating for him to move aside. Staying firm, TJ gave a shake of his head. The man reacted with one swift shove given and unable to stop his momentum, TJ stumbled sideways.

"Leave me alone!" Pixie screamed, kicking, and clawing when reached for. Two large hands grabbed hers and stopped her from scratching. Hauled upward and then dragged several feet from TJ's side, Pixie found herself abruptly thrown back to the ground.

The two-feathered man returned, without a word said, to where he'd been sitting.

In shock, Pixie looked at TJ.

He made a signal for her to remain where she was as he eased back down to the ground.

Trembling, Pixie didn't move from where she'd been placed. *Me and TJ have to get away from these four men.* Her gaze meeting TJ's, Pixie knew that he thought the same as she. An animal howled in the night, the sound eerie. It was as if the animal knew and understood her fear. Curling against the ground to lay her head upon her folded arms, Pixie watched as TJ stretched out. He gazed upward at the stars and ignored the four men. Taking her cue from him, Pixie closed her eyes and pretended to sleep.

"Pixie."

At the soft issue of her name, Pixie opened her eyes. TJ was crouched beside her.

He raised a finger to his lips.

With a silent waving motion, he indicated for her to rise and follow him. Glancing toward the sleeping Indians, Pixie did as instructed. Snatching her purse from the ground, she tiptoed close behind TJ away from the men.

****

"Two Feathers not stop man and woman escape," Crow drawled as the two walked out of sight, their departing forms easily seen. Crow lay on his back with his arms behind his head several feet from where Two Feathers lay awake, watching the two leave.

Two Feathers sat up to drape an arm over the top of a raised knee. "No, go same way we go. Catch easily. Man and woman not get away."

"Two Feathers should punish."

Two Feathers' gaze met Crow's. He didn't respond.

He never understood Crow's quickness to lash out. It was probably why Crow had no family of his own. His woman had absconded, returning to her people after only one year with him, and taking their child with her, only stating that she was unhappy and lonely away from her people. She had seemed happy until the last few months before her flight.

With her people and theirs on friendly terms, and her tribe offering their protection, Two Feathers' father had refused to intervene on Crow's behalf, leaving Crow unable to bring her back.

In fairness to his blood brother, Two Feathers had never seen his friend be cruel to his wife, only indifferent.

Lying back down, Two Feathers gazed upward toward the heavens and he studied its stars. His feeling of resentfulness toward the woman's male companion confused him.

He had never before felt such an emotion.

It was why he hadn't stopped their leaving. He needed time to think. Rationalize what was happening.

His father would be glad to hear the bison were coming their way, with his and his companions' help. The past winter had been hard. It was why he and the others made this trip. To force the bison to move their way earlier than they usually did. Two Feathers frowned as the image of his son rose. Yes, the winter had been brutal on them all. Home was twenty complete day and night cycles away and he'd be glad to get back. He missed his son.

Chapter Five

"I can't believe we haven't seen a highway or a house or any form of civilization, and we've walked all night without stopping. My phone is still not getting any reception either, and now it's about dead."

With disgust, Pixie tossed her phone into the depths of her purse and then wiped at her brow.

The day had heated fast once the sun rose to its full majesty. She was thirsty and painfully so.

The rolling plains around them stretched out as far as the eye could see, dotted here and there with rows of trees, although Pixie still didn't see any homes or any sign of destruction from the tornado.

TJ stopped walking.

It had been a slow process, their running away. Although the more he moved, the more he seemed to gain his strength back. Now though, he seemed to lose all steam.

"Let's rest," he stated.

Pixie halted, continuing with her complaint.

"There were homes everywhere along the interstate the other day so I don't understand why we aren't seeing any of them now or at least some sign of their destruction. There should at least be debris."

"I think we were taken further than we realized. We weren't just lifted and then dropped," TJ responded. His words were soft.

Pixie's gaze met his and she frowned. "I wonder how far then if that's true?"

TJ's gaze was steady. "How about so far away that we were thrown back in time."

"What?"

"I think we were dropped back in time, Pixie. Something happened and we fell through a time window."

With disgust felt, Pixie jerked her gaze from TJ's.

"You're as crazy as those men we left behind if you think that, TJ. And if you're trying to joke, it's not funny." Pixie scanned the horizon. *There had to be homes, people, something out there? Maybe they had walked the wrong way?*

"Look around you, Pixie," TJ, demanded. He jabbed at the air.

"Doesn't the area look different? Seem different? Feel different to you?"

Drawing her gaze to the man beside her, Pixie snapped back her reply, "Since I haven't lived in Oklahoma, past or present, how would I know what it's supposed to look or feel like?"

With a jolt of shock at seeing TJ's jawline tighten, Pixie realized that he did actually believe that they were in another era. With concern, she reached out to feel his forehead, and he jerked back from her touch.

"I'm not feverish, damn it!"

Pixie, stricken, abruptly stepped backward.

"Open your eyes, Pixie. See the world around you. Everything is different and those men we left behind aren't crazy. They are authentic and living in their time. We are the interlopers here. We are the crazy ones."

His breathing had grown heavy.

Pixie took a step toward him. "Let's sit down," she suggested quietly as she took hold of his arm.

He resisted.

"Come on, TJ. Let's sit a while," she begged.

He seemed to wilt.

Helping him to ease to the ground, Pixie moved to sit along beside him. She looked around to make sure no ant dens were about as she did so. She had noticed several as they'd walked that day.

Lying back completely, TJ closed his eyes. He lay still and unmoving. Silently, Pixie studied him. "Are you in a lot of pain?" she finally asked in concern.

"Just tired, Pixie, tired and confused."

"We'll rest as long as you need to. If those men were going to come after us, they could've caught up to us a long while back."

"It might be best if they did come after us. Maybe we would survive then," TJ murmured.

"We'll find help, TJ. You've watched too many science fiction movies. You're stressed and not thinking clearly is all."

"Your phone is still not working?" he murmured.

"No."

TJ didn't open his eyes.

After a moment, he took a deep breath. "Last night, as I lay awake, I realized there were no satellites in the sky, and no lights from any home, and that no planes passed over us. Oklahoma City has a major airport. When the tornado lifted us, we were just outside the city."

Pixie didn't respond.

TJ needed medical attention.

Furrowing her brow, Pixie looked out and scanned the horizon. Everything did seem different somehow, quieter. Turning to state as much, Pixie realized that TJ was sound asleep. Taking her phone from her purse, she examined it. It still showed no signal picked up.

Pixie stared at the thing. *Don't start thinking crazy, girl. Your phone isn't working because of the tornado, that's all.*

With a shake of her head, Pixie dropped the useless device back into her purse. She yawned wide, and the action made her jaws pop. She was exhausted herself.

Curling beside TJ, she positioned her purse under her head and promptly fell asleep.

****

Waking to stretch and then turning over to her other side, Pixie frowned as she stirred.

She could hear the low murmur of male voices. It was what woke her, she realized. Abruptly sitting up, she looked around.

Had help arrived?

Disappointment flooded through Pixie when the men they had left behind the night before strolled up to where she and TJ rested. She didn't move. She watched as they began to prepare a place for a fire, their movements precise and knowing. The sun was now low in the sky and the air noticeably cooler. None of the men tried to communicate or even looked her and TJ's way.

Pixie licked at her lips and then grimaced at the stinging sensation left behind from the action. Her lips were sunburnt and swollen, and she was thirsty, parched in fact. She and TJ must've slept the afternoon away.

The men held the same type of birds in their hands that they'd roasted the evening before. They began to prepare the game to be cooked. What Pixie desired was the water that they carried, water to soothe her dry throat.

TJ rose to sit alongside her, and he licked at his lips as she'd done. They'd not thought to bring any water with them.

"Water," Pixie croaked.

The men idly looked her way.

"Water," she rasped again and held out her hand for the bag that dangled from the hip of the man nearest to her. He paused in what he was doing as his eyes went to the fingers that she stretched toward him. Ignoring her request, he turned back to his task. Pixie dropped her hand back to her side.

The others ignored her as well. It seemed that they deferred to him.

Pixie's embarrassment rose. She would not beg if that was what he wanted.

TJ remained silent.

"Aren't you thirsty?" she hoarsely rasped.

"Dying from it, but we'll get water when and if they want to give it to us," he replied.

"They're barbarians."

"They want us to know that we're dependent on them."

Pixie looked toward the Indian with the feathers stuck in his hair, his profile harsh. The one she'd asked for the water from. He was paying attention to their low conversation she instinctively knew, although he never once glanced their way, keeping to his task.

****

Two Feathers felt his frustration rise as the man and woman conversed. He could understand nothing of their words. He felt shame he hadn't immediately given the woman the requested water. She needed it. Her lips were swollen and cracked, and the man's were in no better shape. She scratched at her scalp as her companion spoke to her. She was unclean. Tomorrow they would come upon the stream he and his companions had passed in their travel and she could bathe, they all could.

Two Feathers walked toward the man and handed his water skin over to him. His gaze made contact with the woman's as he did so. Her scornful glance didn't surprise him. She didn't understand that he had their life in his hands. He watched as the man drank deep, and then with his nod of approval given, the man passed the water skin over to the woman.

When she was done, she held it up for Two Feathers to take. As their fingers touched, she croaked, "Thank you."

Two Feathers started in surprise, understanding her words.

"Water it is good. Two Feathers give life," he responded back. The woman's gaze met his. At her blank expression, Two Feathers knew she didn't understand what he'd said. She looked to her companion and gave a shrug. Her nonchalance shown at his gift angered him. She was disrespectful of his generosity. Two Feathers felt his companions watching, judging his response, wondering why he didn't put the woman in her place. Punish her. He questioned the fact himself. He returned to where they stood. They appeared embarrassed, spinning back to preparing the meal.

"Should Two Feathers beat respect into woman?" he demanded of them.

Too Little and Rock relaxed.

"No," Rock stated in his raspy voice, damaged from a long-ago combat with warring neighbors, his gaze meeting Two Feathers'. "It not respect woman give if Two Feathers beat. Anger and fear woman give, and if anger win, Two Feathers have to watch back."

Crow silently turned the roasting meat. Two Feathers studied him until he glanced up. "What say, Crow?"

"Crow say leave woman be for now."

Crow's response surprised them all.

"What?" Too Little jabbed, causing Crow to stiffen and his lips to curl back into a snarl.

"Too Little, shut up," Two Feathers ordered. "Go and check our surroundings then we eat."

****

"Whatever game they're playing, I don't think that they plan to harm us," Pixie stated as she watched the men talk. It seemed for a while that they argued amongst themselves.

"What makes you believe that?" TJ responded.

"I don't know. However, we did get water and I bet they feed us again same as last night."

TJ stared at her as his brows came together. "You think the tornado lifted and dropped us into these men's laps and they instinctively know that you're a privileged rich girl, so they won't harm you?"

Pixie frowned. "I didn't say that."

"You believe it though, don't you? You are always taken care of. No worries for the rich princess."

Pixie's mouth went slack. "That was uncalled for, TJ. And you're just jealous because I didn't have to eat from garbage cans, or have a mother who's stoned out of her head all day."

"And you're a stupid, spoiled bitch."

Pixie shot to her feet to stare down at TJ. Curling her fists, she worked her mouth, her words of insult stuck in her throat.

Whirling, she stomped to the other side of the camp, and slamming her purse to the grass, plopped down onto the hard ground.

The Indian men looked from her to TJ.

Pixie glared across the open space toward them. They could all just mind their own damn business. The short Indian returned from wherever he had been and spoke to the one who seemed in charge. At the other man's nod and guttural response, he took the meat handed to him and turned to amble toward her.

With triumph, Pixie slanted a barbed smile at TJ and accepted the offered meal.

As she ate and everyone around her devoured what they held, Pixie's tears rose, a third night out in the wild, and her and TJ at each other's throats. Making it worse, they were with strange men who couldn't be understood in their language or their behavior.

Were she and TJ their captives?

It seemed they were and yet at the same time not.

When the sun peeked over the horizon the following morning, Pixie jumped up from where she'd slept. She had made a decision during the night, and with determination, she swiped at the dirt she'd accumulated on her person. She then snatched up her purse and began to walk. She didn't look toward TJ or the other men, and didn't care if they saw her leave. She was leaving and good riddance to them all. She didn't need any of them. She would find her way home on her own.

A single male voice shouted out. It wasn't TJ's.

Pixie kept walking. A bit faster though.

At the firm clasp of fingers to her shoulder, Pixie spun swinging her purse. Satisfaction rose within her at its hard contact to the man's face whose hand held her in place. He dropped his hand from her shoulder, his surprise reflected as he stared at her.

Spinning, Pixie took off at a run. Suddenly, Pixie pitched forward and unable to stop her momentum, she grunted at the ground's hard contact as she rolled through dirt and grass. Her feet swept out from under her had sent her tumbling forward. Dazed, Pixie turned to look up from where she lay.

The man who'd pursued her stood over her. He grasped her forearms and yanked her up from her fallen position.

"Woman not hit again," he ordered.

"Let. Me. Go." At Pixie's sharp, precise command, the two-feathered man stilled, and he glanced downward at his hands, he lifted them from her. Pixie stepped backward.

"Yeah, you better listen," she snapped. Her smugness rose. He knew who was in charge here.

Whirling, she took off.

Her shoulders firmly clasped again, the man halted her departure, and she was rotated about to face him.

"I said for you to let me go," Pixie challenged.

"No."

Pixie stilled, the man had spoken his native language and had before she realized. In confusion, she met his gaze. "I understand you," she stated in surprise.

The man nodded.

"How...?"

His fingers tightened.

"When touch, we understand."

Pixie looked at his lean fingers holding her in place. Her gaze traveled upward from them. The man before her assessed her same as she did him, she realized.

"Take your hands off me," she demanded.

"Woman not order Two Feathers."

"Okay, please take your hands off me."

"No."

Pixie twisted attempting to remove his grip.

"Why woman thrown from sky?"

Stilling, Pixie looked upward to stare at the man who restrained her. Were they to converse as if he weren't holding her captive?

"Are you for real?"

"Two Feathers stand here does Two Feathers not?"

"Good grief, are you an actor or what? And how can I understand you now when before I couldn't?"

The man shrugged. "Why Master of Life unhappy with woman?"

"Master of Life?"

"The One who make all things."

"The One who...? Are you talking about God? Look, I got caught in a tornado, I prayed, and here I am. Tell me where here is?" Pixie indicated the area with her chin—given the man refused to loosen his hold.

"What tornado?"

"A twister, you know, a whirling wind. It lifts you and destroys everything in its path?"

"Ah, yes, the whirling winds."

"Who are you?" Pixie felt her unease rise. His questioning, the way he spoke, it wasn't faked. TJ couldn't be right. It wasn't conceivable.

"Two Feathers. Son of Chief. Who you?" he countered.

Pixie's knees went weak. It couldn't be possible.

"Pixie, my name is Pixie Black."

"Who man with Pixie Black?"

"TJ Jones."

"Not Pixie Black's man?"

"No."

"Good. Pixie belong to Two Feathers, given by Master of Life."

"What!" Pixie struggled against his hold. "Let me go you crazy nut!"

The man laughed, and it seemed he gave a genuine chuckle. "Two Feathers like. Woman make good companionship."

Sputtering, Pixie drew in a sharp breath. This man scared her.

"Look, Two Feathers. I just want to go home, okay?"

"Where home?"

"New York."

"Two Feathers not know this place New York?"

Ceasing her attempt to get him to release his grip, Pixie stared. TJ's hypothesis rose again. This time it held and it startled.

"What state is this?" she asked.

Her breathing supply seemed in short order and gulping, Pixie sucked what air she could into her lungs.

"Two Feathers not understand question."

"What is the name of this area, the state that you live in? What do you call it?"

He frowned, and then with a tilt of his head indicated toward the northeast. "Come from long distance. Search for buffalo for tribe. Not know name this place."

Pixie's horror rose. It couldn't be. He had to be an actor.

****

Two Feathers watched as the woman slumped. *Why woman made unaware?* he wondered. He lifted her to cradle her within his arms and then turning, walked back to the others to where they had watched and waited.

The woman's companion limped toward him. He spoke. His words made no sense.

"Crow, take woman's pouch, lay pouch there," Two Feathers ordered, indicating with a tilt of his head where he wanted to place the unconscious woman.

As Crow tossed the pouch where commanded, Two Feathers gazed down at the female that he held. She was light in his arms. Her personality made her seem a sturdier person. Laying her on the ground and then positioning her pouch under her head for support, Two Feathers took one of her hands within his. Her life pulse was strong. He felt relief at its steady beat.

Her male friend shuffled over to his side and Two Feathers looked up at him before rising to stand beside him. He grasped the man over the collarbone with his fingers.

"Woman okay," he reassured.

The man the woman called TJ abruptly halted his angry tirade.

"Man, understand Two Feathers?" Two Feathers asked.

"Yes. How? I don't understand...."

The man seemed dazed and confused. Two Feathers looked down to where his palm lay on the man's frame.

"I see," the man mumbled, although his puzzled expression didn't change. His gaze circled to encompass Crow, Too Little, and Rock.

"Are you men actors?"

"Two Feathers not know what actors mean? We are of the Master of Life. He create all peoples."

"Who are you?" the man stuttered.

"Name Two Feathers."

When the man just stared, Two Feathers lifted his arm to indicate his companions. "We leave our people to find buffalo. Now push animals toward village. Our people wait for us. Wait for kill."

"I was right! Shit, I was right!"

Two Feathers recoiled at the screamed words.

Crow, Too Little, and Rock circled. With a raised hand, Two Feathers let them know all was okay. Crow walked up to stand alongside him. His skinning knife, he palmed.

"Crow kill man for Two Feathers," he stated, his scowl fierce.

The woman's friend scrambled backward. His gaze jumped between them.

"No need to kill, Crow."

"Why man yell strange words?"

"Don't know. Loco maybe."

Crow gave a snort of scorn and his gaze swept over the man. "Crow don't like."

Two Feathers laughed. "Crow like no one."

Crow looked toward him. "We blood brothers since childhood, Crow like Two Feathers."

With affection, Two Feathers laid his hand on Crow's shoulder. His bond to the man by his side ran deep. When young boys bent on proving their manhood, they'd saved each other's lives many times.

"Tomorrow we travel on toward home. Man and woman seem well enough. Two Feathers grow tired of this delay."

"Crow tire of it too," Crow responded.

Chapter Six

Pixie tripped over her feet as they dragged, each one feeling like a leaden weight attached to her legs. As soon as the sun had shown its first few rays of light, she'd been woken and forced to walk.

She and TJ hadn't spoken since their ugly words and the day prior was a foggy memory. She had slept the entire day after her attempt at leaving.

Pixie drew her gaze upward to look ahead to the savage who walked in front of her, his steps sure and confident. A fit specimen of a man he was, and she hated him. Yes hated him. She directed all her anger toward him and clung to it. It gave her the energy to move, to do as he ordered.

"Yes, I hate you," Pixie stated aloud unable to hold her tongue.

The one called Two Feathers turned as he paused, and his gaze connected with hers, questioning. Pixie stopped her walking.

"You don't understand, do you? Well, let me repeat myself. I said that I—Hate—You. How do you like that, Mr. Dumbass who can't even understand what I'm saying!"

The man before her looked at her for a moment before he shrugged, and then turning about, resumed walking. The others paid her no mind except for TJ, who now limped toward her, his determination obvious.

The short Indian who'd kept pace beside TJ curiously looked their way. He continued walking also.

TJ halted beside her, his gaze direct and firm. "Pixie, honestly, you can't talk like that. You'll get yourself hurt or even worse killed."

Pixie snorted. "Oh, so now you speak to me. And they can't understand what I say so why do you care anyway?"

"Look, I'm sorry for what I said out of anger at you, but you said some really hateful things to me, too."

They moved again after their leader turned and sharply motioned for them to follow him and the others. Pixie wiped away her tears that sprang forth, her dragging steps now in sync with TJ's. How had she and TJ landed in this mess or even survived the tornado?

Pixie took a breath.

"I shouldn't have said what I did to you, and I'm sorry for that."

Giving a nod at her apology, TJ didn't respond. His steps measured and determined.

Pixie knew the day had been hard on her, but it must've been extremely hard on TJ. Still he'd managed to keep pace with everyone and without complaint.

"I don't understand this mess we're in, TJ."

"Me either. Here we are though."

"Exactly where is *here*?"

"I'm trying to figure that one out."

TJ was a history buff and a history teacher, and Pixie realized what his animated expression meant. He found it exciting, the thought of their being back in time. She didn't give a damn where *here* was. She just wanted home and civilization.

They stopped to rest exactly four times that day and Pixie was positive they'd walked a hundred miles. More than likely closer to thirty, she had to admit, though it felt a hundred. Her feet, legs, back, and shoulders ached. Even her lips hurt.

The sun was setting when the narrow stream of water came into view, and the man she despised, their leader, signaled for all to halt for the night. Pixie flopped to the ground.

The four Indian men began to prepare a fire and filling their water containers. Once their tasks were completed, they waded out into the shallow stream to wash, no whooping, no hollering, just a quiet undertaking of cleaning of bodies.

TJ followed their example.

Pixie's object of hatred strode from the water and the rest of the men followed. He walked up to her and pointed a finger toward the water.

Pixie didn't budge. He gestured toward the water again.

"No. You can just smell my stink, Mr. Dumbass."

At TJ's sudden stiff posture, the man before Pixie frowned. He looked between her and TJ, and Pixie knew the instant the man realized that she'd insulted him. In a flash, jerked to her feet, he flung her backwards into the water. Going under with a splash and swallowing the dirty liquid, Pixie attempted to stand. She couldn't, held down by large hands, hands that scrubbed at her body. Finally pulled upward, Pixie sucked in precious air before shoved back under the water again. Her eyes made short contact with the man she'd labeled Mr. Dumbass.

"You ass!" she screamed when finally lifted clear of the water and set to the water's edge. The other Indian men laughed. Pixie thought even TJ laughed. The man before her laughed. Her anger soared at the sound and she clawed at the man. A fingernail caught the corner of his eye.

Instantly, he slapped her hands aside.

In the background, Pixie could hear TJ yell for her to stop, however, she couldn't, intent on plucking out her tormentor's eyes. She made a dive for him again. His bellow of anger rose when she made contact and clawed. The skin on his face peeled and collected under her fingernails.

Landing on her butt at his backhanded slap given, Pixie slowly raised a hand to her cheek. It throbbed, her temple to her chin. Her anger was gone now, and replaced by misgiving. Pixie stared upward at the man, a man who heaved with his anger. The other Indian men had stopped laughing and even TJ grew quiet with his screams for her to calm down. Pixie's gaze circled to them. They all stood unmoving, watchful.

Scrambling upward to her feet, Pixie swung her gaze back to the man before her and her heart gave a quick pitch forward.

His long fingers flexed around the handle of his hand-honed knife, a knife previously in a pouch at his side, but now in his hand. The same knife he'd used to skin those poor animals.

Turning, Pixie fled.

She had made a mistake, her mouth as always two steps ahead of any common sense that she may have. When her feet hit the embankment on the opposite side of the body of water, Pixie clawed at its grass covering, intent on climbing the small incline. She gave a shriek, and thrashed wildly, at the grasp to the back of her head as fingers tightly coiled into her hair. She was pulled back down the incline.

Flipped around to face her assailant, Pixie glimpsed a lifted hand. In that hand the reflected dying rays of the sun glinted on the blade of the knife. The man's lips were drawn back. His teeth exposed. Pixie grabbed at his hand. Her scream for mercy echoed. "Please, don't kill me! I'm sorry!"

****

Two Feathers stilled. His anger was powerful, but her words sank into his awareness. His heart slammed against his chest wall, and his body shook with his rage. It took all his willpower not to bring down the knife he gripped. No woman ever fought him, much less wounded.

"Quiet," he ordered. The noise the woman made unnerved him. He could barely see from the eye that she'd pierced, and his face stung where her fingernails had stripped away his skin.

Her screaming immediately stopped.

The woman's fear remained palpable. Its essence encircled him. Her fingers gripped his and held tight. The whites of her eyes were extreme, her irises a dark brown flecked with the green of early spring.

What he'd almost done sickened him. He never lost control. Did the Master of Life look downward and frown?

Two Feathers forced his body to relax. He took several deep breaths. The act helped to lessen the molten fury that flowed through him.

No matter how much this woman provoked, he'd not kill her, he decided as he looked down at her.

"Two Feathers not kill this day," he rasped out. He reached with his free hand to remove her fingers from around his fist. The woman held fast refusing to let go.

Forcibly, loosening her hold, Two Feathers placed his knife back into the pouch where he carried it. He let his fingers glide over the knife's handle as he hardened his expression. He reached out to touch the woman's arm. He may have decided that he would never kill her, but she needn't know.

"Before Pix speak, Pix touch Two Feathers. Two Feathers punish, maybe kill if no understand words Pix say."

The woman's eyes widened. Two Feathers hadn't believed that they could get any wider. She stepped back away from him, and he let her. She looked toward the others and then back at him. Silently at his nod of approval, she walked past all who'd observed their violent confrontation.

The man TJ fell into step beside her.

He said something to her and she snapped back at him. She turned to look backward.

Two Feathers frowned. He laid his palm over the handle of his knife as he took a step forward. She had disobeyed his instructions.

She bolted toward him, grabbing at him and wrapped her body around his.

"I just told him to shut up. That's all!"

Two Feathers felt a surge of awareness of her femaleness. She shuddered with fear, clinging to him. Her body pressed against his.

"Don't kill me!"

Lifting her with his hands to hold her still, Two Feathers turned so that his back was to the others and with the woman in front of him. The others view blocked from her emotional breakdown. She kept her gaze locked with his as she continued to beg him for mercy.

"Calm," he directed as he stroked her backbone. Why did this strange woman arouse a protective instinct?

With her forehead flopped against his chest, she took several deep breaths, and Two Feathers felt her terror recede. Gradually, her shaking ceased.

Abruptly, she lifted her head and dropped her arms from around his waist. Her eyes she kept downward.

"What did he say, your TJ?" Two Feathers murmured.

"He's not my TJ."

"What he say?"

****

"He said I'd better learn to keep my mouth shut."

Pixie lifted her gaze. This man held her life in his hands and she knew it. She was embarrassed at her begging and pleading with him. She took a step back from his touch, and it surprised that he let her.

In that moment, Pixie made a decision.

At the first opportunity, she'd escape this savage creature and his savage friends.

If this were a nightmare—a dream, a coma that she was in—she'd escape from it one way or another. She needed to go back to the same place she landed to find out if what was happening was in truth reality or a dream.

Unwillingly, Pixie reached to touch the bare skin of the man's arm. She was tired and extremely so. "I wish to go sit down, please."

Stared at for a moment before he gave a regal nod, Pixie didn't look at the other men as she went and sat on the ground, her jawline tight. Loneliness assaulted her as she gazed into the fire the others built but none looking her way.

Drawing her knees up to her chin, Pixie wrapped her arms around her legs. Never again would she display her fear for all to see. It embarrassed her, her breakdown.

Pixie's eyelids drooped, her stomach full after the offered meal. Had her parents received notification of her disappearance? Maybe they stood around her hospital bed and she was here, in this nightmare, and unaware of their presence. Pixie felt someone urge her to lie down and realized it must be TJ.

His hands were gentle as he guided her head to her purse. She felt him stretch out beside her and she sighed. TJ's kindness made her sorry for her earlier anger at him, and when he pulled her close, giving her his body warmth, she slept, secure in his protection.

****

Their small group walked an unrelenting pace the next day, and Pixie, awakened by Two Feathers at first light that morning, frowned as she realized the growing distance between her and the place where the tornado had dropped her and TJ.

She hadn't spoken much that morning because when she did, she'd had to touch the man who walked beside her, something that brought acute distaste. She wanted to avoid all contact with the brown savage.

It worried Pixie that she couldn't explain to TJ what she planned. *He seems to be enjoying himself*, she thought, her frown slashing deep as she watched him.

TJ kept a palm on the Indian's shoulder called Too Little as he and the short man conversed, looking to be fast friends. Anger rose in Pixie at TJ's easy acceptance of their situation. Who knew what their future held in this place if they didn't try to go back to where they belonged.

Stumbling, Pixie righted herself. Her shoes were not made for a long walk that was for sure. She'd had sneakers in the car and had planned to change into them when she and TJ arrived at the park that day.

Two Feathers looked her way.

Turning her face from him, Pixie licked at her lips. They hurt, so dry, so chapped, so cracked. She tasted blood.

A hand grasped her shoulder halting her steps. Looking up at Two Feathers who stood before her, Pixie felt a shiver of fear ripple through her. The man exuded wildness, an un-tameness that unnerved her. Reaching into the pouch that hung at his hip, he withdrew a strip of leather. It looked soft and pliable. He unfolded the small piece, and then dipped a finger into the goo smeared across it.

Pixie took a step back.

What was he planning?

He reached out to halt her movement.

"Bird fat, help lips," he stated.

"No!" In disgust, Pixie turned her face away.

"Yes." Clasping her jaws, the glob of fat on the end of his finger, he spread it across the span of her chapped lips.

Pixie felt instant relief.

The urge was strong though to wipe the concoction away even with its comfort. She didn't want anything to do with this world, dream, or no dream. She didn't dare do as she wished.

"Two full nights lips heal. Two Feathers give more to Pix later."

Revulsion at what was on her lips, Pixie didn't respond. *My name is Pixie, not Pix,* she silently belittled, even though Pixie wasn't a name that she'd ever particularly cared for.

Her curiosity too strong, Pixie couldn't contain her question that had hovered within her all that day. She may not receive an answer. "What do you plan to do with us? TJ and me?"

Two Feathers looked toward the men who continued to walk leaving them behind. His features were solemn.

"TJ do what TJ wish."

Pixie felt her relief wash over her. If TJ could do as he wished, then so could she. A smile spread across her face. The man by her side didn't smile back. Something flickered within the back of his gaze.

"I wish to go home."

"We go home."

Pixie frowned as she gazed up at the man who towered over her. "I mean I want to go back to where I came from."

"Pix can no go back. Past is past."

Pixie's face grew tight as her anger spiked. She tamped the emotion down. "You won't let me go? You just said TJ and I could do as we wish."

"TJ do as TJ wish. Pix Two Feathers'. Two Feathers choose to keep."

Pixie stared. He had stated before that she was his, but she'd blocked it out. She had refused to think about it, until now.

Two Feathers turned and began to walk away.

Pausing, he turned to look back to where she continued to stand. His expression severe, he motioned for her to come forward. Too scared to run and too scared to argue, Pixie obeyed the command.

****

With exhaustion and hunger, Pixie collapsed that evening when they finally stopped for the day. Digging into the depths of her purse, she searched for her mirror. Lightly, she touched at her swollen and chapped lips with a fingertip. She must look a fright.

Unable to find the compact, Pixie slung her purse away. Why hunt for the mirror? What difference did it make what she looked like.

Staring upward in bewilderment when Two Feathers and the one called Crow threw the animals they'd killed that day down at her feet, Pixie drew her legs away from the carcasses.

Two Feathers bent to pull her up to stand beside him. "Pix clean and cook."

"No."

At once, his gaze sharpened and his fingers tightened around her arm. She had angered him.

Pixie tried to pull her arm free from his grasp.

He turned and grated out, "Crow, take others go to buffalo. Make sure animals travel right direction."

Crow stared at Pixie in obvious contempt before he turned to do as ordered.

Pixie flicked her gaze upward at Two Feathers, and her panic rose. Once again, she'd spoken before thinking.

She looked toward TJ.

"TJ, don't you leave me here alone. Don't you dare!"

Too Little and Rock grasped TJ's shoulders and forced him to walk with them. He strained to look backward.

Two Feathers remained silent until Pixie looked at him.

"Pix obey when give order. Don't unman Two Feathers in front of others."

"Unman you? I just won't clean those awful things. Besides, I don't know how."

Glancing down at the lifeless creatures at her feet, Pixie felt a ripple of revulsion run through her. She wanted to kick the dead things away.

Two Feathers withdrew his knife.

Heart nearly seizing, she cried out, "I'll try!"

Pausing, Two Feathers studied her.

Bending, he picked up a lifeless rabbit. "Two Feathers teach."

Pixie watched the poor thing he gripped as he gutted and skinned the animal, his motions effortless. She wanted to vomit. Next, he cleaned one of the lifeless birds and then turning his knife in his hand, he held it out for her to take.

"Pix finish others," he stated. He shook the knife he held when she didn't reach out for it.

Pixie stared at the blood that dripped from the tip of the blade. "I can't."

Two Feathers, his expression firm, placed the knife's handle against her palm and then forced her fingers to close around it.

Pixie felt a moment's impulse as her fingers encircled the handle. It surprised and scared her. She hadn't realized she could think such thoughts. One sharp jab and the man before her would be laid low, maybe killed. She lifted her gaze. If he knew what she was thinking, he didn't bother to move.

Bending, she picked up the remaining unskinned rabbit. The blade of the knife sliced through it easily.

Pixie gave a shudder wanting to cry. With a sniff, she kept at her task. Satisfaction settled into pride in what she finally accomplished. With the rabbit and the remaining bird cleaned, she handed the bloodied knife, handle first, out to its owner.

"Now bury and build fire." Two Feathers made a motion to the animal guts and skins as he took the knife and wiped it clean.

"I don't know how to build a fire."

He shook his head and studied her as if he wondered at her smarts. "Two Feathers teach. Pix have knowledge how to bury remains?" His tone held disgust and his gaze doubt.

Snatching up a nearby stick, Pixie began to rake the animal remains into a pile. Digging a hole, she shoved the entire bloody, disgusting mound down into the cavity. She then covered the mess over with the surrounding loose dirt and twigs. Standing, she gave

Two Feathers a sneer.

She reached out. "How's that? Good enough?"

Without response, the man before her walked several yards away the animal carcasses held in his hands. Turning, he waited for her to come to him. Pixie knew what Two Feathers waited for. With resentment felt, she walked forward and reached out to touch his arm.

"Gather grass and wood, pile here," he instructed.

****

Two Feathers carefully washed the meat prior to hanging the carcasses over the fire he started. His wife, Pretty Flower, explained to him that if her hands and the meals she prepared weren't clean, it made them sick. She didn't know the why.

At the thought of Pretty Flower, Two Feathers missed her and their son. His jolly, little fat son was precious to him.

Glancing toward the woman who watched his actions, he let his gaze move down over her. She was the same size as Pretty Flower. However, that was where their resemblance ended. She seemed younger than what his wife was. Pretty Flower was eighteen summers when she delivered their child and she knew how to keep his household, knew her place. Jerking his gaze from the strange woman, Two Feathers turned the cooking meat. He stood upright and made a motion for the useless female to come forward. Maybe Crow was right, maybe she wasn't worth his time.

"Woman see how prepared?"

"Yes."

"Woman do same. Build fire, cook meals."

Two Feathers watched as the woman's gaze narrowed. She didn't argue, fear holding her tongue. He had wondered earlier if she would follow through on her thought to use his knife on him. He was glad she hadn't tried. He would've punished her severely.

"Clean hands and food always. Filth not good. Make all sick."

A red hue rose and crawled up the woman's neck and across her cheeks. "I know that," she snapped.

Two Feathers held back his smile. She may be scared of him but that didn't stop her from standing up to him. He liked that. He grabbed his water container when washing her hands she wasted too much. Tomorrow they would come across more water but now they needed to conserve their remainder. Pulling the container's leather string tight, Two Feathers studied the strange woman who baffled him and held his interest. He touched her arm.

"Why woman know nothing of survival?"

"You wouldn't understand so I won't even try to explain."

Realizing her condescension, Two Feathers wanted to slap her to the ground. Turning his back to her, he walked several paces away, his muscles rigid. He wanted to please the Master of Life, but this trouble he didn't understand. What had he done in his twenty-five summers that warranted his punishment of the past year?

Squatting, Two Feathers watched the woman turn their meal as he'd instructed. She was a fast learner. His gaze traveled the length of bare legs.

The others walking back into the camp drew his attention. The man called TJ had his hand on Too Little's shoulder as he and Too Little talked nonstop. It seemed they'd become fast friends.

Two Feathers understood several of the words asked of Too Little. *Where do you come from? What's the name of your tribe?* Earlier, Two Feathers noted that he could understand more of their strange language even when he and the woman weren't touching. Before long, he'd be able to communicate without any connection. It confused him the woman and the man called TJ. How had they appeared as if from nowhere? And why did they know nothing of day to day survival?

Two Feathers wanted to ask questions, but his pride wouldn't allow it. He didn't believe that the two came from the heavens as originally thought, yet if they didn't come from the heavens, then where were they from and how had they appeared as they had?

Crow met his gaze and walked up to squat beside him.

"All fall for Two Feathers, aye."

Two Feathers looked at him in question.

Crow slung a hand out toward the woman. "Crow believe Crow come back to battlefield. Woman obediently cooks, instead."

Chapter Seven

Pixie tried to scoot away from the man lying so close beside her, his body heat fusing with hers. He had insisted she lay beside him even when she'd argued against it. TJ informed she'd slept *beside* Two Feathers the night before, not *with* him, when she'd looked to him for help in her argument against the demand. Frowning, Pixie stared out into the surrounding darkness.

If what TJ said was true, she'd cuddled against Two Feathers during the long hours of the previous night. This evening they lay under a large tree, its branches generous over their heads.

TJ was excited by their experience. His hand motions earlier, wide and expressive as he relayed that he believed they were in a period of history before any white settlers. Too Little and Rock had informed him they'd never before seen people such as them. Pixie didn't care. All she wanted was home. She missed all the lights, the people, and the cars. It was too quiet where she was. She loathed this place, and she loathed the man who lay beside her. She was going home, she resolved, her jawline tight. Come hell or high water, she was returning to civilization and sophistication. Back to where a person didn't have to kill what they ate every damn day.

The next morning it rained.

Pixie, her tears blending in with the downpour, walked behind the man who controlled her. Unexpectedly, he and the others halted. She glanced toward TJ and his confusion matched hers.

Grabbing her arm, Two Feathers yanked her to the ground then sprawled along beside her. The other men followed suit with TJ copying their actions. Pixie could tell TJ was thrilled while she was scared senseless. She watched him reach out to touch Too Little's arm. "What is it," he asked the other man.

Pixie understood the words "unknown tribe" that Too Little answered back.

"Quiet," Two Feathers ordered. It seemed that he didn't even breathe.

As the group passed by them, Pixie and the others were silent and still, blending into the grass. It was a large group. The men and women in the group chattered, as the children darted in and out among the walking adults. A tribe relocating it seemed.

Pixie's heart pounded as the seconds and minutes passed. She shook so much that she wondered how the earth didn't move and alert the passing group. Two Feathers' hand squeezed hers, and Pixie lifted her gaze to connect with his. He ran a thumb back and forth across the skin on the inside of her wrist. Mesmerized, Pixie couldn't move. Minutes, hours ticked.

"Pix can rise now."

"What?" Pixie responded.

Two Feathers stood and pulled her up beside him. He turned to the others. Embarrassment flooding, Pixie made a show of brushing the accumulated mud and grass from her legs. She kept her head down as the falling rain did a better job of washing the grime away.

She hadn't even realized the group was gone. So magnetized by the man by her side all she'd known was his touch that slowly, moved over the inside of her wrist. Even now, her breathing seemed labored.

"Tribe go opposite way. It is good. We walk again."

Pixie frowned. They weren't touching and she'd understood everything said.

Did he understand her when not touching?

Straightening, Pixie stared at Two Feathers' back. She didn't reach out. She had understood Too Little earlier also, and without even realizing it.

"We don't have to be connected. You can understand now, can't you?"

Two Feathers turned. He caught hold of her arm, and he shook it. "Woman instructed touch Two Feathers when speak."

His frown stretched.

Pixie hesitated. "I said this rain is terrible."

Two Feathers watched her for a moment and then gave a slight nod of agreement.

"We go," he stated. His hand dropped from her arm.

The rain ceased and the sun came out and Pixie's smile spread. When Two Feathers glanced her way, she quickly wiped the expression away. She didn't know why but the thought that she could understand the savage and him not her, made her happy.

****

Two Feathers stretched his tired muscles as the group settled in for the night. That evening, all bellies were full. Fourteen more suns and they'd be home. They had been able to bathe in a natural rock basin of water, left behind from the recent downpour, and it felt good to be clean. The mud had itched.

The woman glanced his way from where she stood, and with a gesture of his hand, Two Feathers motioned for her to come to his side. She acted as if she didn't notice his command and turned her back to him.

Crow watched him as did Rock and Two Feathers sighed. He couldn't allow the woman to disobey his instruction, not in front of the men. Standing, he stalked to her and grabbed a fistful of her hair. He pulled her to where he'd been resting.

"Sit," he ordered.

She sat although her gaze held banked anger. Two Feathers watched as she swallowed several times. She wanted to scream at him he knew. She held her tongue, though. It was good. The strange woman was learning.

When he reclined beside her, she scooted away. Sitting back up, Two Feathers reached out and buried his fingers into her hair, and pulled her back to his side.

Her anger blanketed him.

He massaged the back of her head as Crow and Rock watched him. They smiled. They thought he punished her. When they turned away, satisfied he'd put the woman in her place, Two Feathers withdrew his hand. She sat stiff and unmoving. He indicated for her to stretch out beside him.

"Good grief, the man's a strange savage," she mumbled as she obeyed.

With a raised hand, Two Feathers encircled her wrist with his fingers. They engulfed it. Her guarded gaze rose to his. He had understood 'man', 'strange', and 'savage', the 'good grief' words she mumbled puzzled him.

"Pix touch when speak. Two Feathers not instruct again." He tightened his fingers and let his features grow unkind.

"If you try to force yourself on me, I'll fight you," she vowed.

Jerking his hand away, Two Feathers frowned. He had never attempted to have unwanted relations with a woman, much less, where others could watch. He let the woman inch some space between them, her eyes glued to his.

Two Feathers' senses hummed in acute awareness with her accusation, her every move now sensual and noticed. Stretching out onto the ground, he tried to settle in for the night. Each time the woman shifted, he tensed.

****

Pixie forced her body to relax.

She didn't know why she'd accused the man by her side. He hadn't made any advances under the cover of the night so far. With embarrassment, Pixie realized the *why* of her words. It was she who was sexually aroused not him. She had been aware of him since early that morning, after the passing of that other tribe. She had watched his leg muscles the rest of that day as they'd walked, lean, smooth muscle everywhere, and no fat anywhere.

Good grief, I've got to get back to the normal world and the faster the better, Pixie's thought flashed.

She didn't believe TJ would try to go back with her to where they landed. He seemed to blend in with the harsh environment. He had come alive. He walked and talked with more confidence. He was surer of himself. Pixie had never seen this current side of him. His metamorphosis was an odd thing to witness.

Two Feathers' breathing slowed and Pixie knew that he slept. She inched sideways to put distance between them. His friend, Crow, prowled the area, and Pixie watched him through lowered eyelids.

He had seemed friendlier that day and had even hoisted her over a rough spot when Two Feathers had gone ahead to scout for food and a resting area for their group. At the time, she'd worried Crow held her arm a bit too long. When Rock spoke to him, he'd released his grip and turned away as if nothing had happened. Too Little asked if she needed water breaking her study of the man.

Too Little was a funny individual.

He always had some comment to make as they walked and pointed out this or that of interest that he found. That day, Pixie understood much of what he said.

Unlike Too Little, Rock stayed quiet only speaking when spoken to by the others.

If there's an opportunity to escape tomorrow, I won't hesitate to take it. Upon that thought, Pixie yawned, and let her eyelids fully close.

****

In confusion, Pixie squinted up at the early morning sun as she woke to a quiet camp. Who would have thought that she could've slept so soundly? She blinked several times. It seemed as if she'd just laid her head down. She yawned. It was then that Pixie felt the ground shake and jumping to her feet sought the cause.

In that same short span of time, she realized that she was alone and whirling, she looked for the others. None were found nor the reason for the earth's rumble.

Chapter Eight

At the last minute the bison turned, the maneuver successful. For a moment, Two Feathers wondered if they'd all be trampled, and he never to see his son grow into adulthood. The bison could be a violent creature, ferocious and brutal when angered.

TJ laughed beside him. "I'm alive!"

Two Feathers smiled. "Yes. TJ escape."

"No, I mean, this is the life! The life man!"

Not understanding, Two Feathers frowned.

TJ continued. "The future sucked the soul out of me. I belong here. Here, I connect."

Even more confused, Two Feathers shook his head. The man was peculiar. He turned and walked toward Crow.

He informed Crow, "Two Feathers fetch woman. Crow and others continue toward home. Two Feathers catch up."

Crow studied him and then flashed a knowing smirk.

"No," Two Feathers responded.

"Crow would," Crow grated.

For a moment, Two Feathers felt anger spike at his long-time friend.

"Two Feathers not use woman that way. Crow forget Pretty Flower and Two Feathers' promise?"

Crow's smile disappeared.

Turning, Two Feathers stomped away.

When he came to the campsite he and the other men left hours earlier, he gazed around it. The woman was gone. At first notice of her absence, he'd been alarmed. TJ assured that morning that she wouldn't run away without him.

Studying the ground, Two Feathers knew there'd been no struggle. Lifting his gaze, he stared in the direction the woman headed. He didn't rush to gather her back; instead, he began to stroll in the same erratic direction as she'd gone. He would let her run as far as she could.

Dusk fell and Two Feathers watched the woman from a distance. He had wondered about her sanity when she left the safety net of him and the others, and now he could only shake his head. The woman shivered with obvious fear as she sat huddled against the tree by her side. Alone and with no idea of what she was doing. She had no weapon for protection, no fire, and he could hear her stomach rumble even from this distance. It rumbled with the same hunger, he was sure as those animals that cried out in the night. The coyotes howled again, and the woman jumped to her feet. Her back pressed to the tree as her gaze searched the area around her.

With a smile, Two Feathers rose.

The growing darkness would cover his approach. He had waited long enough for her to feel the emptiness of the evening and to know isolation.

Letting the twig under his foot snap, Two Feathers stepped forward. At the sound, the woman shrieked and began to scale the tree she'd cowered against just moments before. Two Feathers watched as she kicked out at the feel of pressure from a tree branch against her leg as she scrambled upward. She tried to peer down to see what it was that touched her, while at the same time she stretched and reached upward searching for another tree branch to ascend.

Earlier, he'd watched and listened as she spoke aloud her

thought that she might sleep up in that tree to be away from predators. She had scoffed aloud at her fear deciding to settle at its base instead. Now the tree height, he knew, seemed a refuge.

Suddenly, she was falling, arms and legs flailing, and her cry of distress echoed out into the night. Landing on her backside, she grunted at the ground's hard contact when she hit.

Two Feathers pounced straddling her, and he howled in imitation of the animals of the night.

Screaming and swinging her fists while she pitched her hips upward at the same time, he plummeted to the ground beside her. Surprised with the unexpected and swift response, he lay unmoving.

The woman straddled him as he'd done her. A fist connected with his jawline and then another and another. Two Feathers began to laugh and he drawled as he caught her fists midair, "It is unmanly, Two Feathers not able hold mere woman down."

The woman on top of him stilled and then her laughter bubbled up from her belly.

Two Feathers continued, "Woman should be punished for actions." He didn't mean the words. He delighted in her unexpected behavior. She always surprised him. Disentangling himself from her limbs, he sat up.

She scrambled right back up onto his lap and exclaimed, "I've never been so terrified in all my life! Well, except for the tornado. I'm so…so…glad to see you!"

Astonished at her ease with him, Two Feathers encircled her waist with his arms. Holding her to him, he scooted backward so that he could lean against the tree she'd thought of as a refuge.

She curled against him and chattered on as if they were long-time lovers and friends.

"When I saw that I was alone this morning, I decided to escape from you. As the day passed, I realized that I had made a huge mistake in my thinking process. Ha! I didn't think before I took off, so there was no thought given to it. I had no idea where I was going anyway."

She paused to take a breath and then continued, "I ask you though, what made me believe that I had a hell's bell's chance I could find the exact place where I'd landed? And then be lucky enough to go back to my time because of it?"

She looked at him in the shadowy night as if he had the answer for her. Two Feathers gave a shrug. He didn't even understand what it was she rambled on about.

She continued. "What's the possibility of that happening? Returning, I mean?"

Two Feathers shrugged again. Her words baffled him. His hand, as if it had a mind of its own, slid up her bare leg. Two Feathers tensed. Her leg was satiny and soft to the touch. He wanted to trace more than her leg. He should lift her from his lap.

Abruptly, she stopped talking and she took a deep breath. She looked directly at him as if she just remembered him.

"Where are the others, and why was I left alone this morning?"

Her question surprised him. She spoke and acted as if they were intimate of one another. He responded in kind. "They travel on. We needed to turn buffalo with early morning, and Pix slept sound. TJ promise Pix not run away."

She stared at him. "I swear I want to kiss you so bad that I think I'm going to do just that."

Two Feathers' indrawn breath was unstoppable. He was shocked. He had known no woman who spoke this way.

She raised her arms to encircle his neck.

He didn't move. In truth, he couldn't.

She leaned in close and then sighed when their lips touched, the sound reflected the same instant pleasure he felt.

Two Feathers almost copied aloud her sigh, his muscles jumping. Catching his groan back in time, he moved his hand further up her leg. He tightened his other hand against her waistline. It took all his willpower not to throw the bold woman to the ground and mount her. Relieve his tension.

Abruptly, she turned so that she straddled his hips, her knees bent on each side of him. She settled her feet up under her thighs. Two Feathers didn't move a muscle at her audacity, shocked into stillness. She sat snug against his man parts, parts that bulged.

She laid her palms against the sides of his cheeks. "I'm so glad that you're here. I thought of you today."

Could she not feel his need, his pounding heart?

She leaned in and kissed him again, no restraint, no hesitation given, same as before. Her lips firm, soft and sweet, moved over his. Two Feathers' heart thundered. In a daze, he palmed the back of her head to hold her in place, taking over the intimacy she'd started. It felt as if his heart would burst from his chest.

He wanted this woman, had desired her since he'd first laid eyes on her. She took his mind from his sadness. He forgot all others when around her, forgot his promise to Pretty Flower.

Two Feathers threw the bold woman aside as he lunged to his feet. Disgust washed over him at his weakness.

"Woman act in shameful way so Two Feathers not punish for running away?" he demanded.

Springing to her feet, the woman called Pixie quickly backed away from him.

She wouldn't meet his gaze.

Her hands she twisted together.

He had blurted the first thing that he could to distract himself from her sexual appeal, and now Two Feathers wondered if in fact her actions had been ulterior. He grabbed hold of her arm to halt her steady, sliding movement away from him.

She didn't reply to his question only stood stock still at his touch. In anger, Two Feathers shook the arm that he held.

"Pix answer Two Feathers. Does woman act in shameful way so Two Feathers not give deserved punishment?"

"Yes," she cried out. "Yes, I acted as I did so you'd forget! There, are you happy?"

Tightening his fingers on her arm, Two Feathers tempered his rage. The woman may not desire him, but he desired her and his weakness disgusted him. She played a game, and he'd forgotten Pretty Flower with it.

"Sit," he ordered.

He forcibly yanked her to the ground when she didn't move. Quickly, she scooted backward from him to hug against the tree trunk, its overhead branches a witness to his weakness. The woman didn't look up and kept her head bowed. She drew her knees up to her chest to wrap her arms around her legs as if to draw within herself. Unable to control his action, Two Feathers' gaze skimmed the outline of those bare legs.

The strange attire that she wore he could easily remove. She had admitted contrived desire and still he wished for what she offered. He was tempted to know her thoroughly. It was an insult she didn't desire him only feared his punishment, though what angered him the most was the lust she'd managed to instill in him. She had almost made him break his promise to Pretty Flower. He would not be tempted again.

Turning, Two Feathers stalked several feet away, his back kept to the woman. Staring out into the moonlit darkness, he breathed deep. If he turned, he knew he'd search for a view of the woman. He wanted to touch her, to absorb her scent, and to see if the rest of her was as soft as that one leg. It was a want which hurt physically.

****

Pixie positioned herself so that she faced away from the savage that prowled the area. How stupid was she? Very, very stupid, she decided. As always, she acted on impulse with no thought given about consequences. She may have only known the man for a few days, but who was in her thoughts and who was it she had wished beside her as the evening grew late? She felt safe with him, which she didn't understand, especially when their interactions were so…explosive.

Pixie felt prickles behind her eyes. Putting her knuckles to her eyelids, she pressed against them to stop her tears.

When she'd come to the realization that trying to recapture the moment that she had landed in this bizarre world, was bizarre in itself, she'd halted her escape attempt. Deep down she knew that she was lost anyway and with no idea which way she needed to go.

When coming across the tree grove and never before seen small body of water, she'd stopped walking entirely. With a certainty, she was lost she had decided. Expecting a rescue at any time, she'd twiddled away the day waiting for the men to find her. As she waited, she'd washed herself in the pool of water and shaved her legs.

Pixie grimaced, repulsed by her action. Yes, she'd shaved her legs. Moreover, who was it that she'd wanted those legs smooth for—him! What kind of idiot carried a razor in their purse?

Her embarrassment high, Pixie covertly watched as Two Feathers stomped by her once again. He kept his face turned away not looking in her direction.

As night had fallen, she had started to believe that no one searched for her. She had even wondered if they had left her behind on purpose. It had terrified her. She had been so acutely relieved to hear Two Feathers' familiar voice that she'd acted on it. When she'd kissed him, it felt wonderful. Desire had sparked immediately. Shame made her lie when he'd showed his revulsion of her touch by wiping at his mouth after throwing her aside.

"Two Feathers leave."

"What?" Pixie looked up. Two Feathers now stood before her, his stance wide. He seemed so angry.

"Two Feathers not wait till light. Leave now."

Slowly standing, Pixie waited.

"Woman follow behind Two Feathers. Not touch Two Feathers again."

Pixie's temper flashed. She fought it. It won. How dare he act so insulted! Enough was enough. She had no wish to touch him now anyway and they didn't need to.

"What? Like this?" Reaching out, Pixie grasped hold of Two Feathers' arm the way she had when they had needed to communicate.

"Or like this?" She snaked her palms down his bare sides to clasp his lean, barely, covered hips. Looking upward, Pixie met a narrowed gaze. *He's going to kill me now for sure*, she decided in horror.

He seized her hands and she believed he was to sling them aside. Instead, he yanked her toward him.

"Two Feathers don't desire Pix," he snarled.

"Well hell, I don't desire you either," Pixie retorted back. She did though. Heaven help her, she did. Two Feathers crashed his mouth against hers. A sound like a moan emerged from him. He jerked their hips together.

Sinking to his knees, he dragged her to the ground with him. Pixie didn't fight.

In fact, she leaned into him.

It was right where she wanted to be.

Chapter Nine

Trudging behind the silent man who walked with long strides ahead of her, Pixie fought her shame. *Thoroughly fucked not once, but twice, and I enjoyed it, savored it all night long,* she thought in disgust. At one point in the prior night, her mouth covered by his was only to stop her cries of pleasure that joined the animals in their howling. Pixie didn't believe there was one area on her body not explored by Two Feathers and that hadn't delighted in his touch. Two Feathers hadn't been rough and had even seemed to want her to enjoy their lovemaking. Now with the light of day and with his behavior since, she felt used. Tapped and discarded.

Her purse slipped from her fingers to the ground as she walked, and Pixie let it lie.

When they caught up to the others that evening, she couldn't meet TJ's gaze. Silently, she walked up to stand beside him.

Two Feathers continued to ignore her as he had the entire day. He spoke to his companions though upon entering the camp. The three men didn't look her way.

"Are you okay?" TJ asked from beside her.

Nodding and unable to stop her emotional response at his voiced concern, Pixie's eyes teared.

"Did he rape you?" TJ's voice was hushed, his distress evident in his gaze.

Turning her gaze toward the aloof man who had used her and then cold-shouldered her, Pixie shook her head. "No, TJ, he didn't have to rape me. I was a willing participate. I'm just as you've told me over and over. I'm stupid and spoiled, thinking the world revolves around only what I want."

Reaching out, TJ patted at her back, his action awkward. "No, Pixie, you're not stupid. I'm sorry that I called you that. You haven't had to face the ugliness of life that's all."

Two Feathers' dark gaze rose to hers before it slid to TJ's hand. Pixie stepped away from TJ's touch. Two Feathers studied her for a moment longer before he turned away. Pixie's heart pounded. He no longer desired her, his expression, though, had let her know that he felt he owned her.

TJ stayed by her side as they traveled onward the next morning, speaking low and ignoring the men. Two Feathers not once looked their way or separated them as he had before, and Pixie couldn't keep her gaze from straying to wherever he was until she realized that Crow watched her.

"Can you understand them now without touching?" TJ asked her as they walked. Pixie nodded.

"I can, too," TJ continued. "Strange."

Pixie grimaced. Her attachment for the man who walked ahead of them was *strange*. TJ's easy acceptance of the world they had landed in was *strange*. Every damn thing about the situation was *strange*, if anyone bothered to ask her.

"Too Little says their tribe has moved to new lands."

Pixie's gaze moved toward the man TJ talked about, although she didn't reply.

"He's married with four children, two boys and two girls. He also has a large extended family."

Pixie jerked her gaze toward Two Feathers. Was he married? That possibility hadn't entered her mind.

TJ continued talking with no mention made of the others marital statuses. Pixie wanted to scream out her frustration. She wanted to know Two Feathers' marital status although she wouldn't ask.

She was ashamed of her preoccupation with the man.

"We stop for night," Two Feathers suddenly stated, halting his smooth, walking motion. "Two Feathers find food. Others make camp."

With his abrupt statement, he turned away, no glance given toward her. Watching him leave, Pixie felt her heart shrivel.

The day had been long and tiring.

Crow sauntered up. "Woman start fire."

"I don't know how."

Frowning and his gaze narrow, Crow stared at her. "Woman gather fire items needed. Crow start fire."

Pixie looked around. Dried buffalo chips and some not so dry lay scattered about on the ground within the open area. Strolling about, Pixie gathered up an armful of the dried ones and then walked back to where Crow waited for her.

Taking two stones from his side pouch, same as what Two Feathers carried, he motioned for her to drop what she held. Pixie did as instructed, and then watched as he bent on one knee to strike together the rock pieces that he held. Sparks flew. He blew on the dried pieces of grass placed over and around the buffalo chips.

No matter how hard she tried, she never seemed to be able to get that blasted spark.

"Woman not make good wife," Crow stated as he stood, a flame ignited behind him.

He looked at Pixie as if telling her something important.

"Two Feathers need slave, not wife, need caregiver for son. Two Feathers not want second wife," he continued.

Well, there it was, her question answered. Married and with a child. Resentment rose in Pixie at Two Feathers and shame at herself. Shame felt that she had given no thought to his having a wife.

"Woman be Crow's wife if Two Feathers agree," Crow said, his voice low and muted. He drew closer glancing at the others as if not wanting any to overhear his words.

Pixie stared. "Why would you want me if I'm not wife material?"

Crow's gaze slithered down over her, and Pixie wanted to slap his face. Experience held her hand. Two Feathers must've informed the men of what had occurred the night before. The thought made Pixie want to gag. She couldn't stop her hate-filled gaze when Two Feathers strolled back into the area. He seemed to pause in his step, before he dropped what he carried at her feet.

"Clean and cook," he ordered before he turned away.

Stepping away to do as ordered, Pixie worked on their meal. Crow watched her from a distance, and her gaze connected with his.

Hours later, the camp was quiet, except for the occasional snore. Pixie gazed up at the stars, wide-awake. The men slept sound.

She had been ordered to lie beside Two Feathers. Her argument to the contrary cut short when she'd told him that she wanted to sleep beside TJ.

A lump rose in Pixie's throat and she forced it down. She blinked rapidly as she stared at the stars above her. She couldn't stop her angry thoughts that filtered.

Is this your idea of funny, God?

I pray for rescue from the tornado and you give this answer?

****

Two Feathers lay awake and knew that the woman by his side did also. He had betrayed Pretty Flower and it cut deep. He had given a vow that he'd never take another wife or have relations with another woman, and he'd broken that vow. A vow given the day Crow had found Pretty Flower and brought him to her resting place.

For the past year, it had been easy. He hadn't looked at or

even desired another woman, until now.

Now his senses were alive and he craved Pix as he'd craved no other, maybe even more than Pretty Flower.

Two Feathers slung his arm across his eyes. No. Pretty Flower was the mother of his child. Pretty Flower was whom he wanted. Whom he'd always wanted.

Pretty Flower's laughter echoed and Two Feathers' tears slowly rolled down the sides of his face.

Chapter Ten

Pixie's mouth dropped opened at the sight of the bustling village when she topped the hill that she and the others climbed that evening. Along the full length of the valley below, a sprawling, bustling community spread out before her.

Twenty days of walking and she'd begun to believe that they'd never reach their destination. Two Feathers and the other men had been excited that morning. Their home was close they'd said. Pixie's palms sweated as she stared down into the village. A fine tremor seemed to take hold of her body.

"Would you look at that, Pixie," TJ breathed by her side. Someone below spotted them and a shout went up toward their group. Pixie followed close behind Two Feathers as he and the others walked faster toward the crowd of people at the bottom of the hill. Naked children encircled them when they reached the village, their chatter and laughter loud, their brown bodies glowing with health and sunshine.

Pixie found herself searching each child's face looking for any resemblance to the man who strolled ahead of her. He patted the head of one or two as he passed. He didn't stop to lift any.

Too Little let out a shout of happiness and took off toward a lodge where a woman stood with a child resting on her hip. Several children ran up to him, their expressions animated and their shrieks of joy escalating. The woman's gaze widened at her notice of TJ, and then she slowly looked over to Pixie.

Rock, who stood beside Pixie, hoisted a child up onto his shoulders, his laughter deep. The girl grasped a handful of his hair as she screeched with laughter.

Crow veered to the left of the surging crowd. He didn't lift or greet a child and none greeted him. Suddenly, he stopped and reached backward and gripped Pixie's arm. Pulling Pixie close to him, he mouthed in her ear for her hearing alone, "Two Feathers forget Pixie. Crow wouldn't if Pixie were Crow's woman."

In the chaos around them, Pixie let her gaze meet his.

He loosened his grip on her arm then spun to walk away.

Moving her gaze over the jostling crowd, Pixie searched for Two Feathers. He had forgotten her just as Crow had stated. He had left her behind to greet his wife alone.

TJ was free to do what he wanted while she was somehow stuck with Two Feathers—for him to do what with exactly? To be a slave, a woman on the side when he grew tired of the same ol', same ol' with his wife? A child clutched hold of her knee, and Pixie flinched away from the touch. The girl fled her cries of outrage loud.

TJ stood still as he drank in the sights and sounds, and Pixie grabbed at his arm. His expression, when he turned, reflected the same mindboggling experience that she felt.

"Don't leave me, TJ. Please don't leave me."

Wrapping his arm around her shoulders, TJ shook his head. "I won't."

Too Little turned and he motioned. "Come, friend, come," he shouted out.

Pixie moved when TJ did, determined to stick to his side.

"Too Little's wife," Too Little stated when they approached. He included Pixie and TJ both in his introduction to the woman who stood beside him. Pixie flashed a friendly smile. She needed a comrade in this wacky place.

The woman didn't respond back in kind.

Pixie dropped her gaze, more insecure than she'd ever been in her life.

Turning, the woman entered the dwelling they all stood before. Too Little motioned for TJ and Pixie to follow his wife inside it.

"Too Little's home. Welcome," he stated when they stepped forward. As Pixie entered the low passageway, she wondered how Two Feathers' greeting to his wife was playing out. Did he lovingly kiss her and tell her how much he'd missed her?

Pixie forced the vivid image away.

Upon fully entering Too Little's home, Pixie's first thought was that it was a larger dwelling than she'd believed, and second, that it was bursting to capacity. Several unlit fire pits lay scattered about within the rectangular area with people lounging around each one. All who sat within the interior of the home shouted out, "Too Little, welcome!"

Chaos reigned as the people within the lodge rushed forward chattering at once. The children ran about screaming with laughter. Pixie hugged against TJ at the surge of adults that came their way.

Too Little took the frenzied scene in stride. Bombarded with questions about the trip, the buffalo, and the two strangers with him, he fired answers back right and left, his smile never wavering.

Food, animal skins, and weapons lay atop short platforms that lined the interior wall of the home; the large structure formed from malleable tree limbs, joined, and secured together making the home sturdy. The frame of the lodge encased in buffalo hides and the bark of trees, leaves, and branches. The home had dried mud packed thick at the base of the floor, to secure the people from vermin, Pixie assumed, or maybe rainwater runoff? Several of the buffalo hides had been laid back to let the sunlight stream in.

The hole in the ceiling, Pixie knew was to let the smoke out from the fire pits scattered about within the home. The women within the lodge encircled her. Some reached to touch her hair. Some pulled at it. Some chattered with excitement, yet didn't reach out.

"Ow," Pixie gasped and slapped at the hands that roughly pulled at her hair. The women laughed. Enjoyment gotten from her panic it seemed.

Too Little's wife came forward. "Leave," she ordered the crowd. When the women scattered, she turned toward Pixie, her expression as solemn and unsmiling as earlier. *Maybe that's her permanent countenance*, Pixie thought in bemusement.

"Why hair short? Punished for wrongdoing?" the woman demanded.

"No," Pixie stuttered.

Too Little's wife patted the tip of a finger against her own chest. "Brave Bird."

She pointed toward Pixie. "What woman called?"

"Pixie Black. And this is my friend, TJ Jones." Pixie pulled at TJ's arm causing his attention to shift from the mayhem around them to her and Brave Bird. He seemed dazed.

"Friend?" Brave Bird's gaze sharpened and she frowned. Pixie nodded.

"Too Little!" the woman screeched, causing Pixie and TJ both to jump in fright.

The wave of bodies that encircled Brave Bird's husband parted and Too Little hurried forward.

The home emptied. Silence left behind in the sudden wake.

Brave Bird stood with her hands on her hips, her anger evident. Too Little frowned and he glanced between Pixie and TJ as if wondering what'd been said.

His wife pointed a short, stubby finger toward Pixie. "Why husband bring strange woman to Brave Bird's home? Husband want woman?"

"Too Little not wish for woman," Too Little responded.

"Why brought to home if husband not want?" Brave Bird snapped.

Too Little sputtered then pointed toward Pixie's ankle. "Woman Two Feathers'. See, woman wear mark."

"Wait a minute," Pixie interjected. TJ clasped her arm. His action halted her heated words of denial at being Two Feathers' woman.

"I don't want your husband," Pixie meekly stated instead.

"Why woman not desire husband?" Brave Bird demanded insulted it seemed.

Pixie stuttered. Good grief she was confused.

"Too Little good man, good provider to family." Brave Bird drew herself up to her full height apparently in full insult mode.

"Two Feathers call out. Hear argument."

Everyone swung about to meet Two Feathers' gaze. He dwarfed the entryway of the lodge.

Now it was Brave Bird's turn to stammer.

Coming fully into the home, he walked up to Pixie to grasp her forearm. "No worry, Brave Bird. Woman Two Feathers'. Two Feathers take to home now."

Pixie wanted to claw at his fingers that Two Feathers had wrapped around her upper arm. She didn't want his touch in any form. TJ let his hand drop away from her other arm, and Pixie swung her gaze to meet his. His gaze was apologetic in return, and she knew that he wouldn't come to her defense against the man by her side.

"Thank you for nothing," she murmured, hurt lacing her voice.

"It would do no good," he stated back.

"Too Little, continue to show new friend our ways." At Two Feathers' statement, Too Little nodded his head in agreement. His wife stayed silent.

Pulled toward the home's exit, Pixie strained to look back at TJ. He avoided her gaze. Bitterness rose in Pixie, and its acidity spread, tightening its grip around her heart. Her gaze swung to the man by her side as they exited the lodge. She couldn't stay quiet and began to beg. "Please, leave me with TJ. I've no wish to go with you."

Two Feathers' stride grew wide as he dragged her along beside him. Pixie struggled to remain upright. She continued her begging. They reached a lodge sitting at the edge of the village, and he slung her inside it, away from the scrutiny of the ones who'd watched their procession.

Stumbling forward through the home's doorway, Pixie met the stare of a young woman who sat within the center of the home. She held a sleeping child within her arms and her gaze glowed with a warm welcome. She was striking. *Breathtakingly beautiful*, Pixie thought, jealousy rising. Long, black hair hung straight and loose and draped to the ground around her hips. She stood. Her movements graceful as her gaze met Two Feathers'.

Remorse rose in Pixie as the memory of the night she and Two Feathers shared together flashed. She had not given a moment's thought that he could be married.

"This is woman Two Feathers speak of?" his wife asked him. He nodded.

Pixie wanted to disappear into the ground, her humiliation complete. How could Two Feathers present her to this beautiful creature?

His wife walked forward, and with a smile, she stretched her arms out, offering to hand Pixie the baby that she held.

Pixie jerked backward, horrified. She would not hold this woman's child as if she and the woman's husband hadn't been intimate together.

The woman frowned and pulled the child back to her bosom. She shook her head. "Fawn don't trust. Fawn keep Three Feathers."

Two Feathers took the baby from his wife's arms, and with tenderness, he bent and kissed the sleeping infant's forehead.

"Two Feathers keep."

"Brother, it not wise."

In confusion, Pixie listened to their exchange. This beautiful woman was Two Feathers' sister? Not his wife as she'd believed?

"Woman not hurt child. If woman does, woman suffer much

pain."

Two Feathers' gaze rose. The crystal reflected within their depths left Pixie in little doubt as to the truth of his words.

"Fawn watch with woman during lightness of day," his sister demanded in response.

Two Feathers nodded his agreement.

Giving a glance in Pixie's direction, the woman left the home.

Two Feathers turned. "Pix care for Two Feathers' child and home now. Live in home with Two Feathers."

"Where's your wife?"

With a frown, Two Feathers glanced down at the infant in his arms. "Wife die. Pix not speak of wife again."

"Well dead or not, I refuse to take care of her child or her home. I could not care less about either one."

Pixie knew as soon as the words left her mouth that what she'd said was horrible, and she wanted to take them back. She held her tongue. She wouldn't give the man before her the satisfaction of her regret.

Two Feathers stared at her. He seemed almost in shock at her audacity. Without response, he spun and left his home with his child in his arms. Minutes later, he stalked back in empty-handed.

"Pix not fit woman to care for son. Pix no longer Two Feathers'," he rasped.

"I wasn't yours to begin with," Pixie retorted although her heart hit a scared tempo at his words. Where was she to go?

His action so fast she didn't have time to realize what he was about, Pixie let out a scream when Two Feathers slashed her leg with his knife and mangled the tattoo above her ankle. Just as quickly as he'd taken it out, he put the knife back into its pouch at his side.

"Go."

Stretching out an arm, he pointed a lean finger to his home's exit his face a brutal reflection of anger.

Pixie took a limping step forward. Blood left behind with the halting step taken. Two Feathers watched her in stony silence.

No one looked her way when she emerged from the lodge or as she hobbled to the stream of water beside the encampment. Sitting down on the muddy embankment, Pixie stuck her leg down into the swift current. Her breath hissed inward at the sting of cold water that hit raw, peeled skin. The stream of blood that flowed down over the top of her foot and between her toes slowed. Pixie quietly wept as she surveyed her leg and when the sun dipped and the evening grew late, she wept even more.

In the orange-colored dusk, TJ walked toward her.

"Too Little says you're to come to his home. Two Feathers gave you to him," he stated when he reached her.

So now, she was to be handed from one man to the next?

Unable to keep quiet, Pixie spewed her bitterness. "You should've tried to keep me by your side. You should've said I was your woman. You promised you'd stay with me."

Squatting beside her, TJ frowned. He remained quiet. After a moment, he glanced over his shoulder toward the village and its people. He swiveled back toward Pixie, his gaze direct. "You know as well as I do that it wouldn't have done any good for me to protest his taking you from Too Little's home."

His gaze left hers and he studied the fluid river.

He seemed pensive and his words were low. "Life will be easier for you if you try to fit in, Pixie. Our destiny is here now. There's no going back. You can't recapture what is gone."

"How can you be sure there's no going back?" Pixie retorted. She had come to the same conclusion the night she'd given herself to Two Feathers, but she wasn't about to tell TJ that.

TJ sighed. "I feel it, Pixie, deep inside me. What happened was a split-second freak of nature. We were at the right place at the right time. If it hadn't happened, we'd be dead. You heard the car metal twisting around us. I know you did."

Pixie watched the people of the village going about their daily living. Two Feathers strolled through the settlement, his bearing rigid. He never once glanced her way.

"I can't accept this barbaric life or these people, TJ, and I refuse to."

Rising, TJ looked down at her and his voice was sad. "Then I don't know how to help you."

Chapter Eleven

At his father's summons, Two Feathers walked to his parents' dwelling. He tried to keep his gaze from traveling down to the riverbed to where he knew Pix was. TJ now squatted beside her, talking. At their easy comradery, Two Feathers felt his loneliness. The woman made him realize the emptiness of his life. He had been content and happy with Pretty Flower and she with him, or rather, he'd believed that Pretty Flower was as content and as happy in their marriage as he was. She had never complained, always laughing and smiling, until her pregnancy. Her unexpected action still bewildered and shocked him.

Calling out and getting a response, Two Feathers hunched his shoulders to pass through his parents' doorway. Straightening to his full height upon entering the lodge, his gaze met that of his father. The man who'd given him life raised his hand to beckon him forward. Two Feathers accepted his mother's kiss to his cheek. She patted his cheek afterward, and with a soft smile from her, he proceeded on toward Fawn, who sat at the far end of the family home. Three Feathers played contently at her feet. The others in the lodge remained a respectful distance away, privacy given for this meeting.

Sitting beside his father, Two Feathers waited for the old man to speak. As he waited, he stared into the fire built for the night. A coyote howled in the distance, and Two Feathers wondered if one of the animals who answered was its mate.

"Two Feathers find buffalo?"

Two Feathers nodded at the sharp question.

"Distance from village?" His father, never one to say much or to show affection, poked at the fire with the stick he held. He didn't look up.

"Two suns walk away. Able to bring buffalo close," Two Feathers replied just as briefly.

His father nodded. "It is good. Two Feathers rest then lead people on hunt."

His father's gaze rose to his. "Unknown man and woman brought into village. People say woman wear Two Feathers' mark."

At his father's abrupt change of topic, Two Feathers knew the old man had heard all else that had occurred since his arrival home.

"She is Too Little's now. No longer wear mark."

His father poked at the fire again.

Two Feathers waited.

"Father lose first wife and three children."

Two Feathers noticed his mother stiffen at his father's curt statement and change of topic once again. More and more his father brought up that long ago first family as if none knew the history. Two Feathers always felt sorry for his mother. It seemed she'd had to settle to be second best in his father's life: second wife, second sister, second choice.

His father's gaze swiveled to meet his again. "It said man and woman thrown from heavens."

Two Feathers nodded.

"When return from buffalo hunt, bring to lodge, Father wish to question man and woman. Father has much to think upon."

Two Feathers' mother stared across the space of the lodge from where she sat, her gaze on the man she'd loved all her life. Her husband didn't look her way as he poked at the fire, its flames seeming to captivate him. Two Feathers, he'd forgotten or dismissed. Deciding it was both and rising upward, Two Feathers waved Fawn back when she too started to get to her feet.

Walking to his son, Two Feathers lifted him from the hard-packed dirt floor where he'd fallen and now whimpered. It had been almost a full year since his son's birth, and while he'd been absent hunting the buffalo herd, his son had begun his attempt, as all humans did, to rise up from crawling to walking. The boy kicked his feet out, gurgling, wanting to be put back down.

Leaning over, Two Feathers let the boy's small feet touch the ground while he kept one tiny hand grasped within his to hold him steady. As Two Feathers watched the boy's lurching effort to walk, his chubby, round face serious in his attempt, he marveled at the child's perfection. How had Pretty Flower willingly given this up?

"My son."

Looking up at the quietly, spoken words, Two Feathers met his mother's sad and aged eyes.

"Don't harden heart to those who live," she softly stated.

Reaching out, Two Feathers touched a weathered cheek. He loved and felt sorry for this woman who'd given birth to him.

Chapter Twelve

Pixie squirmed at Brave Bird's narrowed stare. She had tried to start the fire as instructed and hadn't been able to manage even one tiny spark from her efforts. Same as the other times she'd tried. She had returned with TJ the evening before to this woman's home not because she'd wanted to, but that she had nowhere else to turn.

"I've never had to do this type of thing before," Pixie said in defense of herself that early morning at Brave Bird's continued, hard-eyed silence.

Inside the lodge, the other women tittered. They had stopped their work to watch her and Brave Bird.

Brave Bird snatched the stones that Pixie held from her hands. "Pixie lazy woman."

"I am not!"

"Pixie burden to Brave Bird. Brave Bird instruct husband to sell."

Brave Bird motioned to another female who worked on her own tasks on the opposite side of the home. When the woman approached, she handed the stones that she held over to her. "Teach lazy woman how to start fire," she ordered.

Pixie, her embarrassment high, remained silent as Brave Bird stomped away. Squatting beside the woman who now kneeled before the fire pit, Pixie watched as a small flame caught hold and the pile of dried grass and leaves erupted. Standing and smiling at her, the woman handed over the stones and walked away.

Staring at the fire for a moment, Pixie got down on bended knee and slowly began to add the small sticks she'd collected that morning. Earlier, she had sworn that she'd done the very same thing as the woman.

Brave Bird hovered over her once again in critical observation and Pixie cringed. The woman was a tyrant.

Above her, Brave Bird thrust out the large bowl that she held. Pixie stood to stare at its contents. Gutted and cleaned fish filled the hollowed out wood container.

"Cook," Brave Bird ordered, shaking the bowl that she held.

"I don't know how to cook that," Pixie reluctantly admitted meeting her gaze.

"Useless," Brave Bird yelled. She lifted her gaze to the other women in the home, and she welcomed their disgust to mingle with hers. They snickered.

Pixie had never felt so lacking as she did in that moment. Everything she did was wrong.

The woman who'd helped to start the fire ran forward and took the bowl from Brave Bird's hand.

"Little Bird teach," she told Brave Bird.

Brave Bird whirled away, muttering as she went to exit the lodge. Its residents seemed to heave a sigh of relief at her disappearance. The woman beside Pixie handed over the bowl she held, and then bending, lifted the flat stoneware that rested beside the fire pit. She positioned the piece across the fire, and with some maneuvering, it remained propped up out of the flames.

She took the filleted fish out of the bowl Pixie held and laid each piece across the flat stoneware all neat and straight.

Looking up, she smiled at Pixie. "See not hard."

Pixie grimaced, feeling like a fool.

"Sister not bad, Sister, no patience though," the woman stated before she went back to the cooking task.

Inspecting the features of the woman beside her, Pixie could see her resemblance to Brave Bird, although a younger, friendlier version than that of the hateful woman who'd just left the lodge.

"Thank you for helping me. I've never had to do this type of cooking before." Pixie caught back her sob of frustration.

"Where are the men this morning?" she questioned and swallowed back the hard lump in her throat.

"Men meet to talk about buffalo hunt."

Pixie didn't say anything. She didn't care about a buffalo hunt. She had looked for TJ upon waking that morning only to find him already up and gone.

"Pixie and Little Bird go, too," Little Bird continued.

Pixie flopped down beside the woman. "What?"

The woman laughed. "Pixie have funny look. Pixie think Pixie hunt? Pixie not hunt buffalo only men hunt buffalo. Pixie cut up meat and help carry back to village. Good for coming winter."

"I see," Pixie replied although she didn't.

TJ stepped inside the lodge, and Pixie wanted to dash to him. Wrap her arms around him. Hold him close. He was familiar. He was from the future. He was from her world. Her face must have reflected her feelings because he paused in his step, his expression questioning.

Pixie dropped her gaze. Her sudden emotion toward him confused her. Did she love him? He walked on toward Brave Bird who'd just reentered the home, and at his low words to her, she looked in Pixie's direction. Pixie stiffened. TJ handed over what he held and then turned and exited the home.

Brave Bird didn't move—her gaze on the bundle in her hands. Turning, she walked to where Too Little and she had slept the evening before, and she buried what she held in her hands behind a buffalo blanket.

She caught Pixie watching her and yelled out, "Do work, lazy woman!"

Pixie spun toward the friendly woman squatted beside her who supervised the cooking fish. "So you are Brave Bird's sister. I am glad to meet you, Little Bird. You already know my name it seems. Do you have any other family?"

Little Bird nodded toward an older man and woman who ambled out of the lodge. "Little Bird's and Brave Bird's mother and father."

She tilted her head indicating the other side of the room. "Little Bird's son and daughters sitting over there on buffalo blanket."

Pixie looked around the inside of the lodge. "Does your entire family live here with Brave Bird and Too Little and their children?"

Little Bird shook her head in the negative. "Two brothers have own families and own lodges. Little Bird second wife to Too Little."

Pixie hid her horror. "Does Too Little have any other wives besides you and Brave Bird?"

Little Bird laughed. "No, Brave Bird no allow. Little Bird's husband killed in hunt and leave behind three children and Little Bird. Too Little take us in. Little Bird help Brave Bird with work."

The rest of that day, Pixie shadowed Little Bird and learned her duties. Twice, in passing as they gathered wild onions and acorns, Two Feathers glanced Pixie's way. Pixie turned her back to him each time. If he didn't care about her, why should she bother with him?

"Little Bird, I'm exhausted."

At Pixie's heartfelt words, Little Bird laughed. It was a nice sound. Little Bird motioned for her to follow her after they stored what they'd gathered that day, their long day of working finally over. Hiding behind several large bushes by the river, they cleansed themselves, and the cold water of the river was a welcome relief to Pixie's aching muscles. Although chilly at first, the water now felt good and its numbing effect relieved the stinging of the wound above her ankle.

"Brave Bird order Sister work Pixie hard today," Little Bird informed as she and Pixie washed.

Pixie nodded. She had suspected as much. She hadn't slowed down or complained as they worked steadily through the day. She'd been determined that Brave Bird would have no cause to accuse her of being lazy.

"Fawn, welcome," Little Bird called out unexpectedly.

Turning her head to look where Little Bird's attention was diverted, Pixie met Fawn's regard. The woman smiled at her.

Pixie tilted her lips upward and back in response. She felt awkward as she recognized the child she'd refused to hold the evening before that straddled Fawn's hip.

He was a beautiful baby.

Alert and awake now, his gaze met hers as if in inquiry. *As bold and direct as his father*, Pixie thought before lowering her gaze to glide her hands through the water that flowed around her. She listened as Little Bird and Fawn conversed. The child kicked out his feet wanting to be put down, and distracted, Fawn sat the boy to the ground. He dashed off at once, escaping her reach.

Pixie lunged when he hit the water going head first under the fast moving current. He chortled when she jerked him upward. Her heartbeat slowed. It was obvious the child thought they played a game. Lowering the boy back into the water, he squealed in delight when Pixie swung him back up.

He slapped at the liquid around him.

Pixie laughed in response, his antics drenching her face.

"Fawn bring Pixie clothes," Fawn informed.

Looking up, Pixie stopped their play.

Fawn unfolded what she held revealing a dress and a pair of moccasins.

"Thank you," Pixie stammered in confusion. *Had Two Feathers sent the items*, she wondered in surprise.

The clothes she wore were rags now and out of place in this community. Maybe he had noticed. She had worried what she would do when they completely disintegrated from her person.

"Crow ask Fawn to bring," Fawn clarified.

"Oh." In shock, Pixie stepped completely from the water. Her shirt and shorts sagged with the water that they held. She was too afraid to undress in the daylight and out in the open, so she washed herself and her clothes at the same time. Who knew who could be watching?

Little Bird displayed no such qualms. Even now, she rose effortlessly from the water and began to dress, no looking about to see if anyone peeped from a distance.

The baby that Pixie held slapped at her face and walking forward, Pixie handed him back over to his aunt. He gurgled happily.

Fawn kissed his round cheek. "Fawn go," his aunt stated sitting the child onto the curve of her hip before she turned.

"Crow must like, give Pixie gift," Little Bird commented into the silence after Fawn's departure.

"How would Crow have a woman's garments to offer to me? I thought that he was single?" Pixie frowned and looked over the garments that she held.

Little Bird swung lengthy black hair over her shoulder to wring the water from the dark strands. Bending down, she slipped on her moccasins before she glanced back up at Pixie.

"Crow have wife and child. Wife leave and take child. Go back to family. Leave clothes behind. Take only what wear."

"Is that allowed? To leave a husband I mean."

Little Bird shrugged a shoulder. "If family agree."

Pixie smoothed a hand down over the dress. It was supple, soft to the touch. "What is this made from?"

"Deerskin."

Slipping the unexpected gift over her head and then down over her shoulders and hips, Pixie worked to pull her top through the sleeve of the dress. Next, she discarded her ragged shorts.

It felt good to be shed of the ratty clothing.

The dress was soft against her bare skin, its hem hitting at her knees. The moccasins were a little big, but better than the sandals she had been wearing.

"We go home," Little Bird instructed, giving her a warm smile. Her eyes danced in amusement at Pixie's obvious pleasure.

"I want to thank Crow for his gifts. I won't be long," Pixie, stated noting that Crow stood alone alongside a lodge as she and Little Bird walked back through the village toward home.

Giving a nod of consent, Little Bird continued walking.

"Is this your lodge?"

Crow tilted his head.

Lifting a foot, Pixie signified the moccasins that she wore. "Thank you for these. I love them and the dress."

Crow smiled, and as he did, his gaze lifted to something past Pixie's shoulder. Turning, Pixie met Two Feathers' direct gaze. He looked through her, passing her in silence.

"Pixie's leg, it heals?"

Turning to face Crow again, Pixie nodded. The whole village knew of Two Feathers cutting away her tattoo, removing his ownership of her and transferring it to Too Little.

"I…I have to go."

"Crow and Pixie see each other with rising new sun?"

In surprise at Crow's request, Pixie agreed. Crow beamed, his straight, white teeth revealed.

Chapter Thirteen

Two Feathers couldn't prevent his awareness of the woman as he passed her. He had known the entire day where she was and with whom, his attention drawn to wherever she happened to be. The dress she wore wasn't the one he'd sent to Brave Bird for her. It was too big. She was of the same build as Pretty Flower and what she wore hung loose on her. He hadn't thought to give her shoes, but it seemed that Crow had.

The lure the female had on him would not win its battle, he'd decided. He had made a promise to Pretty Flower upon her death and he meant to keep it. It was the least he could do. He missed Pretty Flower and thought of her daily. What she had done, he still couldn't understand. Stepping into his lodge, Two Feathers slung his bow and arrows onto the platform that held his sleeping blankets and other daily items.

Fawn looked up in startled surprise, his child in her arms. Walking forward, Two Feathers lifted the boy from her hold.

"My son, he is good today?"

"Brother's son is well."

Two Feathers stuck his finger into the child's mouth feeling around at his gums. "Ah...two more," he muttered.

His son chomped down using those new teeth and Fawn laughed. With a grimace, Two Feathers pried his finger from the child's mouth.

"Brother should know better," Fawn stated, giving a shake of her head.

Looking at the tiny teeth marks left behind on his finger, Two Feathers smiled. "Son fierce, it is good."

"Your woman, she play and laugh with Three Feathers today."

Two Feathers met his sister's direct stare. "Woman not mine," he replied.

"Fawn like Two Feathers' woman as does Two Feathers' son," Fawn continued as if she hadn't heard him.

Before Two Feathers could snap out a rebuttal, Fawn stepped from his home. Two Feathers looked down at his child that he held.

"Three Feathers like woman?"

His son gurgled as if in agreement before he pointed to the floor of the home. "Down," he stated with authority.

With a laugh, Two Feathers lowered the boy to the packed dirt floor. On unsteady feet, the child darted here and there, falling often, but always getting up to try again. It was good, his determination.

****

The next day, occupied with getting ready for the buffalo hunt, Two Feathers didn't see much of Pixie, although he couldn't keep the thought of her from filtering through his meditations.

The entire village bustled with activity. All were excited for the upcoming quest.

Two Feathers could feel the tension building within him also. It always did with a hunt. Not everyone would take the journey. His mother and father and the other elders would stay behind with the children and mothers of infants. It was good this coming chase. They would have meat for winter, blankets to trade, bones for weapons, cooking utensils for the women, and many, many other things. He needed new bowstrings himself.

"Crow ready for journey. Kill many buffalo this hunt." Crow

stopped before him.

Two Feathers sharpening an arrowhead squinted up into the sun from where he sat beside his home to look at him. Not responding, he blew on the tip of the arrowhead that he held. His bow and arrows for the buffalo hunt were different from what he kept stored for other hunts.

"Yes, we bring back much needed requirements," he finally replied.

Crow squatted beside him and watched as he worked.

"Brave Bird talk to Crow this morning. Brave Bird not care for Two Feathers' woman. Ask Crow trade for woman."

Two Feathers tensed but kept his eyes on his task.

"Too Little state price," he questioned after a moment.

"Crow not speak with Too Little only Brave Bird. Price for woman not be much. Brave Bird say woman lazy."

For some reason, anger flared within Two Feathers. He knew Pix wasn't lazy. Ignorant of their ways? She was. Lazy? No.

Brave Bird was the lazy one and intolerable to be around as far as he was concerned. She and Pix more than likely clashed. He hoped that Pix held her ground with the loud and abrasive woman. Too Little let his wife rule his household with a ruthless hand. Maybe that was why he'd given Pix to him. Deep down, he'd known that Too Little wouldn't make advances toward her. He wouldn't dare. Brave Bird would screech loud and fierce, and all in the household would experience her wrath, making it an unhappy household for everyone.

Two Feathers shook off his thoughts. He had no wish to examine why it was he didn't want others to know Pix as he did and he especially didn't want Crow to know her as he had.

He looked at his blood brother. "Woman not lazy, but Two Feathers not believe make good buy for Crow."

Crow's gaze was steady on his. "Two Feathers say woman no longer his, maybe Crow make wife instead of slave."

Two Feathers kept his face impassive.

Rising from his squatting position from beside him, Crow stared down at him.

"If Two Feathers desire woman, why give woman away?"

Two Feathers' fingers tightened around the arrowhead tip that he held. "Trade for woman if want. Two Feathers has no need of her."

With a snort, Crow strutted away.

Two Feathers watched as he and Pix spoke to each other in passing. Crow laughed at whatever it was that she said to him and Two Feathers felt his jealousy rise.

Chapter Fourteen

Turning onto her side, Pixie stared at the wall of the lodge she slept beside every night. She was exhausted and still wide awake. The animal hide that she lay on itched no matter which way she turned. It wasn't buffalo, but something else. Her palms were covered with blisters, and her feet and back so sore that every step, every move that she took, she felt stabbing pain. Sighing, Pixie changed position again, and with a soft moan of pain given, she reclosed her eyes seeking that elusive rest.

Someone coughed in the night.

TJ had shown no patience when she'd tried to talk to him about all that was required of her. She knew there was nothing he could do about it. She had just wanted a sympathetic ear. She had stayed close to his side that evening, and it seemed her action irritated him, as had her complaints. Sound filtered across the home as someone snored and another whispered in the dark. *The whisper is probably Brave Bird telling Too Little how useless I am*, Pixie thought in resentment.

She had watched for Two Feathers that day, searched for him in fact. Why she felt the loss of his person, Pixie didn't understand. The only ones who seemed even to appreciate her company were Little Bird and Crow.

She should be thankful for Crow's sudden attention. He seemed to go out of his way now to be kind to her. When he'd brought her a drink of water as she worked that day, it had surprised her. Even

Little Bird's eyebrows had shot up, but she didn't speak upon it and just watched him. Squeezing her eyelids tighter together, Pixie tried to court sleep again. She sighed a moment later. Counting numbers hadn't helped. Nothing helped. Tomorrow, another journey began, and she dreaded it.

Startled awake at a kick to her back, Pixie jerked upward into a sitting position. She had slept after all. It was morning and time to rise. Stumbling upward, she fought the urge to strike out at Brave Bird. She would love to claw the woman's eyes out for her meanness. Her punishment would be severe if she tried she was sure.

"Be quick, and help Little Bird, lazy woman. We must be on way. Eat and sleep in my home, think don't have to work? Get!"

Hurrying from the enclosure, Pixie noted Little Bird standing beside the lodge and rushed toward her. "I'm sorry, Little Bird. I didn't hear movement so I didn't waken."

Pixie ran her fingers through her hair, trying for some sort of dignity. She must look a fright. Little Bird smiled at her, always pleasant, always easy going, and even in the early morning hours. She was the exact opposite of her sister.

"Little Bird let Pixie sleep in. Little Bird know Pixie tired. Pixie go wash face, take care of needs. Little Bird wait. Leave soon so must hurry."

Pixie nodded as she looked around. It seemed that everyone but her was ready to leave and the sun hadn't even fully risen. Its rays barely peeked over the horizon.

Striding away from the others to hide behind several large bushes on the outskirts of the village, Pixie took care of her morning needs. Afterward, she washed her hands and face in the river, and then smoothed her wayward hair back from her face, running her fingers through the damp strands. Two Feathers' sister, Fawn, stood along beside Little Bird when she returned.

"We go," Little Bird stated. She stretched her hand out for Pixie to take the two strips of dried meat that she held.

Pixie closed her fingers around the food, and bent and picked up the pack indicated she was required to carry. Hitching the bundle high onto her back, she followed Fawn and Little Bird from the village. The two women chattered about the hunt and the excitement they felt as they all walked.

Remaining silent, Pixie worked the tough breakfast meat around in her mouth softening it with her saliva. She found herself searching for Two Feathers within the crowd just as she had searched for him within the settlement the day before. He must've gone ahead as Little Bird had stated he would probably do.

TJ, Pixie noted, strolled along beside Too Little, the two talking nonstop as always. Brave Bird walked on her husband's other side and stayed there as the day proceeded. Crow, it seemed, led the group. He glanced toward her when he passed at his call for the assembly to halt and rest and he flashed a smile at her.

Pixie didn't understand what she felt for him as she tilted her mouth up in response. He didn't seem such a bad person now. Her earlier perception of the man must've been wrong.

He was a better man than Two Feathers, she'd decided. Two Feathers had used her. There was no other word for it. Used and discarded once his sexual need had abated.

Pixie didn't know when she had begun to count her steps that evening on their second day of walking, but she had and now she'd lost her count. The snake that slithered in front of her had made her lose her concentration. Looking up, Pixie surveyed her surroundings.

They should be stopping soon as it grew dark. The second day had certainly been the most strenuous of all. Pixie's gaze collided with Two Feathers' when he strode toward her, emerging from the group ahead that had split from the one that she walked with. It was the first sight of him Pixie had had since their leaving the village. Her pulse leaped when his gaze moved over her.

Lifting her hand, Pixie ran her fingers through her hair to shove the wayward strands back from her face. What did she look like? She had no mirror and no makeup. Two Feathers scrutinized her actions before he turned to speak to his sister.

All around them, the others halted waiting and watching.

Fawn nodded at whatever he said, and Two Feathers walked away, no glance given in Pixie's direction again. Forcing the rejection away that she felt, Pixie watched his disappearing form. It was obvious he didn't care a fig for her. Anger boiled up inside her. Well, bully for him. She returned the emotion.

Fawn moved to where she and Little Bird stood.

"Group make camp here. Brother locate buffalo. Brother say remain quiet, no loud noise, no laughter."

Fawn let the bundle that she carried on her back slide to the ground from its resting place between her shoulder blades. Little Bird and Pixie copied her movement. Select groups around them began to settle as word of the located bison spread. Everyone talked in hushed whispers.

Pixie noticed the men assemble as she sank to the ground beside the bundle she'd dropped. Laying her head on it, she closed her eyes. She was so weary. Why, oh why, were her prayers for rescue from the tornado answered in this way? When she had prayed, she'd prayed for saving in her world, not to be taken from it. She missed her parents and Lynn and all the comforts of the modern world. Everything she had taken for granted, gone in an instant. A thought flashed through Pixie's mind that seemed concrete, valid. *Concentrate on everyone left behind and all will revert to normal.*

Keeping her eyes closed, Pixie focused, and the images of her parents rushed in, their laughter, their anger for her careless attitude toward her life goals, her drinking, her partying. The home she knew from birth she saw as it was the last day she was there. She saw Lynn doubled over with laughter, while at the same time she expressed sympathy, when Pixie tripped and fell on the pavement in front of the handsome cowboy decked out in Western wear. He was so gorgeous that they'd both stared, unable to take their eyes off him and she had done the unthinkable. Sprawled, red faced and on her knees in front of him. He had tipped his Stetson hat at them as he strolled past as if he hadn't seen her embarrassing fall.

Fawn and Little Bird's low conversation intruded. It pulled Pixie back into the world she wished to leave.

Just say, 'All Is Well' three times and everything will be as it was. Pixie realized her thought process was off kilter. She would try what her mind hinted at anyway. Anything was worth a go as far as she was concerned. She wanted gone from this place.

"All Is Well…All Is Well…All Is Well." Opening her eyes, Pixie's disappointment flooded through her. Its sharp knife more than she could bear and she cried out with the pain. Little Bird and Fawn stared at her, their confusion apparent. Embarrassed, Pixie sat up. She didn't try to explain her actions. What could she say to them anyway? How could she explain something that wasn't and wouldn't be for a long time? If ever? Who knew what time world she was in anyway?

Little Bird and Fawn sat down on each side of her.

Quietly, Fawn dug into her bundle to withdraw strips of dried meat from it. She handed several over to Little Bird and then to Pixie, keeping two strips for her own.

"We eat then sleep," she stated as she took a delicate bite from the piece that she held, her gaze assessing Pixie. "New sun bring busy, tiring work."

Pixie shivered with dread for the upcoming event. She hadn't asked any questions. She didn't want to know what the hunt entailed.

Crow walked in their direction, his stride bold and his gaze for her alone. Silently, Little Bird rose to sit on the other side of Fawn leaving Pixie's left side open. He squatted beside Pixie. Fawn passed a handful of the dried meat she'd packed indicating that Pixie was to give them to Crow. Pixie handed the strips over, and Crow's fingers brushed against hers as he took what she held. He took a bite of the dried meat, his teeth strong, ripping the strip in half. He chewed and then swallowed.

"Crow kill many buffalo. Have blanket made for Pixie," he stated.

Pixie met his gaze. He seemed kind now where before it seemed he radiated cruelty.

"Thank you. I could use a blanket," she replied.

With a nod, he stood and walked away. Pixie turned toward Fawn and Little Bird. Both stared at her, neither saying a word.

She frowned. "What's wrong?"

"Pixie want Crow's ownership?" Little Bird asked.

"What? No."

"Pixie agree to it," Little Bird responded.

"I did not."

Little Bird and Fawn nodded. "Yes, Pixie did," they stated in unison.

Looking to where Crow now stood speaking with Two Feathers, Pixie wondered how she had agreed to become his possession. Crow and Two Feathers looked out toward the horizon as they spoke. Two Feathers put a hand on Crow's shoulder. It was obvious the two were close companions.

"Maybe Crow make Pixie wife, not slave," Little Bird stated into the silence. "Crow care to let Pixie know what Crow wish, it good sign."

Pixie didn't respond. Slave or wife, wouldn't it be the same? It would be good to be away from Brave Bird.

Silently, Fawn rose and walked away. Pixie wondered if she had feelings for Crow. She hoped not. She liked Two Feathers' sister.

****

The capture was on—the sun barely up—and early morning dew still glistened on the grass. A silent scream rose within Pixie at the scene unfolding below her that morning. The sound of hooves that slapped against the earth matched her heartbeat as she watched the action from where she and the others waited. All gazes riveted on the woman who now sprinted with all out speed toward safety. No current day runner within Pixie's time would have been able to outrun her. Fawn, a buffalo blanket flapping over her head, raced along the floor of the canyon. The canyon was a natural-made corral for the bison that pounded behind her, the same canyon where Pixie and the others stood along its ridge, watching, and out of the way of the raging surge. In silent anticipation, the men stood ready, muscles bulging with arrows drawn and bowstrings pulled tight. Fawn, seconds before trampled by the herd, disappeared through the small opening at the end of the canyon. The buffalo blanket dropped to the ground behind her during her escape.

Pixie exhaled her pent up breath and then breathed in deep. Her muscles quivered. She had known that the opening for Fawn was there—the canyon's entirety scouted out earlier—but she hadn't believed Fawn would make it in time.

The first arrival bison were bewildered as they circled the canyon as other bison crowded in behind them. Dust and confusion surrounded the animals as they leaped and whirled, wanting out of their natural made cage. The echo of their bellows ascended the canyon walls. Arrows whistled through the air, the projectiles going deep. Pixie saw Two Feathers and Crow—the ones who'd begun the stampede—leap up onto the opposite side of the canyon wall from where she and the others stood, seeming to float up its edge when several of the enormous beasts found their way out. Their released arrows sliced through the air toward the beasts that pounded past them and two fell with their front legs folding beneath them. Before long, all noise quieted and some twenty bison lay dead or dying, the survivors gone as dust flew out from under their hooves at their departure.

The men and women around Pixie swarmed down the canyon wall.

Pixie couldn't move. Sinking to the ground, she watched as Two Feathers hugged his returning sister. Fawn laughed and pointed up to where she sat, causing Two Feathers to look her way. Fawn said something to him, and he turned to bound up the canyon wall.

"Sister hear Pix scream. Wish Pix know Fawn okay."

Pixie put a hand to her brow and found it was wet. She had thought her scream soundless. She didn't rise to her feet. She didn't think that she could.

"How could you put your sister's life in danger like that? You're an uncaring monster to make her run before those beasts!"

Two Feathers reared back as if insulted. "Two Feathers not make Sister run. Sister want honor. Without buffalo tribe starve."

Pixie jumped to her feet. "I hate you and I hate your stupid ways!"

Brave Bird motioned up toward her.

"Woman, hurry, come down here!" she yelled out.

Pixie lurched her way.

"Get in line and do work," she ordered when Pixie reached her. She yanked on her arm to shove her in line beside Little Bird.

"Show lazy woman what to do," Brave Bird ordered before she stomped away. She screeched at someone else a moment later.

Two Feathers passed by his gaze direct and anger-filled.

Pixie ducked her head, embarrassed at her outburst. She knew in her heart that he cared for Fawn and wouldn't have willingly put his sister's life in danger.

"We cut up meat and hang to dry," Little Bird stated from beside her. Pixie nodded as she watched Little Bird's actions. Across the canyon floor, Two Feathers and Crow bent to the task of skinning the bison that lay before them. For a moment, Pixie wondered if she'd gone insane and didn't know it. The world she had been born into seemed surreal, and this one, this one no longer history and something to read about; it had become something she lived, something she suffered. Women lined up alongside of her and Little Bird and all spread out in an assembly line working hard to process the kill the men brought to them.

Fawn hurried up to where Pixie worked, all smiles.

"Brother kill six, Crow only three."

Pixie sliced the meat handed to her as Little Bird had demonstrated. Turning, she hung the long strips over the erected structure beside her. She didn't comment, but she felt proud of Two Feathers, and her gaze slide to where he worked. Her emotion surprised her, and in truth, it angered her. Why should she be proud of him?

Fawn stepped up to labor along beside her. "Brother good provider. Good father," she continued.

Pixie looked sideways at Two Feathers' sister while her hands stayed busy at the task before her. Was Fawn building her brother up for her sake? There was no need. Two Feathers had no care for her so it didn't matter how she felt about him.

Chapter Fifteen

Two Feathers listened without comment as Crow declared his plans to take Pix as wife. It seemed his lifelong friend took delight in detailing to him how the woman had eagerly agreed to his offer. Two Feathers hated the resulting thought that crossed his mind. It was as if Crow expected and even wanted anger from him. The woman kept him angered enough. He didn't want to feel the same emotion toward his blood brother. Two Feathers watched as Crow looked up from his task to search for the woman. Two Feathers knew exactly where she was. Bending back to focus on his work, Two Feathers decided it was his own disquiet over the woman that caused his thought to cross that Crow was more interested in his reaction to his news than that of actually taking Pix for wife. He and Crow were blood brothers, lifelong friends. He would not begrudge his blood brother for wanting a woman he'd discarded. The woman had slaked a need in a moment of weakness, and if Crow, instinctively knowing what happened that night between him and the woman wanted her still, he was welcome to her. He'd had a wife and loved her still. He didn't want another.

With deliberate movement, Two Feathers arched his wrist to slice at the carcass before him. He tuned out Crow's ongoing monologue. Hearing Brave Bird's sudden, shrill yell, he looked up.

Brave Bird bore down on Pix, her intent obvious. Straightening, Two Feathers winced when Brave Bird slapped Pix and she stumbled backward.

Little Bird jumped between her and her irate sister.

Crow stopped his own work to watch the dispute.

"Woman gaze at Crow with much favor if Crow come to her rescue," Two Feathers drawled. He felt unease that it was he who'd put Pix under Brave Bird's hands.

"Brave Bird keep woman working. Woman must have ceased," Crow responded, unconcern reflected.

His jaw tightening, Two Feathers slung down his knife. "None will get any work done watching this spectacle."

Crow's gaze sharpened. He didn't move. Two Feathers moved forward.

"Stop that noise!" Brave Bird turned at Two Feathers' yell, her hand still raised in the air for a second slap to be delivered. Two Feathers had a strong desire to dish out to her the same treatment she'd given Pix.

"None will get any work done with this entertainment. Go to husband's side, Brave Bird, and stay there. Little Bird will deal with the woman."

Brave Bird sputtered as her hand fell to her side.

Two Feathers slung his in the direction where Brave Bird's husband, Too Little, stood. He'd had enough of Brave Bird's meanness and wouldn't tolerant more dished out.

"We've much to do and Two Feathers tire of this delay. Go," he ordered, his voice harsh letting her know to give him no argument. He could tell it shocked Brave Bird, his involvement in their women's quarrel. He didn't understand it himself. At her prompt leaving, Two Feathers swiveled toward Pix. Her face still wore the imprint of Brave Bird's hand.

"Pix obey all Little Bird's direction. If Two Feathers see woman slacking, Two Feathers deliver punishment."

"But...I...."

"Pix cause enough delay. Get back to duties," Two Feathers interjected. He watched Pix stiffen her shoulders, as she returned to the task Brave Bird had interrupted.

If looks could kill, he'd be dead.

Little Bird spun beside her, turning from him, her posture as rigid as Pix's. Two Feathers knew she was indignant over Brave Bird's and his treatment of Pixie. Little Bird was a soft-spoken woman and kind to all. Whirling, Two Feathers stomped back to where Crow had stood and watched.

"Crow never known Blood Brother to become involved in women's disputes," he drawled and a sneer pulled across his face.

"Two Feathers want labor done. Want to return to son," Two Feathers snapped back. He bent to his task and ignored his blood brother. Crow remained upright and silent, as he studied him. After a moment, he focused on his work also.

****

That evening at dusk, everyone sat around their fires with full bellies. Two Feathers found himself scanning the crowd for the woman. He would have denied it if anyone had asked him. He was curious if she and Crow were together this night. He didn't understand his fascination with the woman, and his agitation grew as he thought of Crow desiring Pix as wife.

Rising, Two Feathers left the group of men who sat around the evening fire alongside him. Strolling through his father's people, he stopped to converse now and then before moving on. *Yes, it was a good kill. Yes, winter would be easy, no empty stomachs. No his father hadn't called a meeting with the Council.*

Winding through the people, Two Feathers observed Crow sitting and talking with several men, his hands expressive as he spoke. One of the men laughed at whatever it was that he said.

Pix didn't sit beside him and Two Feathers kept walking. He nodded at the people as he passed them but didn't stop to converse with anyone. He needed, no wanted, to see Pix. It had haunted him all day that she was so upset with him. Fawn noticed him walking through the crowd and tilted her head toward the waterfall that trickled from the wall of the canyon at the canyon's end. Two Feathers began to drift in the direction of the life-giving water. Did his sister know what he was about, his interest in the woman?

Fawn turned back to preparing her sleeping pallet, dismissing him. Two Feathers passed Little Bird. She didn't speak to him and he remained silent as well. The night grew quieter as the distance from the people widened. He drew close to the natural waterfall and could hear its cascading water. He had cleansed his body under it earlier as had the rest of the group. Stepping soundlessly forward, he focused on Pix when she came within his line of vision. Furiously she scrubbed at her head as if she couldn't get it clean, the water that she stood under spilling over her.

Suddenly, she withdrew from the waterfall to climb up and sit on a nearby rock, and she began to sob. She wrapped her arms around her legs as she rocked. She had been an average-sized woman that day she'd landed at his feet those many suns ago. This night however, she was no longer curved in build but gaunt. Had Brave Bird been stingy with food? There was no need. There had been plenty.

Abruptly, she lunged to her feet to look up to where he stood. He must've made a noise. She scaled toward her dress and moccasins. Quickly, Two Feathers stepped sideways, halting her escape and he picked up the garment and shoes that lay at his feet. He held them in his hands.

Pix stood suspended in her flight.

"Little Bird told me that no one would come down here this late." Her tone was accusatory.

Two Feathers pitched the garment that he held toward her. Catching it, she wrenched it down over her head, the material slipping past narrow hips to cover her nakedness. She didn't move afterward and just watched him. Wary it seemed.

"Why are you here?" she finally asked when he didn't say anything.

Two Feathers shifted his feet. "Walking." He pitched her moccasins to her.

Catching the shoes, she snapped, "Don't let me stop you then." She made a move to go around him. Two Feathers reached out, his fingers closing around a wrist as he halted her movement.

"Crow say Pix agree to become wife to him." Two Feathers could have bit his tongue off after his statement. Straining against his hold, she frowned. She didn't deny his statement.

"What do you care?" she asked after a moment.

Two Feathers stepped closer.

"Crow no patience with women."

"Let go of my wrist."

Ignoring the command, Two Feathers tightened his hold, and he took another step toward her. He didn't desire this woman for wife, yet it pained him that she wished to be Crow's. He didn't want his blood brother to know Pix as he did. He didn't want Crow to know her that way *at all.*

"Why Pix cry?"

She stiffened and pulled on her wrist again. Two Feathers held tight.

"Answer Two Feathers. Why Pix cry?" he demanded.

Her anger, a vibrant thing, engulfed him. He felt its heat.

"I hate this life! I wish that I was dead."

With shock, Two Feathers dropped his hand from her wrist. The thought of her demise brought an aching hurt.

"Pix should not chase death," he scolded.

She smacked his chest with a fist and in surprise, Two Feathers didn't move. She hit him again.

"You know nothing," she cried out. "Nothing!"

Catching her flailing fists, Two Feathers pulled her to him. He held her tight against him. She resisted. He held her tighter.

"Two Feathers would not want your death," he countered. His breath caught in his throat. He could barely speak. He had lost Pretty Flower by her own hand and the image of finding Pix in a similar state left him shuddering. Before he could stop himself, Two Feathers reached to smooth her wet hair back from her face. The wayward tresses were soft and silky to the touch, longer than before. Soon she'd be able to braid the thick strands. Lifting her face upward toward his, he searched her gaze. She became still and unmoving. He moved his thumb across her bottom lip and then watched as her eyelids lowered.

"Two Feathers not wish for your death," he stated again. It hurt in his chest that she sought it. Her arms snaked to clasp about his waist and she leaned into him.

"Pixie? Pixie?"

Two Feathers reeled backward. For a moment, he'd thought that he'd cried Pix's name aloud. Little Bird walked forward as she called out Pixie's name again, and her gaze darted between them when she approached.

"Pixie, Little Bird have worry when no show to sleeping pallet. Crow ask Little Bird where Pixie and waits for return," she stated.

"I was on my way back. Two Feathers just happened to walk by," Pix replied. Her gaze questioned Two Feathers as she looked up at him. It seemed that she wanted him to tell her to stay. His facial muscles frozen, Two Feathers didn't react. He should have never sought her out. She was Crow's woman now.

Little Bird looked at him curiously then turned toward Pix. "Pixie stay?"

Pix stared at him.

At his continued silence, her gaze dropped. "No, I return with you," she replied.

****

Stumbling behind Little Bird as Little Bird turned to walk the beaten path back toward the campsite, Pixie wondered why Two Feathers had bothered to seek her out. He hadn't admitted to it. She knew though that he had. She had wanted him to demand that she stay with him. It offended and hurt her when he'd remained silent. When she had first felt a presence and looked up, she'd believed that it was Crow who stood before her. The thought had frightened her. Why it should, she didn't understand. Crow had displayed only kindness since he'd given his ex-wife's clothes to her, and it seemed he believed that she had agreed to become his wife. She would go along with it. What did she have to lose? *Brave Bird's brutality for one*, Pixie thought with a grimace. Maybe with the marriage, she'd have someone who cared for her.

Crow waited for her just as Little Bird had said he did. Little Bird walked on as Pixie stopped before him.

"Where Little Bird find Pixie?" he questioned and his gaze traveled behind Pixie to the footpath she'd just walked up.

"I was covered in blood and wanted to bathe alone. So I waited for the others to finish before I went down to the water."

Crow's gaze moved over her, and Pixie braced herself as nervous energy rose. For a moment, she glimpsed the man whom she'd first met, his gaze threatening and unfriendly. All of a sudden, a slow smile spread across his face and Pixie's unease faded. She felt ashamed. Her edginess was guilt at desiring Two Feathers and not the man who stood before her, a man who wished her for his wife.

"Pixie rest," Crow stated before he turned away. He didn't reach out for her. It was as if he'd already forgotten her as he strolled across the camp area to where a group of men sat. Crouching amongst them, he began to chat with them. He didn't look back at her. One of the men jumped up and made exaggerated moves of shooting a bow and arrow. The group laughed when Crow whooped.

Little Bird shook her head at Pixie as Pixie walked up to her.

"Men, they brag on the hunt. It is always so," she stated.

Pixie didn't respond as she stretched to lie on the animal hide they'd earlier spread out on the ground. Tomorrow would be another exhausting day and she was dog-tired. Little Bird stepped forward to lie down along beside her. It seemed she was fatigued also, her light snore immediately heard. Sighing, Pixie turned so that her back was to her. She had seen and spoken to TJ only once that day. He seemed to thrive in the harsh environment. The scar on his cheek prominent, and in a way, it added to his stature. Pixie closed her eyes in slumber. Two Feathers flitted in and out of her dreams and always beyond reach.

****

Fourteen days more they worked on the slaughtered bison, slicing its meat, laying the pieces out to dry, scraping hides, and gathering and cleaning bones.

Pixie struggled that sixteenth morning to stand fully erect as she looked around at the group of people who had worked so hard. She ached all over. She looked down at her hands. Even her pinkie fingers hurt. Flexing her fingers, Pixie studied them. With the buffalo processed and the cargo loaded, it was time to begin their trip back to the settlement. Giving a heartfelt sigh, Pixie leaned down to pick up the large pack she was required to carry. She had felt sick that morning, unable to keep any food down. Brave Bird smacked her on the back as she'd passed while she vomited her morning meal. She accused her of pretending sickness.

Heaving their bulky cargo onto their shoulders from where they stood beside her, Little Bird and Fawn took off walking. Pixie silently trailed behind them. She was scared that she knew why she'd been ill. It was unthinkable and unwanted. Two Feathers walked past, his shoulders heavy with the burden strapped over his back. Their gazes glanced off each other. Others around them had piled their heavy cargo onto constructed dragging platforms.

TJ called them *Travois* although no animals powered them, only human determination.

Three full days they walked.

At the sight of the village on that third evening, Pixie almost crumpled to the ground to sob out her relief. The older men, women, and young children who'd stayed behind set up a wail at their spotting them. Children ran forward, their cries of welcome ringing through the air. A feast was quickly prepared, and as the ebbing daylight blanketed the village, laughter rang and the beat of drums sounded.

Everyone seemed to be energy-filled with the return home.

Sitting beside Fawn and Little Bird that night, Pixie fought to keep her eyes open as the night's festivities wore on. In a stupor, she watched TJ, Two Feathers, Crow, and several other men participate in a competition of throwing a smoothly rubbed pole, suspected from a result of years of use, toward a round wheel-like object. The one who got the pole within the target or closest to the target won each round. Yawning behind her hand again, Pixie missed seeing Crow's winning throw. The crowd responded. Some groaned with disappointment, while others yelped in approval, the latest played round making Crow the overall winner for the night. Jubilant in his victory, he laughed loud and cut his gaze her way as Two Feathers slapped him on his back in congratulations of the win. Pixie thought Crow seemed overly smug. By her calculations, he'd won by a hair's breadth over Two Feathers. The two men remained standing close and talking together even as the others dispersed from around them.

Oh, thank goodness, Pixie thought when some of the women who'd been spectators began to extinguish the fires that lit up the long pathway of the game. Stumbling upward, she stood quietly beside Fawn and Little Bird who'd risen to their feet also.

TJ strolled forward, his profile hazy within the sudden dimness.

With surprise, Pixie listened, her eyesight adjusting to the darkness as he asked Fawn if he could walk her home. Fawn agreed to his request and they strolled away.

Little Bird turned toward Pixie, and her features showed her exhaustion. "We allowed rest and sleep late. We not have to rise with new sun. Old mothers who stayed behind take care of families for us."

Raising her hand, Pixie hid another wide yawn. She would have no problem sleeping all the next day, maybe several days if allowed.

"We go?" Little Bird questioned her.

Pixie nodded in agreement, ready to call it a night. Crow appeared from the darkness and she sighed. She had no wish to converse with the man even though somehow she had agreed to be his wife. His arrogant attitude grated on her as tired as she was.

"Crow walk Pixie to lodge," he stated when he stepped up alongside her and Little Bird. Little Bird turned to look toward him, her face solemn. He frowned. "Crow need no approval from Little Bird."

"I wish to walk with Crow," Pixie interjected. She just wanted sleep. Crow preened at her stated preference for his company.

"Little Bird inform Sister Pixie with Crow. Keep trouble away for Pixie," Little Bird stated before she pivoted to walk away.

Pixie barely heard her as Two Feathers walked up to where she and Crow stood. He carried the game pieces under his arm. Why did he capture all her thoughts when he'd made it plain that he didn't want or even care for her? Pixie felt the urge to cry.

Two Feathers halted before them. Uncomfortable with her thoughts, Pixie shifted her feet lowering her gaze when he glanced her way. Crow stood too close to her. He smothered her with his nearness. Pixie wanted to slide away from him. She didn't.

"Good challenge this night," Crow stated.

Two Feathers tilted his head in agreement. "Crow won fair."

He looked like he wanted to say something else. Instead, he turned and walked on.

"Best warrior won, Blood Brother."

In surprise, Pixie glanced upward. Crow's quietly drawn out words seemed cloaked in resentment. In puzzlement, Pixie searched Crow's features. An undercurrent of hostility seeped from him. He appeared to have forgotten she was by his side as he stepped forward before he paused and turned back toward her.

Chapter Sixteen

Stretching her legs out to their full length, Pixie turned from her side to lie on her back. Unmoving, she gazed up at the ceiling of the lodge that was her home until she and Crow married.

Turning her head, she looked across the space of the dim interior of the home. Just as Little Bird had said, all who had went on the hunt rested that morning. She seemed to be the only one in the lodge awake. It surprised that she had woken so soon. She'd believed that she could sleep forever if allowed.

Sitting up, Pixie eased to her feet and then slipped on her shoes. Stepping lightly, and carefully, around the sprawled and unconscious forms scattered throughout on the floor of the home, she strolled from its enclosure.

Lifting her hand to her forehead, Pixie shaded her eyes from the glare of the morning sun. Standing at the lodge's entryway, she glanced around. The village was quiet and empty. Turning, Pixie took off toward the river, her steps hurried. With so many sleeping in, she could enjoy a bath with little fear of passersby, a luxury hard to come by with all the people always around.

Hiding behind bushes that grew along the riverbank, Pixie yanked her dress up and over her head to sling it aside. Hopping on one leg and then the other, she untied her moccasins and kicked them off her feet. The water, when she waded into it, instantly brought chill bumps. It took a moment for her to adjust to the cold.

Pixie felt almost wicked as she leisurely washed using the

sand that she grasped from the bottom of the riverbed.

Bending her head, she scrubbed at her scalp until it felt squeaky-clean. Next, she cleaned her teeth with the twig she had pounded on one end, fraying it. Little Bird called it a chewstick when she made hers. Reaching for the leaf of a nearby bush, Pixie plucked it and stuck it in her mouth. Chewing for moment, she then spit. She didn't know what the bush was but its leaf's juices gave a burst of morning freshness. Hearing people beginning to stir, Pixie scurried to pull her deerskin dress back on. Running her fingers through her hair and squeezing out its excess water, she hummed. A modern upbeat tune emerged and the sound shocked her. It abruptly died in Pixie's throat. How could she experience happiness in this place? Sitting on the flat surface of the rock that jutted up from the ground beside her, Pixie dusted the sand from the bottoms of her feet. She pulled on her moccasins and tied their strings tight around her ankles giving each a firm tug as she did so.

The flat rock under her butt was warm and relaxing, the sun's heating of it a blessing after the cold shock of the water.

Hearing a splash, Pixie turned toward the sound. She froze. Two Feathers bathed several yards up-stream from where she sat. She should leave. He strolled from the water and then paused noting her. Pixie devoured his naked form. It was sleek with an absence of fat and toned to perfection. Abruptly, she turned her face away embarrassed by her behavior.

Two Feathers halted before her moments later fully dressed. Pixie kept her gaze lowered and focused on his moccasins. Why had he walked her way?

"Pix should eat more. Pix too skinny. Not healthy."

Outraged, Pixie jerked her gaze upward.

"Did you hide and watch me bathe?" Her tone held her contempt.

Two Feathers' gaze slide down over her.

"Pix one who watch," he drawled.

Jerking her gaze from Two Feathers', her embarrassment high,

Pixie looked out over the water. It was true. She was the voyeur, not he. She swallowed and her throat ached. She refused to look at him again. The silence stretched uncomfortably between them. After a moment, he said, "Two Feathers collect Pix and TJ in short time. Bring before father. Expect be ready."

Pixie wanted to demand why. Instead, she gave a nod of understanding.

Turning, Two Feathers strolled away.

Stumbling to her feet, Pixie watched him. *Glance back,* she thought. *Show a little interest, just a little.* On impulse, she took a step forward thinking to call out to him. Pixie paused. Two Feathers' bearing was inflexible, his stride wide. Her shoulders slumped. He didn't look back. If he had, she would have gone to him and confessed her suspicion of her condition.

"Two Feathers is to come and collect TJ and me this morning," she informed Brave Bird moments later having returned to the woman's home, and ordered to go collect water.

"Why?" Brave Bird demanded in response, her fingers splayed out over the curvature of her hipbones. Her gaze was narrow with suspicion as if Pixie lied to her.

"I don't know why," Pixie replied.

Reaching out with a swiftness that shocked Pixie, Brave Bird pinched down hard on her arm. Jerking her skin from underneath the woman's fingers, Pixie's anger spiked. She had had enough of this woman's meanness. She raised her hand ready to strike. Brave Bird's gaze sharpened, although she didn't move. It dawned on Pixie that Brave Bird coveted her striking out, expected it in fact. Forcing her clenched fist back to her side, Pixie flexed her fingers. Brave Bird wouldn't get a reason to punish not today.

"Pixie nuisance," Brave Bird snapped. She whirled to stomp away leaving the lodge.

Trying to see the back of her arm, Pixie abandoned her attempt. What was one more bruise after so many? A burning sensation began to spread as feeling returned to the numbed area.

TJ hurried toward her upon entering the empty lodge. Brave Bird must've immediately informed him of Two Feathers' summons.

"What's up?"

While she'd lost weight and struggled with this brutal environment, TJ it seemed thrived. Before long, except for the lightness of his hair, he'd be indistinguishable from the other men.

"Two Feathers is to collect us to take us to his father this morning."

"Why?"

Pixie gave a bitter laugh. "How would I know? I just do as I'm told."

TJ paced.

"What's wrong with you?" Pixie demanded watching him. TJ stopped in his tracks. He spun to face her. Pixie thought he'd paled.

"I've messed up."

Giving a snort, she retorted, "Oh really? I thought that you did no wrong."

"Dammit, Pixie." TJ's shoulders slumped.

Pixie's curiosity rose. "What have you done that demands an audience of us both, if I might ask?"

"I think it's because I kissed Fawn last night after I walked her home. I didn't ask her permission. I just did it."

"Well crap. Why should I be included in this summons then?"

Brave Bird entered the home.

"Two Feathers wait," she stated. She gestured toward the outside of the lodge. Her gaze followed Pixie as Pixie passed by her.

Pixie didn't understand the woman's absolute hate and dislike she displayed. The woman had loathed her from their first introduction. Two Feathers spoke to neither her nor TJ at their stepping from Brave Bird's home. TJ drew close to Pixie's side as they followed behind their silent escort and reaching out, Pixie touched his hand. Whatever happened, they'd face it together. Squeezing her fingers, he directed a tight smile toward her and then loosened his grip from hers.

Two Feathers halted at the entrance to the largest lodge in the village. All others fanned out from it. His home sat not far from his parents. Pixie remembered it as she glanced toward it, although she hadn't been on this end of the village since evicted from the home. His face impassive, he called out for permission for entry into the lodge. With it given, he made a motion for TJ and Pixie to go before him. Abruptly halting upon entering the home when TJ did Pixie felt Two Feathers bump into her. She sensed his hand on her lower back before he walked around her.

"Come, sit by fire before Two Feathers' father," he ordered them both.

The old man, who he called Father, studied them as TJ and Pixie did as instructed. The old man poked at the fire and then made a sharp motion for Two Feathers to sit down beside him. Pixie felt Two Feathers' tension as he lowered his form beside that of his father's. His features didn't reflect any emotion, although Pixie sensed his conflict. She couldn't stop her gaze from flicking between the two men, one old, the other young, their relation obvious.

Two Feathers' mother and sister walked out from the shadows of the home to settle down beside Two Feathers. Pixie hadn't realized any others were in the lodge until their coming forward. Pixie let her gaze circle the home and noted several others were present although they appeared not to give attention to the small group gathered around the fire pit. TJ watched Fawn while Fawn's gaze darted around the room avoiding any connection with his. Pixie's fear spiraled. She didn't want to face whatever this coming punishment was to be.

No one moved or spoke.

Two Feathers reached down to lay a hand over his mother's

slender fingers. The touch was light and Pixie didn't think anyone else noticed. The old man looked directly across the fire toward TJ.

"Chief ask if man fall from heavens?"

TJ's gaze slid from Fawn. Pixie could tell the old man's question confused him. It did her.

"Yes," TJ answered. His gaze flicked back toward Fawn. Fawn studied her hands.

"How possible?" the old man asked.

TJ gestured toward Pixie. "We were caught up in whirling winds and the winds cast us to this place."

The old man frowned.

"Man and woman not live with Creator? Not know Creator of peoples?"

His expression mystified, TJ shook his head. "No. We were in a far off future place when the whirling winds picked us up and dropped us at your son's feet."

Pixie noticed that Two Feathers studied her and TJ, his gaze puzzled.

The old man covered his face with the palms of his hands.

"No knowledge of family if not from Creator," he moaned and he rocked in seeming despair. In confusion, Pixie slid her gaze toward Two Feathers' mother. His mother's face was stiff as was Fawn's. *Weren't they the old man's family?* Pixie wondered in bewilderment.

"All go!" the old man stated and he jerked to sit upright, clearly agitated.

Rising to his feet, Two Feathers indicated for Pixie and TJ to stand. His mother and sister rose also. Outside the lodge, he put an arm around his mother's shoulders.

"Father is worse," he stated.

"He calls out in the night for them now," his mother replied. Seeming to collect herself, her expression back to its normal disciplined smoothness, she turned and reentered the lodge.

Chapter Seventeen

It had been fourteen days since her and TJ's bizarre meeting with Two Feathers' father. Pixie knew the exact days, because she'd counted, and she hadn't seen or spoken with Two Feathers since. He had disappeared two days later after a meeting with several of the village leaders. Crow had been included in that meeting, although he never stated where Two Feathers had disappeared to or why, and Pixie didn't dare to ask him. Each day though, she watched and searched for his return and each day that passed, her misery deepened. TJ was just glad that his misstep hadn't led to any punishment.

Crow had begun his courtship in earnest after Two Feathers' disappearance, and Brave Bird's smile was huge these days. Her selling price high for Pixie her sister had informed and Crow was meeting her selling price. Stepping from the lodge that early morning hour as she had the past fourteen mornings to meet Crow, Pixie frowned.

"Why, woman, not happy? Crow pay much to make wife." Crow seemed to catch himself at Pixie's startled look toward him. He had not spoken so harshly since the first days she'd known him. He took hold of her hand as if in regret and Pixie breathed in. She dreaded what she needed to tell him, but he should know the truth before he gave Brave Bird any more demanded items.

"Crow, I have something to tell you. If you decide not to marry me, I'll understand."

Crow's fingers tightened around hers.

"We walk. No one hear Pixie speak," he stated in response.

"I'm pregnant with Two Feathers' child." Pixie winced. They stood by the river's edge, the village, and its people behind them. Her words sat suspended in the early morning mist. They seemed harsh, no smoothing of the truth for the man by her side. Watching Crow, Pixie couldn't read his emotion. His expression didn't reflect surprise at her intimacy with his friend.

"Two Feathers know of child?" Crow didn't look at her his gaze locked on something across the river.

"No," Pixie responded.

He turned toward her. "Pixie not speak to Blood Brother. Crow raise child as own."

Pixie frowned in response. "Two Feathers should know of my pregnancy, Crow. It's the right thing to do."

In her heart, Pixie wished it were Two Feathers who stood beside her and excited at her news. She didn't believe that he would be though. She avoided Crow's gaze.

Crow jerked her chin up so that their gazes clashed. "Two Feathers love only Pretty Flower and her child. On quest seek vision from Pretty Flower."

So now, she knew why Two Feathers had disappeared. It was always about Pretty Flower. Pixie's words scratched her throat. "Even so, it is right that he should know."

Crow's features reverted to their hard settlement of when she and TJ first landed in this strange environment. For a moment, Pixie thought he looked at her almost with hatred. She tried to step back, to break from his touch. He held her fast.

"If Pixie speak on child to Blood Brother, Crow make Pixie slave not wife. Two Feathers take child either way, leave Pixie behind for Crow."

"I won't say anything," Pixie assured him. The way he looked at her scared her. Crow's mouth softened at her promise and the brutality across his features faded. He slid the backside of his hand down the curvature of her cheek.

"Two Feathers not want Pixie. Crow do," he stated.

What Crow said was true. Two Feathers didn't want her, and to have this unknown, living, breathing baby ripped from her arms when born was unthinkable. She wanted and loved the child already.

"I'll be your wife, Crow, and I'll stay quiet. I promise. This child will be known as yours."

Crow smiled and a satisfied expression settled across his face. Pixie pulled back from him. He allowed their connection to be broken. The cold morning air suddenly felt, Pixie shivered as she rubbed at her upper arms. "I must go. Brave Bird will be angry with me for wasting the morning away."

"Go. Crow not keep."

Crow's demeanor was changed. Seeing it, unease filtered through Pixie.

"I'll make you a good wife, Crow. I promise."

He walked away.

Pixie's instinct urged alarm.

Dismissing the emotion, Pixie turned to begin her chores. Much needed done that day and she wanted to get to it. Besides, it was understandable that Crow was upset. He still wanted to marry her and that was what was important. He must have a care for her if he desired her for a wife even knowing what he did.

That evening with the darkness of the night edging across the land, Pixie startled from her duties jumped in fright at a sound heard. Quickly, she swiveled toward the sound. Two Feathers emerged from the grove of trees that grew along beside the settlement and he walked in her direction. Resentment and rage flooded through Pixie at his sudden reappearance. She turned fully toward him as she watched him. Not once, it seemed, had he given her a second thought after their night together. The soft leather leggings and top that he wore molded to his form. Pixie knew they were soft because she'd helped Fawn one day to mend them.

"Did you have your vision of your precious dead wife?" Pixie sneered when he drew close about to pass her by. She couldn't stop her voiced bitterness. With two long strides her direction and a quick grasp of her upper arms, Two Feathers yanked her toward him. The gathered firewood that Pixie held in her arms scattered, falling about their feet. Pulling her through the haphazard mess and into the tree grove he'd just emerged from, Pixie's head snapped back onto her shoulders at his shake given to her. Her teeth rattled together in her head.

"Don't ever speak of Two Feathers' wife again," he snarled down at her. Rage seeped from him.

Pixie couldn't respond. Fear choked her.

Two Feathers dropped his hands from her shoulders and stepped back. He turned to leave. Taking a step forward, he abruptly stopped, and then pivoted back toward her.

"Pix provoke Two Feathers with words."

Pixie realized that he was going to kiss her as he took a step her direction. She could see it in his face. She wanted it, desired it. She strained forward. She didn't dare to reach out. In the end, Two Feathers closed the gap between them. Grasping a fistful of her hair, he tilted her head back, his fingers against her scalp. His gaze searched hers. Pixie sensed that he sought to step back away from her. He pulled her into his arms instead. When their mouths melded, it felt right. It was where she was supposed to be, where she wanted to be. Pixie encircled her arms around his waist and held fast. Her hands had a mind of their own as they caressed and touched his bare skin under the top that he wore. His skin was warm and smooth to the touch. She'd missed him so much, thought about him day and night. His grip of her hair tightened and her back hit the tree behind her at his aggression. He pressed against her, his desire obvious.

"Woman...," he murmured his mouth over hers, his breathing heavy. "Woman make Two Feathers lose self."

Lurching backward, he turned and stormed away.

Gulping in the cold air around her, Pixie shuddered. She didn't understand what had just happened. Why kiss her, his desire obvious, and then leave as if he hated her? Bending low at the waist wanting to cry out in humiliation, confusion, and hurt, her throat burned. She would not cry. She would not. Stumbling from their hiding place, she went back to her work. Brave Bird probably waited and who knew how much time had lapsed.

Pixie winced when she noted that Brave Bird did wait for her. The woman stood at the entrance to her lodge as she approached.

"Come here, lazy woman!" Brave Bird's shrill order echoed across the village and heads turned.

"Where Pixie be?" she demanded when Pixie drew close.

"I've been gathering firewood for the evening fire." Pixie tilted her chin to signify the armload of wood that she'd regathered and now carried with her.

Brave Bird scorned back at her, "Brave Bird believe lazy woman hide and sleep. Brave Bird be glad trade complete with Crow. Lazy woman always trouble for Brave Bird."

"Well the feeling is mutual," Pixie snapped back unable to stop herself. Did everyone have to attack her this day? Brave Bird's hand struck her face before she could duck. Drawing her hand back ready to strike her again, Too Little, walking from behind their home ran up to wedge himself between them.

"Why women fight?" He looked at his spouse his agitation evident. He was such a strange little man, easy to be around, and always friendly. *The exact opposite of his bitch of a wife*, Pixie thought.

"Stupid slave talk back. Brave Bird not allow disrespect."

Pixie remained silent when Too Little cut his gaze her way. It'd do no good to try to defend herself against his wife.

At a movement close to the lodge, Pixie looked past his shoulder. Her gaze connected with Two Feathers'. Hurt rose in Pixie at the hostile look he returned to her. Breaking their eye contact, he dismissed her and strode forward. It was as if earlier they'd had no passionate interaction at all. As if he hadn't kissed her like a man drowning. Pixie's resentment swelled. Yes, of course, he'd take Brave Bird's side and any others against her. He spoke as he passed. "Too Little, Two Feathers expect woman healthy and well."

At Too Little's quick nod, Two Feathers continued on his way.

"What Two Feathers mean?" Brave Bird demanded.

"Two Feathers trade for woman." Too Little gave a nod toward Pixie.

Brave Bird snapped back at him, "Brave Bird agree trade with Crow. Crow pay much. Not give back items."

Too Little put a hand on her shoulder soothing her agitation. "Two Feathers pay more. Whatever Crow give Two Feathers say Two Feathers give twice."

Pixie, stunned at their exchange, turned to stare at Two Feathers' retreating back. Her heart gave a funny leap. Maybe he cared for her after all. He had given her away—thrown her away, actually—and now he planned to buy her back at twice what Crow paid? Brave Bird laughed, causing Pixie to look at her in inquiry. Had her hope been so apparent?

The hateful woman drawled, her glee obvious, "Two Feathers need caretaker for child. Sister no time for child, Sister all time care for parents. Lazy woman not chosen for wife as face show want. Lazy woman, be slave still."

Pixie didn't respond.

Frowning, Brave Bird pointed a finger toward the lodge entrance. "Take wood into home. Brave Bird glad lazy slave go from lodge."

That evening, sitting on her pallet beside Little Bird, Pixie tensed at Crow's admittance into the overflowing lodge. Did he know of their changed situation? The adults around her chattered as all sat before the scattered fire pits. Pixie glanced to where TJ and Too Little sat talking to each other on the other side of the lodge. The children within the home played, yelping with laughter as they ran around the lodge's interior. Looking up, as if realizing her unease felt, Little Bird's fingers ceased their movement over the basket that she weaved. Leaning forward toward Pixie, she whispered, "Little Bird glad Two Feathers trade for Pixie. Little Bird never like Crow."

Pixie watched Brave Bird take Crow to where Too Little sat. He rose to his feet and he spoke to Crow. Crow glanced across the lodge toward her before he turned aside and left the home. His expression didn't reveal any emotion he may have felt at their changed circumstances. Brave Bird pivoted to walk her way and Pixie stiffened, ready for a verbal attack.

Little Bird straightened her shoulders as she watched Brave Bird approach. "Sister," she stated firmly when the woman drew near, "husband bring Two Feathers into home."

Brave Bird jerked her gaze to where Two Feathers now filled the home's doorway. Pixie's pulse quickened. He was a welcomed sight. He seemed a safe harbor in this maddening, harsh world even with his anger toward her. Surely, he could have found someone else besides her to look after his son if he'd truly wanted. Whirling, Brave Bird stalked away. A moment later, she marched back to stand before Pixie.

"Lazy woman go."

"What?"

"Go, leave Brave Bird's home. Trade complete this night."

Pixie's gaze met TJ's from where he reclined on his pallet. Suddenly she was scared. He tilted his head in Two Feathers' direction and a smile lingered.

Standing, Pixie took a deep breath. Realizing that her hands shook, she clenched her fingers into fists to hide their shaking. She couldn't read Two Feathers' expression as he watched her approach. Why had he traded for her? Was it only to care for Three Feathers as Brave Bird had insisted? Turning, he exited the lodge leaving her to trail behind him.

The quiet at entering Two Feathers' home was a welcome relief from the loud chaos of the one Pixie had just left behind. Fawn sat beside its one and only fire pit with the child in her lap. She looked up with a welcoming smile.

"Well done, Brother," she stated as she stood.

Two Feathers didn't respond. Walking forward he took the sleeping child from her arms and cradling the infant, he turned toward Pixie.

"Pix care for son. If injury come to child Pix be killed."

"Brother!" Fawn, her shock and disapproval showing, stared at her sibling.

Pixie's hurt ran deep at Two Feathers' belief that she'd harm his child. She had helped Fawn to watch over the child and he knew it. "If you think that I might harm this baby, why would you bring me here to care for him?"

"Crow inform Two Feathers, Pix carry Two Feathers' child. Pix no wish inform Two Feathers Blood Brother say. Say Pix have unlove in heart. Crow warn of treachery and worry for unborn child and for Three Feathers."

In shock, Pixie stared at Two Feathers in disbelief. Crow had set her up.

"Pixie carry Brother's child?" Fawn asked her.

Pixie gave a slow nod.

"Pixie not wish Brother know of child?"

"Crow demanded my silence," Pixie defended.

Two Feathers' face twisted with his disbelief at her response.

"Crow tell truth," he retorted.

Fawn studied Pixie. Hurt coming in waves at her friend's

censor, Pixie reached for the sleeping infant. "I promise to keep this child safe, just as I'll keep your second child safe when born."

Two Feathers let Pixie take the infant from his arms. Cradling the slumbering child against her chest, she looked around. "Where's the child's sleeping pallet?"

"With Two Feathers," Two Feathers responded.

Pixie stared. "If I'm to keep this child safe, I'll sleep next to him, but not you."

At her abrupt declaration, Two Feathers' scowl slashed and he drew a breath.

"Make bed here," Fawn interjected and she walked toward a rolled buffalo blanket. Shaking the roll out, she laid it close to the lodge wall. Turning, she laid another buffalo blanket down on top of it. Straightening, she gestured for Pixie to come forward. Pixie laid the slumbering child down between the two soft furs and then she sat down beside the boy.

"Fawn go home now," Fawn told her gently, her hand on her shoulder. She looked up at her brother for his approval. He nodded in agreement. Squatting before the fire pit after his sister's departure, Two Feathers studied the fire in it that glowed with color. His back straight and rigid, he ignored Pixie, and the silence between them dominated the lodge. Crawling fully dressed over the slumbering child so that she laid facing Two Feathers, Pixie pulled the infant close. Two Feathers' silence continued. The furs were warm and cozy and even as Pixie fought to keep her eyelids open, they closed.

****

Without looking at the woman, Two Feathers knew when she went to the dream world. Leaning forward, he stabbed at the fire before him. After a moment, he set aside the stick that he held. The fire would endure, its coals lasting the night. Rising, Two Feathers went to his sleeping pallet. Stretching out on top of his buffalo robes, he lay wide-awake, and restless. His gaze drifted to the woman. The fascination she continued to hold over him puzzled him. He didn't understand it. Even with her requested deceit of Crow, he'd felt a compulsion to defend her when the Council looked at him in question at Crow's revealing of her condition. There was no censor in their gazes toward him. She had been his at the time of conception to do with, as he wanted. Their censor lay at her feet. For her to withhold knowledge of his growing seed was a serious wrong.

At his return from his vision quest, the Council members demanded an immediate meeting. They had given him his requested time, they stated, and now, they wanted a decision made. His father falling further and further from reality could no longer lead the tribe.

The Council listened quietly that morning as he had revealed his vision to the collected group. Smoke curled in the air as the pipe of harmony passed from hand to hand.

The eldest member leaned forward, his gaze meeting his at the end of his disclosure.

"When look across river, Pretty Flower and woman called Pixie walk hand-in-hand, companions?"

Two Feathers nodded. He hadn't liked it, his vision. Pix was not fit to touch Pretty Flower. What he hadn't revealed was that his wife's features had remained muted while Pix's, the woman he couldn't keep from overtaking his thoughts, had been sharp and clear. It had grieved him. Coming out of his thoughts to glance over at the woman again that lay beside his son, Two Feathers' insides ached with the realization that his wife's memory now paled. Would he soon not be able to see or sense Pretty Flower?

The elder had continued that morning. "Pretty Flower point to something behind Two Feathers. Two Feathers see nothing. Two Feathers turn back to Pretty Flower, and the woman, Pixie, now alone. Village spread out behind her. Pretty Flower gone?"

Two Feathers gave a nod of agreement. He had grieved at Pretty Flower's disappearance as he'd mulled his vision over. Was Pretty Flower giving approval for his feelings for the woman? He could gather no other sign in his vision and certainly not anything in it that indicated his taking his father's place as Chief of the tribe as the Council members wanted. It surprised Two Feathers when the elder leaned back, his expression thoughtful, his mouth pulling at the pipe of harmony.

Smoke curled.

The elder leaned forward again. "Two Feathers must return woman to lodge. Keep close. Make wife."

Two Feathers shook his head even as his heart leaped in unexpected elation. Its response surprised him.

"Woman is Crow's. Crow trade with Too Little for woman," he'd argued.

"Woman, Two Feathers' path, tribe path, not Crow's," the elder snapped back in response.

The other's murmured their agreement.

Crow, the creases alongside his mouth deep, flexed his fingers. He didn't look up as he spoke. "Take woman. Woman deceitful. Crow no longer wish for wife."

Two Feathers studied his long-time friend and his anger rose in defense for Pix. "Why, Blood Brother slur woman?"

Chapter Eighteen

Pixie tensed upon waking, prepared for her usual morning kick to the backside. Becoming fully alert when none occurred, she remembered and looked down at the child by her side who now gazed upward at her. His eyes wide, questioning.

"Hello," she stated. The child didn't move at her soft whisper. His dark eyes watched her. Lifting her gaze from the child's direct stare, Pixie looked around at the home she'd been escorted to the night before. It was empty of its owner that morning for which she was thankful.

She looked back down at the child. "We better rise, hmm... don't you think? I don't want to be accused of being lazy by your father."

Grasping a fistful of her hair, the infant entangled his fingers into the strands and pulled. Pixie smiled down at him. "Ah. I see. Same as Brave Bird, are you?"

"Up," he demanded.

The childish command darling, Pixie laughed in amusement while doing as instructed. She settled the child on her hip.

"Okay we're up, little boss. Now let's get this day started, shall we?"

Bending before the lodge's fire pit, Pixie raked at the red embers still within it. Adding pieces of the piled kindling from beside the fire pit, flames began to flare and take hold. Pixie added some larger wood chunks.

Done with that chore, and as warmth began to spread within the lodge, she looked around at the interior of Two Feathers' home. What was she supposed to do? Clean, cook, bring in firewood same as Brave Bird's household? Pixie wasn't sure what all Two Feathers expected of her, but one thing she did know: she was to take care of the child she held or experience dire consequences.

"Come, little one. Let's wash you up and then find something to eat. I can't let you go hungry, now can I?"

Emerging from the home with the boy firmly settled on her hip, Pixie walked toward the village's water source. Squatting beside the clear rippling stream, she washed the child's face and then hers. Next, she filled the water gourd that she'd brought with her.

Standing, Pixie pivoted to walk back to the private enclosure of Two Feathers' home. Her gaze collided with Crow's in surprise.

He had come down to the river to fill his own water container. With a frown that she was unable to stop, Pixie dropped her gaze and moved to walk around him. He shifted sideways and blocked her escape.

"Pixie happy Pixie Two Feathers' woman?"

Jerking her gaze upward, Pixie clipped out her reply, "I'm not Two Feathers' woman. I'm a babysitter. Now leave me be."

Crow looked around before he stepped in closer to her. "Pixie be Crow's woman still. Meet Crow in woods."

Pixie tightened her fingers upon the child's waist. He whimpered. Relaxing her grip, she forced the anger that she felt to subside. "What am I to do with this infant if I do as you request?"

Crow's gaze slid to the child. "Bring. We gag. Tie to tree. Him no bother to Crow."

Repulsed, Pixie stepped backward. "Not only do you lie about me to Two Feathers, telling him that I didn't want him to know about his unborn child, but you would also betray him and even worse abuse his child? You make me sick. I am going to tell him what you just said to me. Believe me, I will."

With a narrowed gaze, Crow stood his ground. A slow, cruel smile spread across his face as he stared at her. Pixie trembled at its emergence. Her instinct when she'd first laid eyes on this man was right. She had ignored the subconscious warning.

"Inform Blood Brother. Blood Brother not believe."

Lurching around Crow, Pixie walked with a fast clip back to the security of Two Feathers' home. Once inside, she crumbled. She lowered the child to the dirt floor as he watched her. "So sorry you had to hear what that awful man said."

"Eat," was his lisping response.

"Yes, yes, we will do that. We will eat."

Too fearful of another encounter with Crow, Pixie didn't leave the security of Two Feathers' home the rest of that day. That evening when Two Feathers returned, she couldn't meet his gaze. In some sense, Pixie held anger at him for Crow's behavior. Would he believe her if she repeated what Crow had said?

"Did Sister visit Pix?"

Giving a nod, affirming Two Feathers' question to her, Pixie didn't look up, her courage to reveal his friend's deception wilted. Two Feathers walked forward toward the platform that held his homes personal belongings. He laid his bow and arrow down in an empty area. He didn't look her way as he spoke again.

"Two Feathers kill rabbits. Leave one outside lodge for Pix. Two Feathers take others to parents then return to home."

Silently, Pixie gave a nod at his statement although she didn't think that he noticed. She watched him turn and stroll back outside the home. Going to the doorway, Pixie noted the animal left behind on the ground. Sighing, she gathered the items needed to begin the tedious chore of gutting and cleaning their evening meal. Would she ever get used to this way of living? Always it was a day-to-day, hand-to-mouth existence. No dashing to the grocery store to grab what you needed for your meals, or popping in at a restaurant when you were too tired to cook.

"No, Three Feathers," Pixie called out later when the child she'd cared for that day lurched on unsteady feet toward the home's fire and the now roasting rabbit she'd positioned over it.

"No. No. Hot. Hot." Pixie chanted as she steered his attention and form from the allure of the flames.

"No. No. Hot. Hot." He repeated. He furiously, shook his head his face a picture of serious reflection. Pixie laughed, and once started, she couldn't stop. The child stared and then joined her in her laughter, his chubby cheeks rising, crinkling up the skin around his eyes. His black hair, thick and sticking out over his ears, gave him an adorable, tousled look.

Wiping at her wet cheeks, Pixie bent over toward him and she tapped at the end of his nose with a fingertip as she cooed, "You are darling. Do you know that?"

He nodded in solemn agreement causing her laughter to erupt again. His father entered the home, and Pixie abruptly straightened, her merriment dying as quickly as it had started. Two Feathers looked between her and his son, his gaze questioning. He walked forward to sit before the fire and rotated the cooking rabbit.

"Fawn say, Fawn not need keep guard over son. Say, Pix give good care."

Pixie had known Fawn was checking up on her when she kept dropping in throughout the day. She hadn't minded and hadn't resented Two Feathers' caution. Walking forward, Pixie readjusted the meal. Three Feathers tottered forward to wrap a chubby arm around her leg. His father plucked him up to settle him on his lap.

Silently, both males watched her as she worked.

Unable to keep her thoughts to herself, Pixie blurted, "I am glad that you bought me back. I'm thankful not to be Crow's woman."

His surprise reflected on his face, Two Feathers studied her. He didn't respond.

Embarrassed, Pixie shrugged a shoulder. Two Feathers' expression didn't invite confidence in her that if she informed him of his friend's behavior it would meet favorably in her direction. Now she wished, she'd kept her silence, but she'd wanted him to know her gratitude. More importantly, she'd wanted to test the waters. Two Feathers didn't ask why she was thankful as he silently considered her. Pixie directed a timid smile his way.

"Anyway, I thought that you should know."

****

Watching the woman as she busied herself with their meal, Two Feathers wondered at her motive behind her words. Was she trying to trick him into believing that she cared for him? Brave Bird revealed she'd expressed delight to become Crow's wife and had relished Crow's price paid for her, bragged about it in fact. Two Feathers couldn't deny that the unexpected statement hadn't brought a leap of joy. As he began to eat what she silently handed to him, he paused in the act. His gaze rose to hers to where she now sat. Of course, the woman was glad he'd brought her back to his lodge. Crow hadn't been pleased with her pregnancy or with her asking for his deceit to a blood brother and she knew it.

She had thought Crow weak with desire willing to bend to her will. She gave another one of her slight smiles toward him as he continued to consider her. The smile angered him. The woman protected her own skin, thinking to deceive him.

"Crow glad not have Pix in Crow's home with Pix's treachery. Two Feathers owe Blood Brother much for telling Two Feathers truth."

His words punitive, Two Feathers watched Pix's smile fade. Hurt flashed across her face. At his sudden emotional softening, he hardened his heart. Scheming and trickery were her skills just as Crow had stated. He couldn't trust her. Dropping her gaze, she shifted sideways away from him. Abruptly standing, she walked toward his home's entryway.

"Where Pix go?" he challenged.

She didn't turn around, only pausing in her step. Her soft, hesitate words fell on his ears. "I need to gather water from the river."

"Go," he ordered.

Her shoulders straight and rigid, she went to pick up the water gourd and then exited his home.

****

Pixie wanted to scream her hurt and anger at Two Feathers. Oh, she'd tested the waters all right and received his answer loud and clear. If she repeated what Crow had said to her earlier that day, she'd be accused a liar. She'd had to bite her tongue to keep from shrieking out the truth. Why couldn't Two Feathers see his friend for what he was? Crow was an emotionally cold and calculating man.

Squatting by the river's edge, Pixie plunged the gourd that she held down into its clear blue water. She wished it were Two Feathers' neck that she gripped. The man wore blinders.

"Two Feathers believe?"

Almost jumping out of her skin, Pixie lunged upward to whirl around. Crow grasped her upper arm as she stumbled backward nearly falling into the water. She had done it again, so lost in thought that she hadn't heard his approach. No others were by the river's edge, all settled in for the evening. Pixie let her gaze challenge Crow's. She would not allow this man to know her paralyzing fear of him.

"When I choose to tell Two Feathers, he'll believe. Now release my arm and get out of my way."

Crow released his grip of her arm only to clasp his lean fingers at the base of her neck. He arched his body toward hers and those same fingers tightened, hurting, and he grated, "Crow give orders not Pixie."

He didn't look around, seeming to have no fear of anyone

noticing her and him. Her heart pounding, Pixie knew Crow could feel its rapid pulse beneath his fingertips. He stroked the base of her neck with a thumb and then swooped to capture her lips with his.

Pixie attempted to pull back. Crow seized the front of her dress binding her to him. His lips devoured, tasting, nipping, spittle clinging. Pixie gagged and thrashed straining backward. Crow tasted of buffalo meat and she could smell his body odor. It wasn't strong, but forced up against him his odor repulsed her. Abruptly released, Pixie wiped at her mouth with the back of her hand. She wished she dared to spit in the face of the man before her. He would kill her on the spot if she did. Crow issued a low laugh and dragged her against him once again, and with one hand on a breast, he squeezed it, hurting.

"Woman nothing to Crow or Blood Brother," he declared and his lips slid over the outer shell of Pixie's ear as he spoke. With a shove given to her away from him, Pixie landed on her backside in the water.

Crow strolled away.

Struggling to stand upright as cold water swirled over her, Pixie found her footing and stood. Scrubbing at her mouth again, she watched as Crow meandered through the settlement. He not once looked back at her. It seemed to Pixie that he didn't have any concern whatsoever, if anyone in the village had observed his actions. Cupping her hands full of the swirling water, Pixie brought them to her mouth. She swished, then spat, then repeated, and repeated, and still she tasted Crow's vile scent. Reaching down to gather up a handful of sand from the river's floor, Pixie scrubbed her body. Shivering as the night air swept down over her wet head and skin, she stepped from the water to pick up the dropped water gourd. Her hands shook.

When she reentered Two Feathers' lodge he glanced up from where he was placing Three Feathers onto the child's nighttime pallet. Pixie turned from Two Feathers' questioning gaze. Her teeth chattered. Whether they did from Crow's brutality or the cold, she didn't know, but she was beginning to shake all over and she couldn't stop.

"Pix fall in river?"

"Yes, that's what I did," Pixie snapped back. She laid the blame for Crow's assault at Two Feathers' feet. Yes, it was wrong, but she did it anyway. Frowning, Two Feathers straightened fully to watch her. Three Feathers snoozed away, his chubby little face relaxed, his fingers curled against his cheekbone. Oh to be so innocent and cared for and watched over. Pixie wanted to weep. Why couldn't she have someone to care for her and to watch over her?

Placing the water gourd that she held down beside the inside of the doorway, Pixie lurched toward the warmth of the fire. She spread her hands out over its heat as she squatted beside it. With no change of clothing, did she spend the night in her soaked garments?

"Undress."

Startled, Pixie met Two Feathers' gaze. *Did he read her mind*? "I don't have anything else to wear."

He walked toward her. "What Pix do with Pretty Flower's things Two Feathers give?"

"I didn't receive anything from you."

With a frown, Two Feathers squatted beside her. "TJ not give to Pix? Two Feathers send with him."

Shaking her head, Pixie met Two Feathers' direct and questioning gaze. She touched the hem of the soaked dress.

"I didn't receive anything from TJ. Crow gave me this and it's all that I have."

Disbelief seemed to grow in Two Feathers' gaze as he studied her and Pixie felt her anger rise.

"Why would I lie?"

"Pix trade to make life easier. Not want Two Feathers to know. Maybe Two Feathers ask Brave Bird of this."

Pixie's shoulders slumped. *I'm always to be untrustworthy.*

"Ask her. I don't care," she retorted.

"Pix sleep with Two Feathers tonight."

Pixie snapped back, "No!" Shoulders now rigid and hands at her side, Pixie couldn't keep the revulsion she felt from her tone. Crow's groping was enough for one night. Pixie realized the instant anger of the man before her.

"Yes, Two Feathers give warmth. Not want Pix sick."

"No." Pixie shuddered.

Grasping her arm, Two Feathers pulled her upward with him. In one swift move, he had the water-soaked, buckskin dress that she wore pulled up over her head and flipped out to dry beside the fire pit.

"Go," he graveled his gaze narrow.

He pointed to his bed when Pixie remained unmoving, her arms wrapped tight around her naked chest. His aggressive stance gave no room for argument, and sliding between Two Feathers' buffalo blankets, Pixie couldn't stop quaking. She knew her shuddering now wasn't completely from the cold or the ordeal with Crow. No, it was her dread at what Two Feathers wanted this night of all nights. She was tired, so very tired of all that had happened since the tornado. Every day since had been a fight for survival, and every day an ordeal, she had to work through.

"Do your pawing quick," she blurted when Two Feathers slid in beside her. He was angered already. What was more anger? Another bruise on her person or another scar, she was getting used to them. He paused in his movement to look down at her before he rearranged the top buffalo blanket so that it covered both their bare shoulders. When he reached to drag her toward him, Pixie's tears spurted. She gulped trying to hold them back. The raw emotion gained momentum despite her fight to rein it in. She hated knowing that she couldn't stop what it was Two Feathers wanted and hated that the man by her side didn't have feelings for her. All he wanted was to slack a basic need. Would he take her all the while he wished that she were his dead wife? Pixie's weeping increased. She tried to muffle the sound, afraid of waking the child.

Shame rose that she was jealous of a dead woman. Leaning back to frown down at her, Two Feathers smoothed her hair away from her face. Several moments passed, and when he didn't speak or make any other movement, Pixie's tears slowed. Would he now punish? Cautiously she met his gaze. Silently, he wrapped his arms around her and positioned her so that he could hold her close, and then to Pixie's amazement, he rested his chin atop her head. The stillness of the room pressed as they lay beside each other only their breathing heard. He shifted and his foot touched hers. She tensed. It startled when he began to hum. With her cheek pressed against Two Feathers' bare chest, Pixie listened. It was a low melody, the tune soothing, calming. The palm of his hand passed back and forth over the span of her back.

Pixie's eyelids began to droop.

"Two Feathers, I...," she murmured. Her body had ceased its uncontrollable shivers warmed by the one pressed against hers. She couldn't focus. Her thoughts floated. The dream world reached up to drag her down into it. Pixie struggled to resurface back to awareness. She wanted the man by her side to know her gratitude for his bringing her back into his home. Her mother's image drifted by and then her father's, and Pixie tried to call out to them both. She could see them, but they couldn't see her. Her tears rose again.

Two Feathers' humming continued.

Images of the past flickered and flowed and always beyond reach.

Brave Bird's cruelty pressed down on Pixie as did Crow's

viciousness. The present world ruled. No longer did she have autonomy. Always there were others prodding and telling her what to do. Had that other life existed at all? Had she just dreamed it up to escape? *No, don't leave,* Pixie cried out in her dream world trying to grasp and hold on to it a little longer.

****

Abruptly, opening her eyes, Pixie lay unmoving. Something had waked her. Listening, Pixie didn't move. Light filtered into the lodge and the man by her side slept. The cold of the early morning caused her breath to rise visibly into the air above her. The fire across the way had burned down to only a few red embers left. Soon even those would be black with no heat left.

Rising onto her elbow, Pixie tilted her head toward where Three Feathers lay beside the lodge wall. The child was sound asleep, snuggled underneath the buffalo blanket his father had wrapped around him. He was warm and cozy. Glancing down at the man who slept beside her, Pixie moved her gaze over high cheekbones and a strong jawline. Two Feathers' features relaxed in slumber made her wonder just how old he was. He looked younger asleep than when awake. It was his eyes, Pixie realized. His eyes made him seem much older than he must be. Asleep there was no haunting sadness to see.

Lifting her hand, Pixie touched a scarred shoulder. Funny, she'd never noticed that jagged line before. It must have been a deep cut, she mused as she studied it. Two Feathers had several scars across his back, but this individual one she'd somehow missed. Pixie wondered at the stories behind each of his wounds. Her attention shifted to the tattoo he sported on his shoulder. Both of his upper arms displayed that single, large, black feather. Pixie lightly traced the design on the arm closest to her with a fingertip. She had admired the matching patterns before. Three Feathers sported the same tattoo as his father, as did four women within the village although theirs were much, much smaller versions than Two Feathers' and on one shoulder only. Pixie knew the women were Two Feathers' slaves. They didn't live in his home though. They stayed at his mother's house. They were proof of the brutal period she now lived in.

Letting her hand slide up and over the tattoo, Pixie studied its design. The pattern was intricate and a perfect depiction of the feathers he sported in his hair. The design was much finer and nobler than the feather motif she'd had tattooed above her ankle.

Pixie frowned at her thought.

An ugly scar now left behind where that tattoo had been.

Lifting her gaze up from the tattoo she inspected, Pixie gave a start of surprise.

Two Feathers watched her.

With embarrassment, she turned to pull away.

"No," he murmured and his hand gripped her wrist. He spread her fingers against his breastbone maintaining their body contact as his gaze searched hers. "Pix...?" His morning voice husky and low rippled over her.

At a sudden deep voice calling out for admittance to the home, Pixie jumped with fright. It was Crow. Two Feathers, gave a low laugh, and positioned himself to where he could sit up, and he called out Crow's permission to enter the home. His gaze remained on her as she struggled to a sitting position.

Pixie quickly dragged the buffalo blanket upward to cover her nakedness just as Crow stepped through the doorway. She caught his sharpened regard. Ducking her head, Pixie tightened her fingers over the edge of the blanket. Crow's look of disdain made her burn with shame. He thought that she and Two Feathers had had a night of debauchery. As Crow's steps brought him closer, Pixie raised her gaze in defiance to meet his stare. Who was he to judge if they had? He was cruel and untrustworthy, a backstabbing person who masqueraded as a friend.

"Does woman's scent make Two Feathers forget duties?" Crow scoffed at the man who sat beside her.

Pixie felt Two Feathers' muscles tighten.

"Blood Brother go too far," he snapped in response.

"Council demands Two Feathers' presence," Crow fired back.

"Let Council know Two Feathers arrive soon."

Pixie kept her gaze forward not looking Crow's way. She wished that she had the nerve to tell Two Feathers of his deceit, to spill all in the moment, and let the chips fall where they may. Crow pivoted leaving the home, and Pixie slowly breathed. She hadn't realized that she'd been holding her breath.

With two fingers firm on her chin, Two Feathers forced her to look toward him.

"Crow accept Council's instructions for Two Feathers to bring Pix to lodge," he told her. He ran the ball of his thumb across her chin and his gaze followed his action. So, she'd been ordered back into his home. He hadn't willingly bought her back from Too Little. Pixie felt her hurt rise.

"You best go. I don't want to be accused of keeping you from your duties." Her tone was shrewish. She couldn't control it. Looking everywhere and anywhere except at the man by her side, Pixie was glad she hadn't gushed the night before about how wonderful it was that he'd bought her back and that her marriage to Crow had been stopped. Her face burned in humiliation at the thought that she almost had. She had almost kissed his damn feet.

Two Feathers' fingers tightened on her chin before he dropped his hand from her. Rising and dressing in silence, he turned and exited the home. Pixie knew he would visit the river first before he attended the meeting. He was meticulous in bathing.

"Eat!"

Turning toward Three Feathers who'd risen unnoticed, and now tottered toward her, his little face determined in his single-mindedness, Pixie replied, "You're a demanding little thing aren't you. Just like your father."

Two Feathers' son nodded firmly.

Giving a genuine snort of amusement at the chubby cuteness of the child, Pixie reached for her dress that Two Feathers had tossed toward her and she pulled it on. She rose to her feet. "Let's rebuild that fire and get you bathed. Then you eat, mister."

"Eat," was the demanded response.

Chapter Nineteen

As Two Feathers stepped into the dimness of the Council hut, he wondered if the man whose seed had brought him into the world would recognize him. His father's shoulders, once wide, now seemed narrow. He sat slumped over, his face pensive, as he waited along beside his peers. The same peers who planned to vote him out as their tribal leader that morning. His father's blank gaze rose to his, and Two Feathers realized the private hell of the man before him. His father a man always wanting and never able to let go of that first family killed in a raid by another tribe. He had never let his hatred heal. Hatred that now consumed him, eating at and destroying from within. His father refused to connect with, or even accept, the son born from his second marriage. A marriage demanded of him by tribal leaders and family tradition. With a resigned sigh, Two Feathers sat down before the shell of the man who had sired him. The Council members realized that his father could no longer lead and his status would end this day. Two Feathers dreaded the coming confrontation his words were to bring.

"Council pleased Two Feathers arrive," the eldest Council member, stated his tone dry, his gaze direct.

Two Feathers inclined his head in acknowledgement at the rebuff. He had kept the Council members waiting.

His father moved a glassy regard around the circle of his advisors. "Why Council bring this man before us? What crime has he done?"

No one moved. Many dropped their scrutiny of his father to their hands. His father lived in a world of his own now, unaware of his lost intellect and the lost ability to lead the people. It was up to Two Feathers to make him aware of the changing winds.

"The Council ask Two Feathers sit before Chief."

"Why?" his father snapped.

"Council request, Two Feathers, inform Chief must step down as leader of people."

His sharp surprise reflected his father turned to look in question at each of his advisors. They wouldn't meet his gaze. He swiveled his head toward Two Feathers again. The old man's confusion and agitation was obvious.

"Who Two Feathers that Council wish him come before Chief and demand this of Chief?"

"Your son by your marriage to my mother, Runs Fast."

Two Feathers' hurt rose at his father's snarl of outrage and his words that followed cut deep. "Wife and son die long time past at hands of murdering thieves. Chief not recognize Two Feathers' claim!"

Several hours later, Two Feathers emerged from the Council hut. His shoulders hurt and his head ached. When the Council had voiced that from that day forward he was Chief of the tribe, he'd walked out. Pausing outside the meeting hut, Two Feathers could hear his father's continued contention. His father still refuted that he was his offspring. He had even pointed a gnarled finger at Crow, before Two Feathers walked out, stating that Crow, a man he knew well, should take his place as the peoples Chief if they no longer wished him to lead, not the imposter before them.

For the first time in their close relationship as blood brothers, Two Feathers saw something in Crow that puzzled him. Something in his eyes had reaped of satisfaction. Crow abruptly stated that he, Two Feathers, was the rightful replacement when he'd caught his appraisal upon him. His blood brother emerged from the Council hut to stand beside him.

"Winter setting in," Crow drawled.

Two Feathers glanced up at the falling snow. He hadn't noticed the silent flakes. He watched as the woman, Pix, parted from his sister and walked toward his lodge. She entered into it with his son on her hip. She hadn't looked his or Crow's way.

The evening before at her return to his lodge and soaking wet from a fall into the river, he'd felt sympathy for her. At the same time, though, he'd wanted to laugh at her condition. She had reminded him of the baby raccoon he'd once rescued from the river as a child—small and furious, eyes enormous when meeting his.

Coming out of his reflection, Two Feathers replied, "Early snow, winter, long-time cold."

He walked away before Crow could respond.

Chapter Twenty

Pixie sat Three Feathers down onto the lodge floor upon entering Two Feathers' home. The fire inside it glowed warm and inviting. Someone had made sure the fire still burned. She had forgotten again. It had begun to snow as she and Fawn visited. The whole village grew quiet and reflective when the large white flakes started coming down. She had pretended not to see Two Feathers and Crow talking before the meeting hut when she passed them, but she had. Shivering, Pixie wondered what the winter held in store for them all. She dreaded it. Survival was day to day and now they had the cold to contend with, too.

"Three Feathers, what are you up to?" Walking to where the child now stood, Pixie bent and secured the lid back onto the clay pot that he'd managed to remove. The toddler crammed the strip of buffalo jerky that he gripped in his palm into his mouth as if daring her to take it from him.

"You're a brat," Pixie drawled. Swinging the infant up into her arms, she kissed his smooth, round, fat cheek. His arm snuck around her neck.

Pixie swiveled at hearing someone enter the home behind her. Her gaze met Two Feathers'. Quickly breaking their eye connection, she turned to refocus on the child that she held.

"Come. Sit," Two Feathers instructed her as he walked forward toward the fire that burned.

Settling Three Feathers down onto his buffalo blanket to play with his toys, Pixie arranged his items around him. She then rearranged them until she knew she had to stop and talk to his father as ordered. Reluctantly, she walked forward. Two Feathers seemed solemn, as if a weight sat on his shoulders. Fawn stated earlier that her brother attended an important meeting that day. Fawn seemed sad herself all that morning and evening. Pixie hadn't asked any questions, although she'd burned with curiosity. Settling down before the fire across from Two Feathers, Pixie silently searched his features. He didn't say anything as he watched her in return. Pixie dropped her gaze as the silence between them intensified.

"How Pix fall from sky and land at Two Feathers' feet?"

Jumping at the sudden, sharp inquiry, Pixie swallowed. How could she explain something that she herself didn't understand? Spreading her fingers, she studied them.

"Two Feathers ask question," he snapped.

Pixie looked up and gave a shrug of her shoulders at him. "I don't know the answer to give you."

At Two Feathers' narrowed gaze, Pixie knew that Two Feathers thought she played him false. "I can't explain something that I don't understand myself," she clarified.

"Whose Pix's people?" he responded.

Pixie sighed. "You wouldn't understand even if I tried to explain."

At Two Feathers' lunge to his feet, Pixie gave a cry and scrambled backward. Her words it seemed had insulted him. She hadn't meant for them to. Two Feathers didn't come toward her as she expected, but scooped up his child instead and then stomped from the home. Looking around at the interior of the lodge, Pixie's heart pounded. Was she to be punished for an unintended insult? She jumped to her feet. She would not beg for mercy. She would not humiliate herself again with that weakness. Minutes later, Two Feathers reentered the home alone, his face set with doggedness.

Pixie stiffened when he stalked toward her.

"If you want to punish me go ahead, but I didn't mean any disrespect." Her voice quivered. Pixie clasped her hands together before her. Two Feathers paused in his step. In surprise, Pixie watched as he sat back down beside the fire. Reaching up, he yanked her downward to settle beside him.

"Two Feathers ask Pix question. Pix answer," he rumbled. Pixie knew her face must reflect her fear as she quickly straightened to lean away from him. His gaze sharpened at her action.

"Two Feathers not punish Pix. Now explain how fall from sky."

"Can I have my...my...hand back?"

Releasing her fingers, he waited. Pixie grimaced as she looked away from Two Feathers' stern and watchful gaze.

"You won't believe me. It's too unreal."

"Talk."

"I come from a time of many, many suns and moons ahead of the time we're in now."

Two Feathers scowled in disbelief.

"I'm not lying. Go ask TJ to tell you where we come from if you won't believe me."

"Talk."

"TJ and I were driving to visit a friend."

"What this driving?"

Pixie frowned.

Several hours later, Two Feathers added more wood to the fire and he studied its flames. After a moment, his gaze slanted toward her. Pixie raised her hand in protest. "I promise I'm telling the truth. We are from the future."

"Not understand how possible."

"I didn't believe TJ either when he brought the subject up."

Two Feathers reached out to grasp hold of her chin, and he forced her to meet his gaze. "Pix describe strange place where fly in sky with birds, talk through air without person in front of Pix.

Brave Bird and Crow say Pix lie. Two Feathers know Pix lie. Two Feathers suspect tell falsehood this night. Pix try to make fool of Two Feathers?"

Pixie wanted to slap his grasp from her chin, her resentment flaring, at his disbelief of her. He would strike back if she did. She glared instead at the man before her, and refused to answer his question. Let him think what he would.

Visibly, Two Feathers reined in his annoyance. He dropped his hand back to his side.

"Go to Two Feathers' blankets."

Wanting to refuse, Pixie obeyed instead. She didn't remove her dress though only her shoes and his gaze narrowed.

Banking the fire with more wood, Two Feathers looked over at her. Pixie turned her face away when he began to strip bare of his clothes. Feeling him slide between the buffalo blankets along beside her, she rolled sideways turning her back to him.

"Pix face Two Feathers."

Pixie ignored the command.

"Two Feathers punish if not obey."

Quickly flipping over, her bitterness high, Pixie refused to look up. Rising up onto his elbow, Two Feathers gazed down at her. He reached out as if intent on pulling her toward him, but then drew his hand back to his side. Turning, he lay on his back, his gaze directed upward toward the ceiling of the lodge.

"Council believe Pix and TJ from Master of Life. Say must have special power. Two Feathers tell Council not from Master of Life, not special, same as people. Council ask Two Feathers how Two Feathers know this. Two Feathers inform not see any special power. Inform also, when TJ speak with Father, TJ deny come from Master of Life."

"What do you mean the Council believes that we come from the Master of Life? What's the Master of Life?" Pixie couldn't keep quiet. Her curiosity sparked. It seemed she remembered that Two

Feathers had made mention of a Master of Life when they first met.

Turning onto his side so that he faced her, Two Feathers gazed at her in surprise. "Pix not know Master of Life?"

Pixie shook her head.

"Master of Life create all things. Give life, food."

"Oh. You mean the Council believes that we come from the actual heavens!" Pixie laughed at the irony of it and Two Feathers frowned.

"Pix make jest of belief? Make jest of Two Feathers?"

It seemed she'd angered him again.

"No," she quickly interjected.

Two Feathers continued, "Two Feathers now Chief. Council say Pix important to Chief and must bind Pix to Chief. Make wife. Two Feathers not believe Pix important."

"Really," Pixie mocked and then snapped her mouth shut. She should've bit her tongue and remained silent, but his so matter-of-fact statement of her non-importance to him, angered. He rose onto an elbow to stare down at her. Habits that he'd quickly acquired toward her: the stare and the elbow.

"How did you become Chief?" Pixie sputtered.

Two Feathers' expression had closed off. He didn't respond to her question. Fawn had said earlier that day that their father had lost touch with reality. After that one statement, she spoke no more on it and Pixie hadn't pressed. Pixie suspected Two Feathers' rising status was the result of his father's mental decline.

"Ceremony planned for Two Feathers as new Chief in fourteen suns. Pix become wife then," he abruptly stated.

Pixie remained silent.

She was glad to become Two Feathers' wife, though she'd never admit as much. If she and Two Feathers married, then surely Crow would back off and leave her alone.

Two Feathers watched her. "As wife Pix must show respect. No question Two Feathers when in public."

Pixie couldn't stop her self-defense against his demand. "I'm not some stupid person who has no mind of her own, you know."

Two Feathers exhaled and then as if he forgot she was by his side, he murmured, "Pix not Two Feathers' chosen one. Two Feathers only do as Council wish."

Hurt by the quietly spoken words, Pixie remained silent. Would he ever come to care for her? Maybe after their child was born? Pixie wondered if Two Feathers even remembered that she was pregnant. He had not brought the subject up since that first night that he'd fetched her back to his lodge to live. Maybe his first-born was the only child he'd ever really care for. Just as it seemed he could only love his first wife, Pretty Flower. Pixie and her child left out in the cold. No emotion felt toward either of them. He might provide for her and the child, but any love for them, he would withhold.

Pixie swallowed.

It didn't matter if Two Feathers cared for her or their child.

Her child would know love because she'd lavish the poor thing with it.

Pretending at sudden sleep, Pixie closed her eyes. After a moment, Two Feathers rolled to his back.

Chapter Twenty-One

Two Feathers watched as Crow slid down the river embankment toward the animal Crow had just felled. Soon the river that Crow now stood beside would become frozen over and the women would have to break its ice-covered film to gather their water. Winter was coming in fast and furious this season. Skidding down the ridge to where Crow waited, Two Feathers trekked toward him. They had left the village early to hunt that morning before the sun rose. They needed fresh meat for his celebration ceremony as Chief of their people.

"Crow have good aim," Two Feathers stated, complimenting his long-time friend when he reached him. Crow lifted the head of the deer by the tips of its massive rack of horns. They had traveled a ways down the riverbank from their village to track this huge beast. He beamed at Two Feathers.

"Crow chase last winter. Animal elude Crow."

Dragging his knife from its holder, Two Feathers palmed its handle. He waited. It was Crow's honor to make the first cut. Bending, Crow slashed the animal's throat. As its lifeblood flowed, he and Two Feathers gave their thanks to the Master of Life for its sacrifice.

****

Pixie listened as Fawn and Little Bird gossiped. She had felt melancholy that day remaining silent, only responding when directly asked a question. After a while, Fawn and Little Bird both had stopped trying to include her in their conversation. They all three now sat on the ground in front of Fawn's home their chores for the day done, a buffalo blanket spread out under them, and their buffalo robes around their shoulders. It seemed that TJ and Fawn had become an item. Fawn giggled as she spoke to Little Bird about him. Pixie was glad for TJ. Unlike Two Feathers and her, Fawn adored him.

Watching Two Feathers and Crow stroll back into the village, their kills carried over their shoulders, Pixie frowned. How could Two Feathers not see his friend for what he was?

Crow showed Two Feathers a completely different personality than what he displayed toward her, Pixie had to admit, which was why he'd never believe her if she told him all that his blood brother was. Just the evening before, Crow had appeared behind her as she'd gathered firewood, jerking her against him to slobber against her ear. He had laughed afterward and walked away, no one around to see his action. Shuddering, Pixie wiped at that same ear in memory. She needed to be more vigilant. She had thought that she was but still he'd been able to catch her unaware.

Fawn and Little Bird stopped talking to look up at her as she rose upward to her feet. Pixie lifted Three Feathers to settle him on her hip. She adjusted her buffalo robe around her shoulders and his.

"I should go home. Two Feathers may want me to help with his kill," she told the two women.

Little Bird and Fawn smiled their farewells.

Three Feathers fussed, and Pixie lifted him to clasp him high within her arms as she walked. He wrapped his arms around her neck and Pixie's emotions swelled. At least this little man cared for her.

"Are you sleepy, sweetheart?"

Three Feathers laid his head against her neck, and Pixie

patted at his back as she kissed his cheek.

****

Two Feathers watched their exchange and felt surprise when his jealousy rose. How could he be envious of his son receiving Pix's touch? He wanted her to give his son the best of care, demanded it in fact. She and his son disappeared within the confines of his home. He and Crow walked on toward his mother's lodge. His mother would see to all the preparations for his ceremony. Only two rising suns left before the planned celebration.

Seeing his sister and her childhood friend sitting together and talking, Two Feathers grinned. Fawn was happy, her own marriage anticipated after his. He had sought out TJ that next morning after their talk as Pix had told him to do, and the man repeated all that she had revealed of their other life. Two Feathers still was in disbelief of their story although they both told the same strange tale.

****

Laying Three Feathers down onto his buffalo blanket, Pixie afterward started to rise. He wasn't asleep and clutched at her hand for her to stay with him. Squatting back down to pat at the child's back, Pixie hummed to him. His eyelids drifted downward, and she remained by his side to wait for his father. When Two Feathers didn't come to the lodge as expected, Pixie's eyelids began to droop. She stretched out beside the child and promptly fell asleep.

Yawning, Pixie turned from where she lay beside Three Feathers. Sleepily she blinked. Swiftly, sitting up, she stood. Two Feathers sat before the fire in the center of the home.

"I fell asleep waiting. Do you wish me to help now with the cleaning of your kill?" she questioned.

"Mother take care of all for ceremony and wedding."

"Oh." Pixie didn't know whether to be hurt or relieved.

"It is her honor," he continued.

Walking forward, Pixie motioned to the pot that sat inside the fire pit ring but not within the flames of the fire. "I made rabbit stew earlier this day. Would you like for me to dip you out some?"

At Two Feathers' nod, Pixie fetched his eating bowl. Filling it to its brim, she handed it to him. As he ate, she sat down across from him. She didn't know what to say so she fidgeted with the fringe at the hem of her dress.

"Bring Sister to me," Two Feathers abruptly ordered within the silence of the room. He sat his empty bowl down beside him.

Standing, Pixie looked at him in question.

"Why Pix not go?" he demanded.

Whirling, she did as ordered.

"Fawn."

After her quiet call outside the entrance to Fawn's home, Pixie waited.

"Fawn," she called out again at no answer received. At her second call, Fawn walked from the interior of the lodge. With a look of question directed her way, she stepped to where Pixie stood.

"Two Feathers told me to bring you to him," Pixie told her.

"Why?"

Lifting her shoulder, Pixie replied, "I don't know."

"Brother believe he don't have to tell," Fawn responded with a chuckle. "Brother too important now."

At Fawn's poking at her brother, Pixie smiled.

When they entered Two Feathers' home, Pixie was still smiling and he looked at her in question. She quickly sobered.

He motioned toward Three Feathers. "Sister look after child while gone?"

When Fawn agreed, Two Feathers signaled for Pixie to follow him from the lodge.

"Where are we going?" Two Feathers didn't bother to respond

as Pixie trudged beside him. When he turned and headed toward Brave Bird's and Too Little's lodge, her steps lagged, and with bitterness within rising, Pixie curled her fingers into her palms. She must have offended in some way. He must now wish not to marry. She would not go back to that abusive woman's home. She would run from this place. Even caught and punished, she'd continue running until dead. At his call for admittance, Two Feathers glanced at her.

Pixie glared back.

With a frown, he motioned for her to follow him into the home with permission given to enter.

Too Little and Brave Bird hurried forward at their entrance.

Resentment swirling, Pixie stood beside Two Feathers. She stared straight ahead. Why return her to this household? There was no reason for it that she could grasp. Two Feathers reached out to touch her hand. Sliding sideways so that their connection was broken, Pixie straightened her shoulders.

"Two Feathers, welcome!" Too Little called out and as always, a huge, welcoming, beam washed his face. Brave Bird's gaze darted from Two Feathers to Pixie. The woman didn't smile or call out a welcome.

"It is good to see Too Little," Two Feathers responded. He then looked directly at Brave Bird. "Two Feathers wish speak to wife of Too Little this night."

Looking startled, Too Little glanced toward Brave Bird.

"What woman done?" he demanded of her. For once, his expression contained no smile.

"Nothing! Brave Bird do nothing. If lazy say so, lazy lie."

"Pix not speak ill of Brave Bird," Two Feathers retorted his words sharp. Brave Bird reared back. Two Feathers' gaze drilled and held the woman hostage. "Pretty Flower's garments gifted from Two Feathers, why Pix not have?"

Brave Bird shrilled, "Brave Bird know nothing of garments."

With a sharp motion made for TJ to come forward from where he sat listening, Two Feathers then dropped his arm. TJ walked to their group, each step a bounce of energy. Everyone in the home seemed attentive to the happenings within the lodge beside the lodge door.

"TJ bring garments into home, Two Feathers give TJ?" Two Feathers demanded of TJ when he reached them.

"Yes," TJ responded. "I gave all to Brave Bird to give to Pixie as instructed."

At Brave Bird's frightened expression all Pixie could do was turn to stare at Two Feathers. He defended her. He wasn't handing her back over to the vile woman, as she'd feared. Too Little grasped hold of his wife's upper arm. Pixie had never seen the man angry but now it flowed from him in molten waves. Many in the home turned their backs.

"Bring garments now," he ordered.

Brave Bird, intimidated for once, turned to do as ordered. When she returned, she jabbed out the bundle that she held toward Two Feathers.

"Brave Bird hand to Pix," he responded not moving. With obvious venom, Brave Bird did as instructed. As their eyes met, Pixie was relieved that she still wasn't under the woman's roof.

"We go," Two Feathers stated afterward.

Breathing deep the fresh air outside the home, Pixie wanted to dance with joy. She quietly walked by Two Feathers' side instead.

"Thank you."

"Two Feathers not abandon Pix again," he replied.

Staring straight ahead, Pixie didn't reply.

Chapter Twenty-Two

Standing within the interior of Fawn's family home, Pixie watched as her future mother-in-law and sister-in-law floated around her as they prepared her for her marriage, her and Two Feathers' marriage at high sun, and then Two Feathers' swearing in as tribal Chief that same evening.

Fawn circled her. "Pixie beautiful," she declared.

Pixie hoped so. She wanted Two Feathers to see her as attractive. He hadn't reached for her during the nights. She would've been willing if he had.

"Thank you for this wonderful fur." Pixie ran her fingers over the soft, supple pelt that draped her shoulders, a gift from Fawn. The dress that she wore was from Two Feathers' mother, as were the supple and soft boots on her feet. Her soon-to-be mother-in-law was a quiet, compassionate woman. Pixie saw where Fawn had inherited her kindness and her beauty.

"It starts," Fawn stated, turning at the sound of drumbeats heard outside the home. Two Feathers suddenly entered the lodge. His gaze moved over Pixie. Fawn and his mother quietly exited the home. Pixie felt disappointment ripple when, without a word, he reached for her hand. Silently, they walked together out into the sunlight.

The wedding ceremony was short, and Pixie found herself married to the man by her side within minutes. Sitting beside Two Feathers as they shared the meal prepared by his mother and her helpers, Pixie didn't feel wedded. It had all happened too fast. She needed to feel married, wanted that security.

Laughter echoed around her.

The whole village enjoyed the abundant feast that had been prepared.

"I want your feather tattoo now," she voiced.

Two Feathers turned at her statement and he frowned. "Marking done in privacy of lodge, Pix not wish others witness pain."

"I won't show my pain. I'll prove my strength. I want the people to see."

Two Feathers' face reflected his surprise. A trace of respect flickered. He stood. "Two Feathers bring Crow."

Pixie's heart rate dipped. *Crow? Surely, he's not the one to administer the marking? He's the one I wanted protection from, the one to see the mark.* Minutes later, as Crow laid out his paraphernalia, Pixie wanted to cry off. She didn't want his hands on her body. When Crow glanced up to meet her gaze, Pixie stiffened. He expected her to back out, she realized. The people had begun to gather to watch. There was no turning back. It would embarrass Two Feathers.

"I want my feather to match Two Feathers' in size," she demanded.

Crow's gaze narrowed before he bent forward.

Two Feathers sat down beside her, and Pixie felt grateful for his presence.

Her arm suffered as Crow worked, and the minutes slowly ticked. The people who'd gathered to watch began to meander away becoming bored with the passing hours. Crow dapped at the blood that flowed down her arm. His head bent to his task.

"Almost end," he murmured.

It seemed that he took extreme pride in his workmanship. He didn't hurry, even leaning back every now and then to survey his work. All of a sudden, he reared back and dropped his hands to his sides.

"Crow finished," Two Feathers told Pixie when she didn't move. Looking down at her burning appendage, Pixie gazed at a perfect replica of Two Feathers' tattoos on his shoulders now displayed down her left shoulder to the bend of her elbow. Her feather slightly curved just as each one of Two Feathers' was.

No one would question whom she belonged to now.

Pixie smiled and her gaze rose in challenge toward Crow.

When told earlier by Fawn that for her protection she'd receive Two Feathers' mark, Pixie had decided then that she wanted one the same size as Two Feathers'. Crow stood, and bending, he gathered up his scattered work items and walked away. No word said. *Ha, take that*, Pixie thought. Now he would stay away. Two Feathers helped her to her feet and Pixie smiled up at him.

"We go home," her husband told her.

****

Once home, Two Feathers spread salve on Pixie's arm that his mother brought to them. As he worked, his fingertips were gentle over her recent punctures. Pixie studied her husband's features. *Will he ever come to love or desire me as he did Pretty Flower?* She wondered.

Fawn had revealed in confidence the story of his wife's death. She had taken her own life, she'd stated. Hanged herself. If madly in love with Two Feathers as Fawn believed Pretty Flower had been, why take her life within weeks of giving birth to their child? It made no sense. Maybe it was postpartum depression.

In modern times, it could have been recognized. In this era, Pretty Flower wouldn't have known what was wrong with her and neither would have anyone else. Two Feathers looked up and caught her scrutiny of him. Embarrassed, Pixie looked away.

"Friends arrive," he stated.

Hearing their arrival, too, Pixie nodded.

A messenger sent out had announced his change in status as now chief of the tribe. It seemed neighbors had arrived in time to witness the official switch of power.

"We go," Two Feathers stated.

Walking outside their home into the cold evening air, Pixie stared at the gathering crowd. The village overflowed with visitors.

Fawn came forward.

"Brother, Council asks for you."

"Stay by Sister's side," Two Feathers instructed Pixie before he walked away.

"Come, we find Mother," Fawn instructed.

Walking beside her sister-in-law, Pixie was in awe. She'd had no idea that a tribe lived close by.

"Who are all these people?"

Fawn laughed. "Some kin, some friends, my mother's people."

Pixie noticed Crow standing before a woman. He seemed to be arguing with her. The poor woman, she didn't appear too happy to be where she was. Fawn at her awareness of her appraisal of the two, nodded toward them.

"Wife of Crow, not happy in marriage, go back to her people."

So that was the estranged wife. It looked as if Crow wanted her back and she wasn't having any of it.

TJ walked up and a smile split his face as he looked at Fawn. Pixie hadn't paid attention to him the other night at Brave Bird's home, and busy with Three Feathers and her daily chores, she hadn't had time for visiting him for quite a while. *He looks marvelous*, she thought in surprise, the scar on his face giving him a wild, dangerous look. It fitted this environment. Fawn wrapped her fingers around his when he reached his hand out to her. A picture-perfect example of love, Pixie thought with a sharp, jealous pang.

"There is mother. We must go to her," Fawn stated.

The crowd was heavy enough that Pixie and the others couldn't squeeze forward. Fawn's mother didn't notice their struggles behind her as she stared ahead watching the ceremony. The steady beat of drums vibrated through the crowd. Wishing that she could witness what was happening, Pixie stretched upward. A sudden shout went up and the condensed crowd around her and Fawn and TJ parted. Pixie slowly lowered her heels back to the ground.

Two Feathers, with a regal headpiece flowing down his back, stood beside his father. Turning, Two Feathers' gaze met hers and Pixie felt her pride swell. He was the most handsome man in the village. He pivoted to speak to his father when Crow strolled up to stand beside them. Feeling dismissed, Pixie started toward home. She was lonely. She didn't even have the little one to love on this day as his grandmother had gathered him up to be with her. Even Fawn and TJ didn't notice her departure. Arriving at what was now her official home, Pixie gazed at the items stacked at its entrance and which blocked her entry, baskets, blankets, crockery—wedding gifts, she realized in amazement.

Bringing the hodgepodge into the lodge, Pixie placed them where Two Feathers would see them. Glancing around at the interior of the lodge, she exhaled. Outside the lodge, she could still hear the laughter and talking, Two Feathers and the visiting tribe enjoying the feast and the party. Someone had kept an inviting fire going within the lodge and had even laid out a mound of buffalo blankets in the sleeping area. Tempting a married couple to it, Pixie assumed. She turned from the sight.

A container of washing water sat beside the fire. Walking forward, Pixie dipped a finger into the water. Its temperature was just right for a quick wash. Other earthenware positioned close to the fire, Pixie knew, held food. She wasn't hungry though. She breathed deep.

"This is your life, girl."

Pixie jumped. She had spoken aloud.

Tipping her head back to look upward, she whispered, "Was I so bad that this was your answer to my prayer?"

****

Halting before the entry of his home upon his mother's soft request for him to linger, Two Feathers turned.

"Mother?" he questioned. His mother walked forward. The night was late. It seemed she'd waited for his arrival.

"Why Mother stand in dark? Why not home with Father?"

Two Feathers felt sympathy for his mother rise. She was a soft-spoken woman who had always lived in the shadow of another. She stepped before him and studied him. Reaching up to pat his face, her melancholy smile appeared. "Two Feathers have life to live. Live it."

She turned, preparing to leave. Reaching out, Two Feathers touched her arm and she halted, her gaze lifting to his. She laid a hand over his. Giving it a light squeeze, she continued on her way. She had said what she wanted to say.

Entering his home, Two Feathers' gaze fell to the woman asleep on his bed—*no, not woman, wife*—he thought with a smile. Did his mother mean to guide him toward her, to accept Pretty Flower's death? After dealing with his father these past several suns, he'd grasped the wasted life of the man. His father only existed, never living after the death of that first family. Two Feathers didn't want that life. He didn't want to go through the motions of day-to-day living while grieving for the former. He wanted to be in the now—to love—and have love returned. He wanted to enjoy life.

Walking to the woman who that day became his life companion, Two Feathers gazed down at her as she slept. Her newly, tattooed arm, she'd positioned out away from the buffalo fur. Turning from her, Two Feathers went to place more wood on the fire. Snow was falling again, and the night cold with its return. He had been proud of Pix that day, his companion. She had showed strength.

Stripping bare, he eased between the buffalo robes to lie beside her. Reaching out he clasped his fingers with hers and then brought the tips of her fingers to his lips. His feelings this day had softened toward her. She was his future, and as he'd told her so many moons ago, past is past. His life would start again this night with this new wife, a gift thrown at his feet from the skies.

Waking, she turned toward him, and then realizing that he held her hand, she looked up at him in confusion.

"What are you doing?" she inquired.

Freeing her fingers, Two Feathers concentrated on the buffalo blanket that she'd wrapped around her, making sure that their bodies wouldn't touch when he came to bed. She had started that practice after that second night of her return to his home. He hadn't challenged her action before, now he would.

"Release," he ordered.

Holding tight to the edge of the blanket, she didn't move. Two Feathers tugged and pulled it from her. Her hands he grasped afterward and held down at her sides, preventing her attempt to pull the blanket back upward. She watched him. Frightened it seemed.

When she'd wept so hard following that first night in his lodge, he'd been afraid, remembering Pretty Flower. Pretty Flower had become emotional also when carrying their child. Later he had regretted his sharpness with her. Losing his temper over her crying for what she would never say upset her.

"Two Feathers?"

Leaning forward, Two Feathers covered Pix's mouth with his. He didn't want talk. She struggled and then lay unmoving as if ready to endure. Two Feathers breathed deep, slowing his emotion. He wanted Pix with him every step of the way. He wanted *that* night again—their night under the stars—the oneness they'd shared that first time.

Chapter Twenty-Three

Pixie snuggled against her husband.

He slept on. She couldn't stop the smile of contentment that spread and it tugged the corners of her mouth upward. Two Feathers had been disarming when waking her at his arrival to the lodge, his night of celebration over. At first, she'd been afraid, afraid of a careless mating. He had been kind though, whispering how much she pleased him.

Shifting, Pixie felt the soreness of her thighs. A discomfort yes, although not an irritation. Her arm was another matter altogether.

Two Feathers woke at her movement and his gaze met hers.

"Arm hurt?"

Pixie felt shy. "I was just making sure the buffalo blanket didn't stick to it. I didn't mean to wake you."

He didn't reply as he closed his eyes again.

"Why you stare?" he stated a moment later.

Embarrassed, Pixie didn't know what to say. She stared because she couldn't believe how he could drag such hedonism from her. At one point in the night, she'd been the aggressor and he let her. Two Feathers' mouth stretched to form a smile. He didn't open his eyes. Pixie frowned. Did he smile in conceit? She had been vocal in her pleasure.

Unhappy with her thoughts, Pixie closed her own eyes and affected sleep. She sensed when Two Feathers rose to his elbow to gaze down at her. She didn't move. He placed a soft kiss on her collarbone before he moved to her chin to nuzzle there, and he taunted, "Two Feathers know Pix awake."

His lips moved over her neck as he spoke again, "Arm pain wife?"

Pixie gave up her pretense, but kept her eyes closed. "No."

Two Feathers moved his attention to her shoulder blade and she shivered. Opening her eyes, she met Two Feathers' slanted grin.

"Ah...now wife awake," he teased. He shifted giving her some space, his smile leaving although his eyes remained jovial.

"Pix walk through village with Two Feathers after wash and dress and put healing salve on arm," he informed.

"Why walk through the village?" *An after-wedding ceremonial thing?* Pixie wondered as she looked up at Two Feathers in question. *He really is a handsome man*, she thought and she begrudged her thought, although she'd thought the same thing the evening before.

"Speak to visitors before leave. Polite."

"I'm surprised the other tribe would leave this morning, after just one night and walking here?"

Two Feathers gave a partial grin as if he held a secret. "Other tribe not leave till four suns. Two Feathers take wife to quiet place. Stay two suns. Fawn prepare for Pix and Brother."

Surprise held Pixie in place as she stared up at Two Feathers, two whole days alone to get to know him better? Fawn hadn't breathed a word.

"What about Three Feathers?"

"Mother care for son while gone."

Rising, Two Feathers turned to lift Pixie to her feet. Pixie faced him, her hands on his chest.

"What do I need to take with us?"

"Only what wear," he informed.

****

Glancing up at Two Feathers' profile as they strolled through the settlement, Pixie's eagerness for their time alone faded. As soon as they'd emerged from the lodge, he'd reverted to his aloof self. Even now, he walked by her side as if they were strangers, as if the night before he hadn't communicated all those wonderful things. He had never stated why they were going to the place he mentioned. Just that they were. Maybe they went because the people expected it. Glancing sideways at the man by her side, Pixie frowned. He threw scraps of attention her way and she went soft expecting love where none existed. She was a fool.

****

Two Feathers sensed Pix's withdrawal as he conversed with the man in front of him. Her shutdown confused him. Everyone they had encountered that morning accepted her, and none that he'd noticed insulted. He gave his full attention to her when the man before him turned away. Fawn was right. He did need to get to know this woman better. His sister championed her. When she'd brought up the subject of their time alone together, he had balked at first, but Fawn had insisted. Meeting Pix's restrained gaze, Two Feathers frowned. Would two days be enough to understand this woman? He didn't think so. He had thought that he knew Pretty Flower, and her suicide had devastated him to the core. The aftermath of it made him uncertain and wary now of the woman who walked beside him.

Crow was conversing with his estranged wife Two Feathers noticed as he and Pix walked past the couple. He hoped his blood brother convinced the woman to come home and to bring their child back. Crow had stated that morning that he still didn't understand her sudden flight. It seemed he and Crow was in the same predicament with their women. They baffled them.

"We've circled the village and spoke to all who came forward. Now Fawn signals time to leave," Two Feathers informed Pix.

She glanced Fawn's way but didn't respond.

"All is ready, Brother," Fawn informed when he and Pix stopped before her.

"Thank you for doing this, but you didn't need to," Pix told her.

At her tentative smile given to his sister, Two Feathers scanning Pix's face realized she had gained weight, unnoticed by him, and was no longer as gaunt looking. Pregnancy looks good on her, he decided. Now that the time to leave was upon them, he was glad to have her to himself. He felt affection well up. His sister grasped her hand to kiss the back of it.

"Pixie Fawn's sister now. Fawn wish only happiness for Sister."

Embarrassed with Fawn's public display, Two Feathers pulled Pix toward him.

"We leave. Let no harm come to son, Sister," he ordered.

"Son always cared for, Brother," Fawn dryly drawled.

Dropping his hand from Pix's shoulder, Two Feathers motioned for her to walk along beside him. In silence, they left the village and the people within it. All in the tribe was his to rule over now, and the new responsibility weighed heavy on him. Lifting his hand in farewell to his mother, Two Feathers watched her incline her head back to him. His father had disappeared into the family lodge the evening before after his swearing in ceremony as the peoples' new Chief. He had refused to speak with anyone since.

Two Feathers knew his mother fretted over the old man. The mental decline of his father bothered him also, but anger simmered within him, too. His father was a self-serving man and had always been so. His request to enter the family home that morning denied. His mother was apologetic to him in return, although, as always a steadfast supporter of the man who had never loved anyone except that first family.

****

Pixie watched the snowflakes flutter downward to the ground around her. Everything was so quiet and surreal, no honking horns, no phones. There were no distractions except for a tree branch heard creaking here and there. Pixie glanced sideways at the man who walked along beside her. He hadn't made a single comment since they'd left the village.

"How much further?" she inquired.

"Not far." Two Feathers looked at her. "Pix weary?"

"I'm fine. I just wondered."

He stopped walking entirely. "We rest."

"Two Feathers, I only wondered how far we were to walk." Pixie wiped away the clinging snow on her eyelashes. The snow had also begun to collect on hers and Two Feathers' buffalo blanket-covered shoulders.

Holding out her hand, Pixie captured some of the steady falling, large white flakes. "They are so pristine, so quiet. Aren't they pretty, Two Feathers?"

"It is pleasing."

Looking up, Pixie stilled. Two Feathers was looking at her, not at the falling snow. He stepped closer, and reaching out, he brushed the collected white powder from her shoulders and then expanding an arm, gathered her to him. Pixie's blanket dropped from her shoulders as he pulled her under the buffalo blanket that draped around his own shoulders. He didn't say anything as he gazed down at her. The village behind them now out of sight and its people's voices unheard through the tree grove that surrounded them. The scent of smoke drifted through the air.

It comforts, Pixie thought as she curled her fingers into the leather shirt under her palms. She inched closer to the warm body against hers, and savored Two Feathers' heat and his physical strength. She wished for him to recognize only her, to forget that first wife. Was it selfish? Yes. She didn't care. She wanted all that he could give with nothing left over for Pretty Flower. Two Feathers placed a finger under her chin, and Pixie's gaze met his dark, unreadable one.

"Don't take life," he stated.

"What?" Pixie in confusion frowned.

"Pretty Flower take life. Leave all behind. Pretty Flower no talk with husband."

"I don't plan on taking my life." It surprised Pixie that Two Feathers worried about such a thing. Maybe he cared a little.

"I love you." Pixie instantly wanted to bite her tongue. She had thought the words and blurted them. Did she really love him or was he only a safe haven and so she said the words to feel secure?

Two Feathers didn't respond, his countenance solemn.

Slowly, he leaned forward until his mouth touched hers.

An untamed, aggressive storm followed.

Pixie breathed heavy when finally turned loose.

Bending, Two Feathers silently picked up the buffalo robe she'd dropped, and shaking it out wrapped it back around her shoulders.

"Only few steps left then reach destination," he informed.

Pixie looked to where he pointed, and on unsteady legs, she turned to walk with him when he stepped forward.

A small tepee sat hidden when they approached the area that he'd indicated. Two Feathers bent and lifted the structure's doorway flap. He motioned for her to enter through it before him. Rounding her shoulders, Pixie stepped forward. Turning sideways, she allowed Two Feathers to enter the tepee behind her. He dwarfed the area when he stretched to his full height. Animal pelts covered the tepee's dirt floor except around a shallow fire pit at its center. The casually laid out furs gave Pixie pause. They would've cost a fortune at a mall in her time.

Glancing around at the tepee's interior, Pixie noted everything that Fawn had done. A welcoming fire burned within the fire pit and warmed the small space. Prepared food waited for their consumption. Its pleasing aroma filled the area. Buffalo blankets piled high against the tepee wall made an extravagant bed. Fawn had even folded some into pillows. On two pillows, she'd placed wooden stick figures, and their forms resembled humans. Rawhide wrapped around their middles held little outstretched arms in place. The enclosure exuded warmth, coziness, and romance.

A little embarrassed, Pixie glanced toward Two Feathers. She hoped he didn't think she'd put his sister up to this. She and Fawn had talked alone that morning, as he was well aware.

As he looked everything over, he drawled, "Sister Two Feathers think, imagines TJ."

Taking his buffalo robe covering and then hers, Two Feathers laid them beside the tepee entryway to dry. Then removing his shoes, he indicated for Pixie to discard hers. *So domesticated*, Pixie thought as she did what he wanted. However, she knew the illusion was false. Going to the fire, Two Feathers lifted the lids from the stoneware. He looked up at her.

"Hungry?"

Nodding, Pixie walked forward to do her duty. It shocked her when Two Feathers began to ladle out food for them both not waiting on her. Taking the offered meal from his hand, Pixie sat down cross-legged beside the warmth of the fire. Two Feathers rested close beside her. Pixie watched him in wonderment. Behind closed doors he acted different, but in a good way.

He looked up. "Why Pix not eat?"

Pixie took a bite of the meal and then another, and another. She hadn't realized until then how hungry she was. Cleaning her plate, she jumped up to refill it. Two Feathers gave a sudden laugh, and looking up, Pixie realized that he laughed at her. Her embarrassment soared. He made a motion for her to finish filling her plate, his smile wide.

"Pix eat."

Pixie's anger rocketed. "What's so funny?"

Setting his tray aside, Two Feathers rose to his feet and solemn-faced, although his eyes twinkled, he reached for her free hand. "Two Feathers not laugh at Pix again. Not polite."

"Damn straight," Pixie growled. She shook off his hand.

"What damn straight?" Two Feathers' mouth twitched.

"I mean you shouldn't have laughed at me. Why did you laugh?"

Two Feathers laughed outright. "Pix eat so fast look like starved wolf pup."

Mortified, Pixie wiped at her chin. She was supposed to be the civilized one. Her appetite gone, Pixie set the refilled tray aside as she sat back down. Two Feathers sat down beside her to finish his meal. He looked at her a couple of times but didn't say anything. When he'd eaten all that he'd spooned onto his tray, he set his tray aside. Standing, he covered the pots with their lids.

He stretched a hand out to her. "Come, we clean self."

Ignoring his hand, Pixie rose to her feet. Frowning, Two Feathers turned. Coming back into the tepee from their quick wash, he caught her to him to splay his hand over the space where her heart lay. Neither had spoken as they washed.

"Two Feathers not mean hurt in here," he told her.

Pixie stood stiff. As she'd washed her body and scrubbed at her teeth, she'd wondered if she'd lost all sense of decency. Her friends used to say she was urbane. Now she slopped her food, washed outdoors, and felt pampered to have hand-me-down clothes.

"No cry, no cry," Two Feathers stated.

Laying her forehead against his bare chest, Pixie swallowed back her tears. She missed her family and Lynn. Missed the advancements of her time, she even missed the simple pleasure of a warm bath. Lifting her into his arms, Two Feathers carried her to the pile of buffalo blankets. Pixie pushed him back when he started to stretch out beside her.

"No," she blurted.

He frowned. "Pix wife."

"I don't want to be your wife!"

Two Feathers sat up.

Pixie could tell she had angered him. She didn't care. She

turned her back to him. She heard him dress. At his abrupt leaving of the tepee, she flipped back around. All of a sudden, Pixie felt panic wash through her. Would Two Feathers return her to Brave Bird for her denial? He hadn't meant to cause her embarrassment and it was her fault that she'd lost all sense of decorum.

Heart racing, Pixie jumped up. She wouldn't want to live if Two Feathers sent her back to that household. Moreover, she knew that if he did, he'd never again turn to her. Racing to the tepee's entrance, Pixie threw back the shelter's flap and then scrambled through the doorway. Seeing Two Feathers leaning against a tree, she raced toward him. Straightening, he looked around as if expecting an intruder; his hand went to his knife handle. Pixie skidded to a halt in front of him, and she grabbed at his shirt. "Don't send me back to that awful woman!"

Two Feathers' hands covered hers. Pixie held tight to his shirt afraid that he would stipulate for her to step away.

"Why Pix believe this?" he demanded instead.

"Because I denied you and told you that I didn't want to be your wife, but I do."

Two Feathers grasped hold of her shoulders.

"Two Feathers say not send Pix away. Why Pix not believe?"

Wrapping her arms around Two Feathers' neck in gratitude, Pixie stretched onto her tiptoes to kiss the side of his neck and then moved to his jawline as she pressed herself against him. She would whore for him if she had to. She didn't care. She couldn't go back under Brave Bird's control.

"Whatever you want from me this night, I'll give," she vowed.

Pixie found herself back inside the tepee and stretched out on the buffalo blankets with Two Feathers lying beside her. He had pulled her deerskin dress up over her head to throw it across the tent floor. His own clothes shed. When their naked bodies touched, Pixie shivered not in anger, or fear, or a pretense of desire for her own self-preservation. No, she quivered with a fierce, aching need for the man beside her. It seemed every time they connected they devoured each other. Pixie moved her hands to caress Two Feathers' shoulders. The texture of him excited her. She wanted, needed this man. His hands skimmed her bare form, and he seemed beside himself as his lips followed the same course those hands took. He consumed her as he'd done the night previous. Pixie bent her knees. Looking up at her movement, Two Feathers frowned. He seemed angry. Pixie froze. What had she done wrong? Two Feathers raised her leg to touch his lips to the scar where he'd cut out her old tattoo. His gaze met hers again. It was as if he held regret. Pixie's ankle tingled where his lips had touched her skin.

"Two Feathers," she breathed.

Silently, he caressed the length of her leg, and then he stretched upward on bended knee to cover her mouth with his. Pixie found herself flipped over so that she lay on her stomach. Two Feathers' hands molded her bottom as he held her down.

"Let me turn over, Two Feathers. I want to see you."

His fingers skimmed the length of her calves and over her toes. His hands and mouth were everywhere, touching, caressing. Pixie's breathing filled the tepee. When finally spun to face him, he positioned her to bring their bodies together, and Pixie's pleasure surged, almost peaking. Two Feathers was rough, yet tender, silent, yet not, and without words said, Pixie knew she pleased him.

Abruptly, gratification splintered and Pixie cried out, her back arching, her fingers digging into his arms. Two Feathers quickly covered her mouth with his, quieting her cries. His hot fluid flowed seconds later as he moaned against her mouth. Wrapping her arms around his shoulders when he collapsed against her, Pixie held him tight not wanting him to move. This was where she wanted to be. He was her safe place.

****

Rising on his elbows, Two Feathers looked down at the woman

who lay so still beneath him. Tenderly, he tapped at her cheek with the tip of a finger. She kept her eyes closed as if asleep, although she frowned when he withdrew from her to lie down beside her. Opening her eyes, she considered him.

Two Feathers eased his arm under her head. He didn't know if Pix really saw him. Her eyelids drooped downward and closed again as if she were unable to keep them open. Watching her, Two Feathers realized that she was fast asleep, dead to the world and him.

Dragging the buffalo blanket up to cover her and him both, he lay still and quiet beside her. He was tired. It was a good tired, though. It had surprised and scared him when she'd come running from the wedding tepee. His heart had jumped into his throat when he thought she was in danger. When she began to press against him and then vowed she'd do whatever he wanted, he'd lost control. Somehow, this strange and odd woman had become intermingled with his very being. Pulling Pix tighter against him, Two Feathers sighed with contentment. He enjoyed Pix's odd ways and outspoken brashness.

Looking up at the ceiling of the shelter, Two Feathers frowned in thought. No, he silently admitted. He more than enjoyed this woman. He delighted in her. He didn't want to live without her. He wanted her by his side now and always. At his admittance, Two Feathers felt Pretty Flower's spirit leaving, and it grieved him. He wanted to call her back, to ask for her forgiveness. He had thought he could care for no other and had even promised after her death to take no other as wife.

Pix woke beside him, and sitting up, she looked around as if searching.

"Was someone here?" she asked.

Finding his voice, Two Feathers hoarsely responded, "No. No one here with Two Feathers."

Reaching out, he pulled his wife to him.

Chapter Twenty-Four

Two whole days and three nights Pixie and Two Feathers had together, and Pixie wished that they could stay two more. She wasn't ready to go back to that other world. Two Feathers had been loving and kind, and open about his past. He had even talked about Pretty Flower and her death. His grief and shock he shared at finding her dangling from a tree branch. Pixie explained to him about postpartum depression and he wondered on it.

She described more to him about her own life and the modern world that she had lived in. He still wasn't sure how she and TJ could have traveled backward in time, and was awed and unsure of all that she'd revealed. At one point, he became angered over her explanation of the peoples future history.

"Wife, we must leave. Snow is heavy now."

Looking at Two Feathers when he stuck his head though the tepee doorway, Pixie nodded. He was worried and so was she. Crow had walked to their hideaway to inform them that Two Feathers' father was missing.

It was morning, and during the night, a heavy snowstorm had moved in. The snowdrifts outside the tent were knee high when they'd woken and looked out. The light flakes of the past two days a precursor for what now had settled in and looked to remain for a while.

Pixie swept her buffalo robe around her shoulders.

"What about the tepee and its contents?" she asked when she emerged from the shelter. The wind whipped and the cold of it stung her cheeks. Crow stood beside Two Feathers. He didn't look her way.

Two Feathers responded, "Come back for all later. Must hurry and return to village. We lose way if storm continue."

"But we didn't walk that far from the village. How could we get lost?"

Two Feathers started Pixie forward, his hand on her arm. "Gray sky and blowing snow make lose sense of direction."

Struggling through the snowdrifts, Pixie huffed for air. Two Feathers and Crow on each side of her kept their hands on her upper arms, pulling her with them. Two Feathers was right. She had no idea which way they walked, and as the time stretched on, she wondered if perhaps he and Crow had become lost. Her teeth chattered and she was unable to stop their movement as the cold and wet seeped through her leather shoes and up the hem of her dress.

Relief washed through Pixie when the familiar sounds of the village began to drift through the blinding whiteness. Fawn ran up when their small group staggered into her family home. The wind and snow whipped into the lodge behind them as Crow firmly pulled the door shut.

"TJ and Too Little go in search of Father and none return," Fawn informed her brother. Her features were tense with worry as she spoke.

"Take wife home. Crow and Two Feathers leave. Hunt also," Two Feathers, responded.

Pixie looked at Two Feathers.

She didn't want him to go back out in that snowstorm. She knew if she protested he'd be displeased. She placed a hand on his arm.

"Be safe, Husband."

He didn't respond. He turned and quickly gathered up the items he needed. Afterward, he and Crow silently stepped from the lodge. Pixie went to pick up Three Feathers from where he sat and played. His toys scattered around him on the animal fur spread out underneath him. He curled a chubby arm around her neck when she wrapped him within her buffalo covering.

"I can find my way home," she informed Fawn.

Fawn nodded, distracted. Mother hadn't moved. She hadn't looked up when they arrived or when Two Feathers and Crow left again.

Pushing against the wind and blinding snow, Pixie found and entered her lodge. With relief, she uncovered Three Feathers' head letting the buffalo robe that she'd wrapped around them to fall unheeded to the floor. Thank goodness for the fire already built. The lodge was warm. Three Feathers wiggled and wanted Pixie to put him down, and Pixie did as he wished. Stumbling and falling when he took off at a run, he let out a wail of outrage refusing to get back up.

"Let me see," Pixie told him as she bent to inspect his knees. "You're okay, stop your crying."

When he instantly ceased, she picked him up. The wind howled outside the lodge and shivers crawled down Pixie's spine. Sitting down upon hers and Two Feathers' sleeping pallet, she placed the infant onto her lap. She stretched to pick up the bowl that she'd begun to store miscellaneous items of interest in that she found.

"What do you think of this, Three Feathers?" she asked as she pulled from the bowl a small, flat piece of bone. She had collected many of the smooth white pieces. Some long, some short. Pixie held her palm open for the child to gaze down at what she held.

He looked at what she held. He didn't respond.

"Don't you think it would be pretty if I were to punch a hole through the piece to make a necklace? Even scratch a design on it. Your aunt Fawn has several. Hers are pretty."

Gazing up at her in silence, Three Feathers frowned. He wiggled wanting her to let him up. Pixie watched him wobble around the home and her astonishment rose at what she'd just said to the child. Here she was talking about making a necklace of bone when she'd had diamonds in her time. What surprised the most was that the jewelry she planned to make seemed just as precious to her.

Putting away the bowl, Pixie continued to watch the child.

As time crawled and the evening grew later, she worried about the men. A woman called out, and rising, Pixie hurried to the door of the lodge. She picked up Three Feathers on her way and placed the child on her hip as she walked. A woman whom Pixie recognized as a relative entered through the doorway at her request for her to do so. Pixie looked at her in question.

"Two Feathers say fetch wife come to father's home," the woman stated.

"He found his father?"

The relative didn't respond. Instead, she held out her hands. "Give child."

Handing Three Feathers over to her, Pixie grabbed her buffalo robe to sling it around her shoulders. The storm had lessened during her time of waiting and she made her way easily to the other lodge. At calling out and then entering Two Feathers' family home, Pixie paused within the dwelling's entrance. Fawn and Two Feathers' mother sat squatted before two bodies. Their low wails of sorrow heard. All others within the lodge stood quiet, motionless. Pixie felt her sadness rise at their obvious loss. Looking toward Two Feathers, she knew that death had claimed his father. She couldn't see the bodies to know who the other casualty was, a relative maybe.

Two Feathers motioned for her to come forward, his expression drawn. Realizing Too Little's silent and somber statue as Too Little watched her, Pixie screamed, comprehending, and her cry filled the quietness of the lodge. Two Feathers lunged. As she crumbled, he gathered her into his arms striding from the home.

"Not TJ," Pixie moaned. "Not my TJ."

Chapter Twenty-Five

Emotionally detached from the others around her, Pixie sat outside her home and watched the child she was to care for. She had fought her depression, but it lingered, refusing to leave her. Fawn, Pixie knew, silently drifted around the village, although at Fawn walking past her that early morning, Pixie hadn't noticed her appearance until in that moment. Fawn had lost weight. Her eyes hollow. Her shoulders drooped. There was an injury to her arm and Pixie wondered on it. It looked scabbed over so it hadn't just recently happened.

Pixie felt shame rise at her own self-absorption. She had not spoken to her sister-in-law since the day Two Feathers and the others had brought the bodies into the village. While she'd grieved the loss of a friend and her only link to her past, Fawn grieved the loss of two loved ones. How many days had passed since the deaths? Ten? Twelve? Pixie wasn't sure although she'd thrown a small pebble every morning into a container to keep track of her pregnancy days. Two Feathers left her alone, coming and going in silence. The killing snowstorm departed as fast as it had arrived. Just sharp, cold days and overcast skies now left behind.

Standing, Pixie drew Three Feathers to her to hold him within her arms. She adjusted her blanket around his shoulders to make sure that he'd stay warm. Stepping forward, she followed Fawn's path taken and she wondered at the healing injury noted on her arm. Taking the same trail into the woods as Fawn had, Pixie gasped aloud as she looked ahead.

Fawn having bent as if in prayer, suddenly straightened and she sliced her forearm with the knife that she held.

Running forward, Pixie cried out, "What are you doing? Don't do that!"

Turning to look at her, Fawn lowered the injured arm and blood dripped from its wound to the ground.

"Why Pixie follow Fawn? Fawn wish for privacy."

Grasping Fawn's hand within hers, Pixie gazed down in horror at the fresh cut on her friend's forearm. The scabbed over wound above it identical to the new wound Fawn had just inflicted.

"Why?" Pixie gasped.

Fawn pulled her hand from her grasp and tears slid down her cheeks. "Fawn display grief for father and now for TJ."

Sadness overwhelmed Pixie as she gazed at her friend. "I'm sorry, Fawn. Do all your people do this when a loved one passes? I haven't seen wounds on Two Feathers' arms."

Fresh tears spilled down Fawn's cheeks. "Only if want to show outward grief for loved one."

Wiping at her own sudden tears, Pixie swallowed back her sadness. "Don't do this for TJ," she begged. "He would be upset if he saw you harm yourself because of him. In our time, we didn't express sorrow this way and he knows that you suffer his passing."

In the privacy of the woods, Fawn sobbed out her anguish. Pixie and the infant that she held sat quietly by her side and let her sorrow spill. Walking back into the village with Fawn, when her weeping storm had passed, Pixie observed Two Feathers returning from his evening hunt. Her heart skipped a beat of welcome at the sight of him, and it surprised her. She hadn't felt any emotion toward him since TJ's death. Two Feathers' gaze met hers before it moved on to his sister. Pixie saw that he noted the recent cut on Fawn's arm.

"I must go home," she quietly told Fawn.

Nodding, Fawn continued to walk toward her own lodge.

She will be okay, Pixie thought as she watched her. When Two Feathers entered their lodge, minutes after she did, Pixie went and took the small animals from his hand that he held.

"Are these for us, or do I take them to your mother?" At the overwhelming warmth of her feeling experienced for him, Pixie dropped her gaze.

"Two Feathers provide for mother. Pix clean for us."

"I'll leave Three Feathers with you then. Shall I?"

Two Feathers looked toward his son before he inclined his head in permission.

Stepping back out into the daylight, Pixie strolled to the river. Skinning and working to clean the animals that she'd brought with her to the water, she gazed about the village as she worked. Pixie noted the children that played, and their laughter abounded. The children, some with half-naked bodies even in the cold darted here and there, and the adults weaved around their play, going about their business of living, of day-to-day survival. They acknowledged her as they passed and Pixie smiled back in response. She ceased her hands cleaning motion as she moved her gaze over the village and its occupants. TJ had accepted these people and had loved their way of life. Only in that instant did she see their beauty, their authenticity. True happiness flooded Pixie's soul for the first time since the tornado lifted and dropped her and TJ into this primal world.

Had TJ let her see what he'd seen?

Glancing toward the heavens, Pixie wondered. Bending, she began again the chore of cleaning the carcasses that she held. With a feeling of affection for the people who passed, she nodded back eagerly when they called out their greetings to her.

Pausing again, only this time to gaze down at her bloody hands and the animals that she cleaned, Pixie wondered in bewilderment if she loved Two Feathers as she'd told him. She must she decided. It was why, on seeing him come into the village, she'd felt such a rush of welcome for him. He wasn't just a safety net to hang on to, as she'd believed. She had kept the hidden thought that she'd return to her world one day, that these people were unreal and a nightmare to get through only. Frowning, Pixie went back to her work. There was no returning to that modern day world and TJ had always known it. He had told her many times, but she'd refused to accept that reality until today.

Looking up at hearing someone approach, Pixie smiled with warm welcome. "Hello, Little Bird."

"Little Bird happy see Pixie smile again. When friend sad Little Bird sad."

"I'm okay, Little Bird."

She was, Pixie realized. She truly was. She began to clean up the debris around her.

Little Bird leaned toward her and she whispered, "Little Bird hope to expect child soon same as friend."

Pixie felt her eyes widen. Too Little had claimed Little Bird? Brave Bird must be livid.

Little Bird continued.

"Brave Bird not number one wife now. Too Little say he furious Sister make Too Little look bad before Two Feathers."

Pixie rinsed the carcasses that she held making sure that they were clean, her hands and gaze moving over the kill. She shouldn't be happy at Brave Bird's plight, but she was. Dropping the meat into the bowl by her side, she scrubbed up everything around her. Little Bird walked with her back to her home. Little Bird chattered non-stop, her steps light. At Pixie's door, they parted ways, both agreeing to visit with Fawn the next day.

Pixie smiled with warmth at Two Feathers when she reentered his lodge. *Their lodge*, she corrected. He watched her. He didn't smile back. Pixie guessed she couldn't blame him for his aloofness.

She had kept a mental and physical distance from him since TJ's death. Even told him that night that she wished it'd been *his* death.

A female voice called out for permission for admittance from outside the lodge causing them both to turn. Two Feathers gave consent for entry. A relative walked through the doorway into the lodge and he frowned.

"Mother okay?"

"Yes, yes," the relative responded. "Mother wishes Three Feathers with grandmother this night."

Two Feathers handed the child over to the relative.

With their departure, Pixie busied herself preparing the evening meal. Two Feathers went to sit before the fire pit. The strained silence between them grew. Pixie finally stopped what she was doing and went to him. Bending on her knees beside him, she silently waited for Two Feathers to look at her.

"Woman, what is it? Husband hungry and wish to eat meal." Two Feathers' tone was uninviting and his gaze indifferent. Pixie felt a shiver of fear ripple through her. Could he now not even stand to look at her? Absorbed in her self-pity over TJ's death, she hadn't noted his changed demeanor. Had he lost any tender feeling he may have harbored by her hate-filled words that night?

"I'm sorry."

Two Feathers looked directly at her at her apology. He didn't respond. His face muscles tight and unmoving. Pixie continued, "I know that TJ's death wasn't your fault and I'm sorry for my words to you that night. I am sorry also that I haven't given any sympathy to you for your father's passing. Please forgive me. It was all a horrible accident, both their drownings, and I was wrong to lash out as I did."

Pixie saw Two Feathers' facial muscles begin to relax. Reaching out, she grasped his hand closest to her and then brought his knuckles to her cheekbone. She wanted, needed, him to understand how important he was to her.

"I love you," she whispered. She did love this man, this brutal, uncivilized man. Two Feathers didn't vocalize any return affection. He pulled his hand from hers.

"Two Feathers would have punished with beating if others heard disrespect that night."

"I love you," Pixie repeated. She wanted him to know without a doubt how she felt toward him. He allowed her to crawl onto his lap, and his arms encircled her waist, as she wrapped hers about his neck.

"I love you," she repeated. It was good to be close to him again. She had missed his touch. She searched Two Feathers' gaze. Leaning forward, she kissed him full on the lips and pressed against him. He didn't move or respond. Hesitant, Pixie pulled back.

"Does husband find wife unattractive now? Pixie wish to lay with husband."

Two Feathers groaned, and his arms tightened around her waist. "Woman, you make me feel things that I shouldn't."

Pixie moved her lips with exactness over his face, kissing him here and there, and she confessed, "Two Feathers does things to Pixie too...."

Pixie pulled back and looked in astonishment at Two Feathers.

"Do you realize how you and I speak, Husband? We've intertwined our ways."

Two Feathers bent toward her and silenced her and Pixie wouldn't have had it any other way. That night they discovered each other again, the outside world and its demands forgotten.

Chapter Twenty-Six

"Woman…."

Two Feathers' silent laughter curled within him. He was happy. Pix, after admitting her love for him, had changed. She was a good wife, cheerful and wanting to please and now big with his child. He had changed, too. He knew that he loved her deeply.

The cold days of winter were fading, and warmer, spring days were taking over. Their day was a lazy one as they reclined together under a tree.

The tree branches above them were leafing out, the green color of the small leaves replacing the tree's dreary, bare branches of winter. The village had food and no one had an empty belly.

Pix laughed aloud as she tickled his nose again, brandishing the small underdeveloped leaf that she held. Two Feathers pulled her to him so that she sprawled over the top of him.

"I was sleeping," he growled in pretend anger.

She bent to kiss him, not an easy feat given her thickness. Two Feathers' insides coiled with desire. She was his *all*. He didn't tell her such. He was scared to. Frightened if he admitted how much he cared that he'd lose her. Instead, he chose to show his love.

Holding her in place with the palm of his hand, he took over her kiss, his fingers burying into her braid. He moved his palm to cover a breast lush with pregnancy.

"Make love to me," she pleaded against his neck when he finally allowed her to raise, her face flushed.

Glancing around at their hidden spot, Two Feathers was more than willing.

"Wife," he faltered in awe when she cried out her release just as he entered her.

****

Two Feathers noted that Crow argued with his spouse as he and Pix walked back into the village. Two Feathers felt loose limbed and energized. Why Crow's woman had decided to stay with his blood brother instead of returning home with her family, he didn't understand. She didn't seem happy.

Upon her notice of him and Pix, the woman frowned and then turned aside as if ashamed of her audience. Crow glanced up. He reached out and grasped her upper arm, stopping her departure from his side.

"Two Feathers," he called out in a friendly tone as if he and his woman were not just seen in a quarrel.

Two Feathers chose to ignore the obvious also. Pix didn't make any comment as she walked beside him. She watched Crow's wife. Looking back up, Two Feathers realized that Crow's wife seemed fixated on Pix. He frowned. The woman always stared when Pix was in her line of vision. Was she aware that Crow had been prepared to take Pix as wife, and jealous? He would tolerate no abuse from the woman toward Pix. He regretted Pix's verbal and physical mistreatment at Brave Bird's hands. It was his fault by letting his emotions to get the better of him. If he had stayed calm and kept Pix with him as he had desired she'd not have experienced the torment. The deep bruising on her back when she'd returned to his home was his distress to remember.

"Crow," Two Feathers responded.

Crow's glance covered Pix and Two Feathers stiffened in shock at the all-encompassing scan. His blood brother, as if nothing improper had occurred, replied, "Crow plan to hunt when sun fade.

Crow wish for Blood Brother go with Crow."

Pix smiled at Crow's wife.

The woman didn't respond back in kind, and Two Feathers wanted to give a sharp reprimand at her insult. Instead, he answered Crow's request, shaking off his disloyal thoughts of his blood brother.

"Two Feathers gather weapon and meet Blood Brother at lodge."

"I will collect Three Feathers from Fawn," Pix told him when they walked away from the couple.

Two Feathers was curious if she knew the goings on between his blood brother and his returned wife. Their relationship was strange. Normally, he'd not have noticed such a thing, but he was happy and he wanted his blood brother to experience the same well-being. The woman had even sent their child back with her family even as she stayed with Crow.

"Pix, notice wife of Blood Brother not look happy?"

"I'd be unhappy, too, if I was married to that man," Pix snapped back at him.

In surprise, Two Feathers turned fully toward her.

She had not said anything negative about Crow all winter. He had believed that whatever she disliked about his blood brother had been resolved. Crow had begun to sing her praises.

"Wife, Blood Brother now say only good things about you," he admonished.

"He isn't what he seems, Husband."

At his frown, she snapped her mouth shut. Two Feathers watched Pix and a feeling of unease welled up inside him. "Does Pix have attachment for Crow? It is why Crow's woman has dislike for Pix? Woman sees it and Two Feathers doesn't?"

Her expression turning bleak, Pix asserted back at him, "How dare you say that to me?"

"Husband want answer, Wife."

"No! I don't have feelings for that man. I love you."

"It is good."

Two Feathers watched Pix stomp off to gather his son. Why this feeling of disquiet he had, it made no sense? Was he jealous of his blood brother?

"Bah," Two Feathers murmured. *Pix loved him and he her and that was what counted. Would she still love him in the next few days?*

****

Pixie sighed. She felt depressed.

No matter how much she tried to let Two Feathers know that Crow wasn't what he seemed, she always came up against his steadfast devotion to the man.

The winter had been good for her and Two Feathers. It had allowed insulation within their home, warm and secluded, and away from Crow, just her, Two Feathers, and the toddler. Now with the milder weather, everyone was outside and active again, and Crow back to watching her. Shivering in revulsion, Pixie called out for admittance into Two Feathers' family lodge.

"Hello, Mother. I've come to collect Three Feathers," she stated when her mother-in-law welcomed her entrance.

"Daughter took grandchild to river. Mother instruct daughter bring to Pixie when return," her mother-in-law informed.

Pixie smiled at her. "Thank you. I'll go on home then."

Two Feathers' mother turned away, a quiet, sad woman. She had aged since her husband's death. Returning back out into the sunshine, Pixie strolled toward home. Crow's wife intercepted her path.

"Stay away from Crow," the woman commanded. She grasped hold of Pixie's arm and she shook it.

"Stay away," she ordered again. She swept on past Pixie as if worried she would be seen talking to her.

"No worries there," Pixie finally blurted into the empty void. Fawn came into view and Pixie turned toward her. She dismissed the other woman's strange behavior. She would absolutely stay away from Crow.

"Three Feathers can walk you know," Pixie drawled when Fawn drew near.

Fawn laughed. "Three Feathers demand Fawn to carry."

Taking the child from Fawn's arms, Pixie lowered him to the ground to where he had to stand on his own two legs. She held his hand in hers to keep him from darting away.

"He's spoiled rotten," she replied and then, she laughed when Three Feathers wrapped his free arm around her leg and looked up at her as if horribly punished. She adored the little brat.

Pixie looked back up. "Two Feathers says that we have other tribe members visiting in the next few days, neighbors from where you originally traveled from. They sent word that they want to meet with him. Did you see the visitor they sent ahead?"

Fawn nodded. "It is good they wish to come and have talk. Brother build strong relation with them."

"Yes, that's what he told me too. Did you know the visitor? It seemed the Council members were excited after his visit. They kept Two Feathers occupied for several nights."

"Fawn knew man many suns ago before travel to this land to live."

"Two Feathers says that the other tribe wants to live here. Maybe combine with our tribe," Pixie added.

"It is wise to have bigger clan. More protection," Fawn replied.

"That is what Two Feathers said, too."

Three Feathers began to fuss and Pixie looked down at him.

"I better take this little fella home. He looks tired."

"Fawn give bath before bring to Pixie."

"Thank you, Fawn." Pixie picked up the now whimpering child.

"So, I carry you also," Pixie stated a smile given to the toddler.

Three Feathers wrapped an arm around her neck at once happy.

****

When Two Feathers entered the lodge later that evening, Pixie looked up from where she worked. The outside landscape filled with darkness. Three Feathers was fed and now sound asleep lying in his bed across the room from where she sat on hers and Two Feathers' sleeping pallet.

"I was getting worried. Did you find anything?"

Two Feathers went and placed his bow and arrow on the platform where he stored his hunting equipment.

"No, see nothing," he replied.

"Tomorrow you will," Pixie stated confident that he would.

He had seemed reserved the past week, probably worried over the hunting. Pixie felt no concern in that area. Two Feathers was an excellent provider. She smiled at him as her fingers weaved at the basket that she worked on. Two Feathers didn't reply as he went and filled a food platter with what she'd cooked that evening. Sitting beside her, he began to eat and he watched her work. After a time and with his food platter empty, he sat the dish aside. Taking a long drink of water, he set his drinking vessel down beside the platter.

"Pix good wife to Two Feathers."

Cutting her gaze toward him, Pixie smiled. He didn't smile back. Stopping what she was doing, she let her hands fall to her lap. In question, Pixie stared at Two Feathers. He seemed melancholy.

"What's wrong?"

Reaching out, he took the half-completed basket from her lap and set it away. Then turning, he gathered her into his arms and spread his fingers over her extended stomach.

He was tender and loving and Pixie happily followed where he led.

Chapter Twenty-Seven

Pixie watched as twelve unknown men strode into view, strangers to her but not to the tribe. Their welcome into the village called out by all that they passed. A woman also walked with them. Watching her, Pixie wondered at her presence. The men who surrounded her seemed protective of her. Two Feathers stepped from their lodge up behind her and Pixie turned toward him.

"The expected visitors have arrived, Husband."

He didn't acknowledge her statement as he walked forward, his bearing straight. Pixie was proud of him. Her husband looked fierce. He was a strong leader for their people and now would be for the tribe that sought to join theirs. One of the men separated from the small group and stepped before Two Feathers, speaking to him.

Turning at Two Feathers' response, the man gestured toward the woman. She proceeded forward and halted in front of Two Feathers. She kept her eyes downcast. She didn't seem happy although her expression showed no emotion.

****

Two Feathers felt Pix's stare. He had wanted to explain to her, to prepare her, but in the end, he'd decided it was best not to say anything until the moment was upon them. She might be upset at first, but she would accept what was required. The merger would build their tribe. Make it stronger and all safer with it. Turning, Two Feathers' gaze connected with Pix's, and he knew the split-second that she realized what was taking place just as Strong Hand the man before him introduced Blue Jay, his second wife-to-be.

"No!"

Everyone turned at Pix's cry of outrage. Her extended stomach cumbersome to her gait, she darted forward.

"What is this display?" Blue Jay's brother demanded and his gaze drilled into Two Feathers. Pix pushed her way in between him and Two Feathers and the young woman who stood beside him. Turning her back to brother and sister, she looked up. Her gaze narrow and filled with hurt.

"Husband?" she questioned.

"Wife, it must be done," Two Feathers replied, forgetting the others around them. He had not wanted to witness this hurt.

He suffered when Pix did.

She whirled toward Blue Jay.

"I'll not allow this," she yelled in Blue Jay's face. Blue Jay, not expecting her behavior, hastily stepped backward and tripped. She landed on her backside. With hands on her hips, Pix smirked down at her.

Shocked, Two Feathers couldn't move. To dishonor a husband before others disgraced not only the husband but disgraced the wife also. The gathering of men and women stared in silent censure at him and Pix.

Blue Jay's brother scorned, "Does Two Feathers lead people, or his woman?"

Two Feathers boomed in anger, even as he helped his second-wife-to-be up from the ground, his shame before the others felt. "Wife, cease this display at once."

Pix opened her mouth ready to argue. Her gaze darted between him and Blue Jay who now stood by his side. Two Feathers made a sharp motion for Crow and Rock to remove her from their audience. His embarrassment made him turn from her, his stance rigid. He had wrongly believed that Pix would express her anger privately and only to him.

"Take wife home," he commanded the two men. Crow and Rock took an arm each to lead her away. Two Feathers flinched at Pix's stony stare directed toward him.

Blue Jay spoke at his side and her voice grated, although she spoke soft. She dusted the dirt and grass from her dress. She didn't meet his gaze. "Blue Jay ask future husband give Old Wife time to adjust. Blue Jay not wish enter into unwelcome home."

Blue Jay's brother stepped forward, his tone exacting as he motioned toward everyone who listened and watched.

"Strong Hand demand punishment given for disrespect shown to Sister and to tribe. All witness Strong Hand's whipping."

Two Feathers almost struck the man before him. He caught himself before he did as he wished. He resented his future brother-in-law's demand. He knew that punishment was required but not for the reason that Strong Hand demanded. Word would spread of Pix's disrespect to him as Chief of the people, and if he allowed her action to go unpunished, he would lose all respect of the tribe.

"Wife punished by Two Feathers' hand not Strong Hand's," he grated. Spinning, Two Feathers left the group to confront Pix.

"Too Little, place visitors into welcome homes," he ordered as he passed the man.

Pix looked up at his entrance to their lodge, her expression mutinous. Two Feathers quickly lifted a hand and halted whatever it was she was about to say.

"Pix speak quiet so all outside cannot hear."

Her mouth worked. No sound came forth. She crumbled before him, her tears flowing freely. "Why are you doing this? Am I not enough?"

Walking forward to lean down on his knees before her, Two Feathers reached out intending to comfort. Pix jerked backward and avoided his touch. He let his hands fall to his sides. He didn't want a second wife any more than Pix wanted him to have one. He would not tell her that. It would further complicate things.

"Two Feathers do this for tribe, for family, for safety," he replied.

Pix stared at him in disbelief.

"Why not inform me about it then? Why wait until the moment is upon us for me to find out what's happening? Why wait until there was nothing that I could do or say about it?"

Two Feathers scorned in surprise, "Two Feathers does not harken to women."

He enjoyed Pix's outspoken and demanding ways, in this moment though it angered him. She assumed too much. He didn't want this quarrel between them. It was why he'd not told her ahead of time. He watched as she straightened and her hand went to her extended side.

"Does Pix have pain?" His concern rose.

"Oh please and you care?" she belittled. She flapped her hand before his face.

"Go away. Marry your other woman. I want nothing more to do with you. I hate you. Do you hear me? I hate you!"

Abruptly standing at the issued harsh and childish words, Two Feathers stared down at the top of Pix's head. For a moment, he thought to beg her for forgiveness. To tell her he'd fought with the Council members over their decision. He turned away.

****

Pixie felt her new comfort zone shift at Two Feathers' silent departure. It seemed that her opinion didn't matter. Had it ever? She couldn't and wouldn't accept his having a second wife. It would kill her to know Two Feathers shared another's bed. If he wanted that woman, she wouldn't lay with him.

At the sharp pain that spread again, Pixie realized her labor was upon her. It was two weeks earlier than she'd expected. She had kept track of the days. Trembling, Pixie stood. Another pain more intense than the last, shot across her back, and she grabbed at the spot.

"Crow," she gasped, calling out for help. "Crow, come into my lodge."

When Crow and Rock both entered, Pixie gestured toward her extended abdomen. "Please bring Fawn and Mother to me. Hurry!"

Rock immediately backed out of the lodge. Crow remained.

"Pixie call for Crow when Pixie need help," he stated and he smiled. His white teeth flashed.

"No, I...." Pixie gasped as another pain, more intense than the last, hit. "Please, Crow, go tell Two Feathers that I'm in labor."

Frowning, Crow turned to leave. His gaze met Pixie's once more before he ducked and went out through the doorway of the lodge.

"Wife?"

Reaching out for Two Feathers' hand when he hurried toward her upon his entrance to their lodge, Pixie clasped her fingers with his. It had seemed an eternity since Crow's departure. She had begun to believe that either Two Feathers had no concern for their child or that Crow hadn't informed him of her started labor. She was on her knees now panting. He would not be allowed to stay long, his mother granting her wish for his admittance with reluctance. Pixie tightened her fingers around his.

"Two Feathers...promise...promise if I die, that you'll love my child as you love Pretty Flower's."

Two Feathers seemed alarmed at her request and he looked toward his mother. "Mother?"

"Wife not die, Son. Only much pain and believe she die."

"Promise me, Two Feathers," Pixie begged. She feared for her child. Would his new wife love this child as she loved Three Feathers, or would her little one face animosity and repulsion?

"Two Feathers care for all his children equally," he rasped.

Pixie jerked her hand from his.

"Remember your words and live by your promise to me," she

demanded. She turned her face away. He lingered.

His mother urged him toward the doorway.

Pixie almost cried out as Two Feathers stepped away, that she didn't hate him that she loved him. Pain stabbed stealing her words.

"Drink this. It help with hurt," Fawn instructed as she knelt beside her lifting the concoction that she held to Pixie's lips.

Eagerly, Pixie sipped the liquid. She was educated and knew what to expect, but her book knowledge wasn't the same as the actual labor pains that now gripped her. She was to die. She felt certain. She wanted drugs, modern medicine, and modern doctors. Fawn placed a leather strap into her mouth instructing her to bite down on it. Pixie's cries of pain became muffled as she did as ordered. It felt as if someone with large, broad fingers clenched at her back and squeezed down hard: he or she, with each cruel grasp, worked their fingers around her abdomen to her belly button. As the torture wrapped and her stomach muscles tightened, Pixie pushed as commanded, her knees spread wide over the pile of leaves ready to catch her newborn.

Pain cleaved, and Pixie bit down hard on the leather piece in her mouth. *Will my hurting ever end?* she wondered.

Mother and Fawn stood alongside her, holding her hands, supporting her, talking to her, and keeping her in an upright position. Fawn wiped at her brow as sweat dripped down Pixie's forehead and into her eyes to mingle with her tears. The torment began to lessen, and Pixie relaxed, breathing in. She stiffened when the process immediately started all over again. Biting down on the leather piece in her mouth, Pixie pushed as ordered and the cycle repeated and repeated.

With a final push, Pixie felt her child expelled.

Mother swooped to gather the newborn as Fawn gripped Pixie's arm when another wave of pain struck her. Her baby out of sight and with no sound heard, Pixie spit out the strap of leather in her mouth and she cried out, "Mother?"

"Mother inspect baby," Fawn informed.

"Is my baby okay?"

"Baby girl perfect," Fawn assured. Pixie heard the squall of the child's cry and she laughed. Exhaustion swept and her shoulders drooped. Fawn and another relative helped her to stand, and they walked her to her pallet. The other women in the lodge cleaned. Their chatter seemed far away. Fawn and the relative beside Pixie prepared her for rest. Afterward, lying on her bed, Pixie watched as her mother-in-law washed her precious child and then wrapped her firmly in a blanket. Cradling her to her chest, she walked to Pixie to lay her down into her arms.

****

Two Feathers wanted to pace at the sudden quiet behind him. He didn't as others watched him. Instead, he sat outside his home and discussed the merger of the two tribes as if nothing of important was happening within his lodge. He had heard the squall of the newborn, his, and Pix's child.

He had winced each time he heard Pix's muffled groans.

He knew her time for delivery had been close, but it worried him her labor. Her expressed hatred gnawed at him. Did she really hate him? Would she do as Pretty Flower and end her life? *Master of Life*, Two Feathers beseeched under his breath, *give Two Feathers knowledge so not to lose love.*

His mother exited from the doorway of his lodge and Two Feathers rose to his feet. With two long strides, he stood before her.

"Mother? Wife and baby well?" he asked as if it were an everyday thing, his wife giving birth to his child.

"They are perfect," she responded.

Two Feathers felt his unease fade. He straightened his shoulders. It wouldn't do for the newcomers, or his people, to see him overcome with emotion. They would wonder if he were capable to lead, if he were too weak to be Chief. At that moment, he questioned himself if he were strong enough to be their leader. The only thought that he had was of Pix.

"Two Feathers wishes to see wife and child."

"Wife ready for husband's visit," his mother replied. She studied him as if to say more, she didn't. Two Feathers, anxious to see Pix and the baby, turned from her to enter his lodge. On quiet footsteps, he walked toward Pix and their newborn. He hadn't thought to ask the sex of the child. With his heart filled with softness, Two Feathers looked down at his sleeping child and sleeping wife. Squatting beside the pair, he reached out to draw a forefinger down Pix's flushed cheek.

"Wife," he spoke soft. He didn't want to startle her.

Pix opened her eyes to look up at him. For a moment, she smiled but then she frowned and her eyes filled with tears. At her unhappiness, Two Feathers felt his own tears rise. He fought them back. Men did not show weakness for others to see.

"Our baby? Girl or boy?" he rasped.

"Girl," she responded. She dropped her gaze from his.

"It is good. Two Feathers glad for either boy or girl."

"I'm tired, Two Feathers," Pix replied. She wouldn't look at him.

Two Feathers sighed. He reached out to touch his child's soft cheek. She turned to his finger in search for food. He looked from the infant to his wife.

"Two Feathers must marry another, but not wish for marriage."

Pix twisted her face from him toward the wall of the lodge. "Go away," she whispered.

Standing, Two Feathers looked down at the pair, his wife and his child, and his heart was in harmony with Pix's. *She will come around*, he thought as he stood beside her. It was common for men to take more than one wife. All wives accepted it. They even said others helped with the required daily work. Leaving Pix, and their newborn child, Two Feathers strode toward the lodge that housed the woman he was to marry.

His future brother-in-law now walked along beside him.

It was good this union between their two tribes. The merger meant more men to hunt for food and more men to keep the women and children safe. It meant his family would be safer.

Gaining admittance into the hosting lodge, Two Feathers ducked through its entryway. Standing to his full height, he glanced around within the interior of the home.

Chapter Twenty-Eight

Pixie yawned awakening to the sound of the beat of drums. She realized that she was alone as she slowly sat up. Looking down at the baby by her side, Pixie smiled and her heart overflowed with love.

"Sweet, baby girl," she cooed.

At a sound heard at the lodge's entrance, Pixie turned to look.

Fawn stopped in her tracks. "Fawn excuse. Fawn believe Sister asleep. Check on fire. Bring food."

"You don't need to apologize, Fawn. Please, come on in." Pixie smiled at her sister-in-law and friend as Fawn walked on into the lodge.

"Pixie hungry?" Fawn asked.

"Yes, I am." Pixie watched Fawn curiously. She seemed to have a nervous energy about her. Why would her sister-in-law not fully look at her? Drums sounded again and Pixie frowned. Their sound earlier hadn't really registered. Her suspicion rose.

Pixie's sudden thought horrified her.

Surely not?

"He is marrying her tonight? The same night as I've suffered to have his child?"

Fawn didn't reply but she gave a quick nod.

Pixie couldn't believe Two Feathers could be so cruel. *Couldn't he have waited at least one lousy day before taking another wife? One lousy, stinking day he couldn't wait?*

A tear splashed down Pixie's cheek, and she quickly reached to wipe it away. Focusing only on her sleeping newborn, she shut out the beat of the drums outside the lodge. She ignored Fawn as the meal that she held she sat down beside her. She didn't respond when Fawn questioned if she needed anything else.

Waiting for a moment, Fawn quietly turned and left.

As the night wore on and silence outside the lodge took over, Pixie in misery hummed to her child. The stillness of the lodge compressed and her imagination of what Two Feathers and his new wife were doing sickened. It was a physical sickness and one that made her quickly look around searching. The feeling passed and Pixie swallowed.

She looked down at the child she held in her arms.

She wished TJ, her parents, and Lynn could have seen her child. Lynn would've laughed at the thick head of black hair that stuck out everywhere.

****

Pixie cooed to her baby that next evening upon awakening and realizing that there was still no return to the lodge of Two Feathers and his new wife.

"You are as beautiful as your aunt Fawn. Do you know that?"

Her child slept, innocent and unaware of the events happening to her mother. Reclining back down beside the infant, bitterness rose in Pixie at the thought of what Two Feathers was participating in while she recovered from the birth of their child. Where had he and the new wife gone? Had Fawn made a special place for them as she had for her and Two Feathers? Pixie's gaze jerked toward the entryway of the lodge when, as if her thoughts had caused Two Feathers to materialize, he entered the lodge.

The new wife trailed in behind him.

Oh, please, no. No. No. Quick, Pixie shut her eyes and pretended sleep. She wasn't ready to face this new wife or even

Two Feathers.

The two were silent, not speaking as they walked forward.

Pixie listened to their movements as they moved around within the lodge. Her heart struck so hard against her ribs that she was afraid they'd hear it and know she faked her sleep. Pixie sensed Two Feathers' presence when he walked over to stand and gaze down at her and the baby. He squatted beside her. She suffered his touch to her cheek. She wanted to slap it away.

****

Waking the next morning to the sound of movement, Pixie slanted her eyes to look through her eyelashes to inspect the woman who quietly moved about within the lodge. Two Feathers wasn't present. Pixie knew that he hadn't slept with the new wife. He had made a bed away from both of them.

"Blue Jay aware Old Wife awake," the young woman stated in the quiet. Pixie winced. She had slammed her eyes closed when she thought the younger woman had glanced her way. She must have seen her movement. Pixie sat up, her effort trouble-free.

"Don't call me Old Wife. I bet I'm not that much older than you!"

"Not matter," the young woman stated. She seemed smug.

Openly, Pixie stared. The younger girl was pretty, if you liked her sort of features. Long braided hair down to her hips and dark brown eyes with thick eyelashes that framed wide eyes, and full lips—the kind women purchased in modern times, Pixie frowned.

"If you think that you're going to come in here and take over, you're mistaken. I don't care what Two Feathers says or what you two do together. You can both go to the devil for all I care."

The younger woman didn't respond. Spinning, she exited the lodge.

Probably to go tattle, Pixie thought. *Well, let her.* She would tell Two Feathers the same damn thing if he tried to scold her.

The younger girl popped back in the lodge and she carried a

steaming container of hot water. She placed it beside Pixie. She then laid a soft deerskin cloth alongside the container.

"For Old Wife," she stated before she abruptly left again.

Resentful of her kindness shown, Pixie rose. Washing the baby, she checked her out. She was perfect. Wrapping her up, Pixie sat and nursed her and then placed the sleeping infant back onto the sleeping pallet.

Standing, Pixie used the same water to cleanse herself and then redressed. She was sore and tired, but she had no wish to lie back down. She wanted her strength back as soon as possible. No New Wife would show her up. Walking around in the home, Pixie touched some of Two Feathers' hunting gear. Tears rose. She brushed them aside.

"No need Old Wife cry. Husbands have more wives. It is so all time."

Pixie whirled.

She had not heard the young woman walk back into the home. Two Feathers stood behind her. Pixie felt resentment flare at his catching her in her moment of weakness. She ignored him as she continued to walk around inside the lodge. She would regain her vigor as soon as possible so that she could stay away from the two. She would make sure to be anywhere but where they were.

Two Feathers walked over to glance down at their child and when he stooped as if to pick her up, Pixie swooped, halting his movement.

"She's sleeping. Don't disturb her," she snapped. Frowning, he straightened. He looked toward the new wife.

"Blue Jay leave," he ordered.

Blue Jay promptly did as instructed.

Two Feathers looked back at Pixie. "Pix well?"

Pixie looked everywhere but at Two Feathers. "I'm fine."

He sighed, and when he reached to caress her jawline, she jerked back away from his touch.

Without a word said, he turned and left.

In that moment, Pixie hated him, and she hated his new wife. The emotion lessened the sorrow she'd been experiencing. With exhaustion felt, she went to lie back down.

When next she woke, Pixie heard the low murmur of voices, male and female. She didn't move. Fawn was visiting with Three Feathers. Pixie had missed the little scamp. The aroma of a prepared meal wafted through the home. It seemed the new wife had been busy.

Sitting up from where she lay, beside her child, Pixie checked on the infant. She slept content. Her mother wasn't content. She needed some fresh air and to be away from the happy couple. With the baby recently fed and now sleeping, she could step away for a few minutes. Standing, Pixie walked barefooted toward Two Feathers and his new wife. They sat beside each other eating their evening meal before the fire pit. Pixie scowled. Didn't they *just* look cozy, Mr. Husband and his new wife. Pixie sniffed. She didn't care. She glared at the new wife. She ignored Two Feathers.

"I wish to go out. New Wife care for Old Wife's child, if injury come, new wife killed. Fawn report of care given to Old Wife's child." It seemed Two Feathers choked and he looked at his sister. She shrugged. Pixie glared at Blue Jay until she gave a wide-eyed nod of understanding. Whirling, Pixie skirted around Two Feathers to stalk from the home. Upon clearing its entryway, she breathed deep the night air. She had put Fawn in an awkward position. She would have to apologize later.

Two Feathers stepped out from the doorway of the lodge behind her and Pixie took off walking. He followed.

"Where wife go?"

Stopping in her tracks, Pixie turned toward him. "Wife? Don't you mean Old Wife? Old Wife wishes to immerse herself in the river and get away from you!"

It seemed she'd stunned him. Good. When she took off walking again, Two Feathers grabbed her arm halting her progress.

"Don't you touch me," Pixie snapped.

Two Feathers tightened his fingers and he spoke quiet, "If Pix take life, Pix miss all child's living."

Pixie stared at Two Feathers and it dawned on her, an understanding of his fear.

She spoke as quiet as he had. The rush of tenderness felt at his worry she quickly repelled. She didn't want it. "I don't wish to take my life, Two Feathers. I only want to bathe in the river."

Pixie knew that Two Feathers would watch over their newborn, moreover, she hadn't planned on staying gone long. Two Feathers looked around at their surroundings, and Pixie followed his gaze. It seemed they'd attracted an audience.

Blue Jay's brother watched them as did Crow. Pixie turned her back to them, and it surprised her when she heard herself say, "Will you go with me, Two Feathers?"

She didn't like that Crow watched and now that she'd decided to cleanse in the river, she desperately wanted it. A simple cloth cleaning would not do this night. Pixie could tell that she had surprised Two Feathers with her request.

He nodded in agreement.

She stalled. "I want Fawn to stay and watch over my child until we return."

"Go to river Two Feathers inform Sister."

"You will come afterward?"

Two Feathers gave a nod.

Walking on to her hiding place, Pixie sat and waited for his arrival. It didn't seem long before he strolled to where she rested.

"Pix not bathe?"

"I will now."

Two Feathers looked at her in question and Pixie just shrugged. She couldn't admit her fear of Crow to him.

"Two Feathers bathe with Pix."

"I...I...." Pixie grimaced at her galloping heart. Two Feathers helped her to ease her dress over her head and then shucked his own clothing. Taking her hand, he walked with her into the river. Pixie winced when the water hit between her legs and he paused.

"Pix hurt?"

"A little. I shouldn't go any deeper."

Embarrassed at his watching, Pixie quickly bathed. Two Feathers followed suit and they both waded from the water. Shivering, Pixie shook her buckskin dress out and then dropped it down over her head to cover her nakedness.

"Don't," she sputtered when Two Feathers reached to pull her toward him. Lurching from him, she took off back to her child. Entering their lodge, Pixie's gaze moved in surprise to the man who now sat before the home's fire.

Blue Jay's brother sat with Blue Jay and Fawn.

Glancing past her sister-in-law's shoulders, Pixie took in her baby's sleeping form. Two Feathers came up to stand alongside her.

"Why Brother-In-Law visit late in night?" he inquired.

"Strong Hand see Old Wife well. Time Old Wife punished before all," Strong Hand retorted.

Two Feathers reached out and grasped Pixie's arm, when in bewilderment, she opened her mouth ready to demand what punishment.

"Husband talk to Strong Hand," he rasped.

His look gave to her tolerated no argument. Pixie snapped her mouth shut. It seemed Strong Hand's esteem went up for Two Feathers. He gave a nod of approval.

****

Sitting before his brother-in-law, Two Feathers made a sharp motion for the women to leave them. Fawn, eyeing him, took Three Feathers and left the lodge. Blue Jay went to her pallet. Pix stalked to the far wall of the lodge, to where their sleeping pallet was and turning her back, she sat and picked up the now awake infant.

Two Feathers wished all were gone except for him and his two children, and Pix. He dreaded her required chastisement. The merging tribe and his own wouldn't accept anything less. Pix with her behavior had shown public dishonor to the visiting tribe and to him as Chief of the people. He turned toward Strong Hand.

"Wife is well enough as Strong Hand say. With rising new sun punishment witnessed."

Two Feathers noticed that Pix's shoulders tightened. She listened although she didn't look their way.

Strong Hand studied him.

"Strong Hand stay until punishment complete, and then Strong Hand return to home to bring Father and tribe to new settlement."

Two Feathers knew the old Chief waited for word of his daughter's marriage before he moved his people closer. He glanced toward the old Chief's daughter. Maybe he would eventually feel desire for her. Now she left him cold. Inclining his head in acknowledgement of Strong Hand's statement, Two Feathers rose. It was an indication that the conversation was over.

Chapter Twenty-Nine

Pixie stepped from the lodge at Two Feathers' gesture to her that it was time to go. When the early morning sun hit her face, she squinted at the gathered and waiting crowd. It seemed the whole tribe wanted to watch her punishment. The thought hurt.

She hadn't slept any the night before.

After Strong Hand had left, Two Feathers tried to explain to her why the demanded punishment. She had shut him out. Blue Jay had looked at her with sympathy that morning and Pixie snubbed her. Now silently, being led forward by Two Feathers, through the throng of people, Pixie's feet dragged and felt weighted. She almost began to beg him not to punish her, to hell with pride. He looked down at her as if he knew what she was thinking and she saw in his expression what he wanted. He wanted her to stand strong and proud. Blue Jay walked along his other side. Her shoulders thrown back, head held high and her face expressionless.

Pixie copied her.

Brought to a stop before the assembled crowd, Pixie turned toward Two Feathers. She wanted to hide. He rotated her so that she faced the people and then dropped his hands from her. Features solemn, he addressed the gathered crowd. He spoke concerning the new wife and the new tribe to join theirs. He talked about increased protection by the two tribes coming together. Pixie blocked out his monologue as she looked over the heads of the people to the tree tops behind them. Her kneecaps began to twitch and jump. She focused her attention back to whatever it was that Two Feathers was saying when the crowd suddenly looked her way. Apparently, he was wrapping it up and back to why she was brought forward.

"Two Feathers bring Old Wife before tribe to witness punishment. Old Wife insult Chief and welcomed peoples. With public punishment insult gone, and Old Wife with gladness in heart welcome new wife into home." Turning, Two Feathers looked at Pixie.

Pixie stared back. She did not and would not *ever* accept his new wife.

Two Feathers' frowned slashed.

"Pix accept punishment," Pixie whispered. She would never say that she accepted Blue Jay as his second wife.

Two Feathers motioned for Crow to step forward. Pixie didn't look toward Crow. She didn't want to see what it was that he held. She stared instead at a point past Two Feathers' shoulder. Two Feathers turned toward Strong Hand, and to his companions who stood along beside him, and he addressed Strong Hand. "Strong Hand view Old Wife punishment this day. Agree insult to Sister and tribe forgiven?"

Strong Hand inclined his head in agreement.

Two Feathers made a motion for Fawn to step forward. Silently, she turned Pixie so that Pixie's back was to the crowd. She then pulled Pixie's dress down off her shoulders and bared her back. She walked around afterward to face Pixie, and she grasped hold of Pixie's forearms, and her fingers wrapped tight.

Pixie unable to control her curiosity looked to see the thing that Crow held. She tensed when Two Feathers took the lash handed out to him. Its braided length snapped at his hand movement. He had warned what to expect. His warning paled when compared with seeing in person what was to be used on her back.

Blue Jay stood to one side as a witness and Brave Bird had a front row view, Pixie felt mortified. Locking her gaze with Fawn's, Pixie drew a deep breath. She would not cry out.

A crack whistled through the air and Pixie jerked at the sudden sting to her back. Her eyes widened at the shock of the searing burn. Fawn tightened her fingers around her arms. Pixie kept her gaze locked with hers.

After the third strike, Pixie's knees tried to buckle. Pixie wanted to scream her pain for all to hear. Fawn seemed to know what she was about to do, and she squeezed her fingers even tighter and shook her head at her. Pixie clamped shut her mouth. With the fourth assault, her knees folded even as she struggled to stay upright. Fawn grasped hold of her upper arms and kept her from collapsing fully. She pulled her dress up to cover her nakedness.

Pixie heard Two Feathers tell the crowd, "Punishment done."

Grasping her arm, he escorted her to their lodge to where his mother waited. If she didn't stay focused, Pixie believed she'd pass out from the pain. Two Feathers eased her down onto her bedding as his mother walked forward.

"Mother care for Pixie," the older woman informed him.

With a tilt of his head, he exited the home.

Not a word of comfort given, Pixie thought bitterly. So now, she was formally the Old Wife. Hot tears flowed and she couldn't stop them.

"Hush," her mother-in-law, scolded as she eased her dress from her shoulders. She examined her back.

"No break in skin. Hurt several days then Old Wife fine."

Her skin might not be sliced open, but Pixie felt as if her heart were. The new wife strolled in and Pixie turned so that she didn't have to sit facing her. Mother scolded her. Her words quiet and for Pixie's ears only.

"Life easier if accept change."

With that, she left Pixie to the new wife and took Three Feathers with her. Pixie lifted her own whimpering child to her breast. At least the whipping hadn't affected her milk production. Silently and quietly, Blue Jay moved around within the lodge. She pulled her bedding as far away from Pixie's and Two Feathers' as possible. Pixie watched her and felt her bitterness rise.

"Take his bedding with you while you're at it! You can have him. You won, didn't you? I hope that you're happy witnessing my disgrace."

Blue Jay stopped what she was doing to look her way.

Pixie bent her head back to her child. She sensed when Blue Jay walked up to stand before her. Looking up ready to snap at her to get away from her, Pixie paused. Tears shimmered in the younger woman's eyes. Pixie swallowed and her angry words evaporated. Blue Jay reminded her of herself in Brave Bird's home. Hardening her heart, Pixie looked away from her.

"Blue Jay not wish for Old Wife's punishment," the younger woman told her.

Pixie ignored her.

At Two Feathers' entrance into the charged atmosphere, Blue Jay hurried to where she'd moved her bedding. Pixie snubbed his arrival. He walked over to where she sat to squat before her. Pixie raised her gaze to his. Standing, he left the home again.

In puzzlement, Pixie wondered at his action.

****

Two Feathers had seen Strong Hand and his companions off before they left the village. The new peoples would arrive midsummer. Walking into his lodge, he'd planned to inform Pix that they were gone and to ask her forgiveness.

He couldn't speak when facing her. His words had choked at the hostility that radiated from her to him.

Standing by the river's edge where he and she had bathed together the night before, Two Feathers watched the movement of the water. Each strike he'd brought down to her back he'd felt. Crow walked up to where he stood and placed a hand on his shoulder.

"It is good this alliance."

Two Feathers didn't respond. After a moment, Crow walked away.

Chapter Thirty

Pixie watched Three Feathers. *He's getting cranky*, she thought. Tired and dirty from his playing, he came to sit beside his sister. Leaning over he kissed the infant's fat cheek and then patted it with his chubby little hand as if he were so much older. Pixie smiled. From where she sat beside the children under a tree alongside the village, she yawned wide, unable to contain it.

The day had been sunny and beautiful, and it seemed that not only had she become worn out from the day's activities, the children had also.

Seven weeks had passed and she'd healed from the birth of her and Two Feathers' child, and healed from the whipping he'd administered, healed on the outside anyway. Her heart still hadn't mended from his public humiliation.

Rising, Pixie bent to pick up the newborn wrapped up and secure in her covering. "Three Feathers, help mommy to walk home."

Taking her extended hand within his little one, Three Feathers beamed up at her as he stood. Pixie paced her steps to his much smaller tread. They stopped by the river to wash before proceeding on.

Looking down at the toddler by her side as they walked, Pixie sighed. She loved this child as much as she loved her own. It did her heart good that he shunned Blue Jay. Although, she had to admit, Blue Jay never reached out to the boy so that may be why he had nothing to do with her. Blue Jay did her share of work, but all care for the children she left to Pixie.

Pixie was thankful that Two Feathers never coupled with Blue Jay within the home. She didn't know where and when they did, but at night, they slept in their separate pallets while she slept with the children.

Seeing Crow walking toward her, Pixie stiffened. He hadn't said or done anything since her punishment, nevertheless, she felt uneasy around him. He was an enigma, friendly, and at the same time, not.

"Crow see Pixie and children enjoy sunny day?" he stated, halting their progress home. He lightly chucked Three Feathers under the chin. Pixie drew the child closer to her leg.

"Yes, and now I need to take the children home to feed them." Pixie cringed at Crow's glance toward her breasts at her statement.

She edged around him and he let her.

As she hurried away, she held tight to Three Feathers' hand. He scampered beside her before he stumbled. Pixie slowed her pace.

Blue Jay looked up when she entered the lodge with the children in tow. Sadness seemed to overshadow the younger woman's face before her features went bland. That glimpsed expression gave Pixie pause. Shaking off her thought that maybe Blue Jay was as unhappy as she was, Pixie let loose of Three Feathers' fingers, and he darted to his toys.

"I need to feed the children," she informed Blue Jay. She had stayed away most of the day only coming into the lodge to nurse the baby. Now it was time to settle in and stay for the night.

Blue Jay pointed to a covered dish before she turned her back to her. Spooning out some of what the pot held, Pixie called Three Feathers over to her. She handed him the bowl that she held. With a smile, Pixie noted that he picked out with small fingers only what he wanted while he ignored everything else. Turning from him, she put the baby to her breast. When the infant indicated that she was full, she stood to lay her on her bedding. After fussing over the baby for a moment, Pixie went to collect Three Feathers. He'd set his bowl aside and was done eating. Washing his little fingers, she put him to his bed.

Later that evening Two Feathers walked into the silent lodge, and Pixie's heart leapt at his arrival. Its rapid beat both surprised and angered her. She had been numb to his presence since the baby's birth and believed her attraction to the man gone. Why its sudden reappearance this night, she didn't understand.

The basket that she weaved dropped from her hand. Quickly, Pixie retrieved it. Out of the corner of her eye, Pixie watched as Blue Jay stood to gather together Two Feathers' evening meal. He took the offered platter and then sat before the low burning evening fire. He didn't look Pixie's way. The days were warm now and the nights warming. Pixie couldn't stop her admiration of his bare upper form. He wore the same thing as when she'd first met him and her appreciation for his masculinity intensified.

Slamming the basket that she worked on down onto the blanket beside her, Pixie jumped to her feet. Two Feathers and Blue Jay both looked up at her in startled surprise.

Pixie met Two Feathers' gaze. "Fawn asked that I come to see her and I forgot. I go now."

His brows drawing together, he gave a frown. "Wife visit Sister when sun rise with new day not go in night."

"No, I'll go now." Pixie took a determined step forward. She needed some air, needed to get away from this sudden attraction she felt for him.

"Sit," he ordered, his tone harsh.

Blue Jay backed away as she looked between him and Pixie.

Mulishly, Pixie stared at Two Feathers. Did she dare do, as she wanted? He stared back and Pixie knew there would be no relenting on his part. Their words to each other, the most they'd spoken since her punishment, held equal hostility.

Ah, there's my resentment, Pixie thought, relief felt when her rage against the man before her rose again.

Whirling, she planned to go to her bed.

"No. Pix eat with husband this night. Come sit before fire," Two Feathers commanded from behind her.

Pixie spun back to face her tormentor. "I'm not hungry."

"Blue Jay, fill platter for wife," he ordered.

Quickly doing as instructed, Blue Jay held out a full platter to him. Two Feathers made a motion for her to hand what she clasped over to Pixie.

Pixie didn't reach out. She didn't want anything to eat.

"Take it and sit down," Two Feathers ordered. His voice was low. His tone indicated a threat.

Snatching the platter from Blue Jay's hands, Pixie plopped down opposite him. She didn't move and just stared at the food before her.

"Eat," he instructed. He slapped one of the rocks that surrounded the fire with his eating implement held.

Sullenly taking a small bite, and then another, Pixie's non-existent appetite flared. Before long, she'd eaten all that Blue Jay had put on the platter. Wiping at her mouth, Pixie looked up to see that Two Feathers watched her, his gaze softer. Her embarrassment rose at his continued stare. Why, oh why, did she have to find the man so fascinating?

The baby whimpered and Pixie set her platter aside to jump to her feet. Two Feathers quickly rose and met her where the infant lay. Bending, he scooped up the baby before she could.

"She is healthy," he stated, as he looked the baby over.

It seemed he was proud. He looked at Pixie. "Mother must stay healthy. Eat for child."

Pixie swallowed. Her nonexistent appetite and subsequent

weight loss hadn't seemed to slow her milk production. Nevertheless, Two Feathers was right. She did need to be more conscious of her nutrition. Reaching out for the infant, he let her take their child from his arms. Blue Jay had gone to her bed and lay with her back to them. Pixie glanced in her direction when Two Feathers did. He reached out as if to gather her and their child to him. She quickly turned away.

"Don't," she implored.

Letting his hands drop back to his sides, he went to his bedding. Stretching out on his pallet, his arms behind his head, he stared up at the ceiling.

Pixie went to lie down to sleep with the children as she had since his marriage to Blue Jay. Loneliness assaulted her as the night wore on.

****

"Blue Jay not wish for such marking!"

Pixie stared at the woman before her. She had never seen Blue Jay angry before. She had thought to tease the young girl with her words.

When Blue Jay asked that morning if such a large tattoo as what she had on her arm hurt, she'd expressed that it had indeed been painful. Seeing Blue Jay's shudder in response, Pixie's teasing of the young woman had started and it continued the rest of the day.

"You have to receive our husband's mark and it must be as large as mine. Two Feathers demands it. He says that Blue Jay has no choice. When your family arrives, it is scheduled to happen." Actually, Two Feathers had said no such thing and Pixie felt mean for indicating that he had.

Blue Jay slammed down the pot that she held. "Other women not have such large marking!"

Pixie shrugged. "Our husband wants his wives to wear such a

mark. He's strange that way."

Whirling to leave the lodge, Blue Jay mumbled her anger as she went and Pixie laughed outright. She did wonder why though Two Feathers hadn't scheduled Blue Jay to receive his symbol. It had been twelve weeks now since their marriage.

Scowling at her jealousy felt, Pixie straightened up the inside of the lodge, working quietly. The baby had slept through her teasing of Blue Jay and the younger woman's subsequent anger. Fawn had gathered Three Feathers earlier that morning to take him with her to search for eatable roots.

Blue Jay stomped back into the lodge. It seemed she wasn't finished with her argument. "Blue Jay not receive mark!"

Pixie laughed and then she sobered. It was time for her to stop teasing the poor woman. "I'm sorry, Blue Jay. I have been teasing you, and I shouldn't have. Two Feathers never said anything to me about you receiving his symbol. I doubt that you have to have one as large as mine. I requested it. I just wanted to make you suffer for a little bit."

Blue Jay sat down, and she looked at her. She chewed on her bottom lip as if unsure of herself.

"Brother angered when Old Wife make Blue Jay fall before others. Brother say punishment required. Blue Jay say not want punishment. Brother say yes."

"I see," Pixie replied. She went to her child when she woke hungry and whimpering.

"Blue Jay not care for Crow."

In surprise, Pixie turned to look at the woman who still sat beside the fire pit. Blue Jay seemed to want to talk.

"Did he say or do something?" Pixie inquired as she settled the baby against her breast. It startled the sudden shift in their conversation.

"Crow ask if Blue Jay happy. Blue Jay not think, say no, not happy. Blue Jay worry Crow inform husband make husband mad.

Father expect Blue Jay seal bond between peoples. If no children, how Blue Jay do as father wish?"

The younger woman continued to expand on how it worried her, no children from her marriage. How was it her fault, she demanded as she threw her hands up in the air. On and on she chattered.

The baby indicated she was full and Pixie stood. What did the younger woman mean no children? Pixie studied her.

"What do you mean you will never have children? You know that Two Feathers has two children already, so why wouldn't you and he have any?"

Blue Jay directed a frown toward her. "Husband no perform duties."

Pixie couldn't help it. She sputtered. Did Blue Jay mean what she thought she was saying?

Blue Jay continued. "Blue Jay wish to please father. Blue Jay stay silent when father say Blue Jay marry new Chief."

The young woman paused, and then she blurted, "Blue Jay love another! Not wish have new Chief for husband."

"Don't you think that you should've informed your father that you were in love with another before you came here to marry Two Feathers?" Pixie's tone was sharp.

Blue Jay shook her head in response. Her eyes shimmered with tears. "Blue Jay good daughter. Blue Jay obey father."

Once talking, the younger woman didn't stop. Pixie felt worn down by her ceaseless prattle. Pixie bet that she could pick out Blue Jay's father, mother, siblings, and the love of Blue Jay's life without ever having an introduction as the evening wore on.

Abruptly, Blue Jay stood at Two Feathers' entrance into the lodge, and she became tightlipped once more. She flounced to her bed to turn her back to Pixie and him both. Two Feathers looked in question at Pixie. Unable to stop her smile that spread, Pixie gave him a shrug.

Blue Jay had insisted that his menacing silence frightened her. It had frightened Pixie when first experiencing it. However, Blue Jay's fear of Two Feathers wasn't what caused her happiness. No. Her glee came from knowing that he and Blue Jay hadn't consummated their marriage. Two Feathers frowned as he glanced from her to Blue Jay.

Fawn called out and Pixie happily welcomed her into their home. She had forgotten she was to visit that evening. It was perfect timing, her visit.

"Fawn, could you stay and watch the children? Two Feathers and I need to go somewhere and talk privately. I just fed the baby and she'll sleep for quite a while before waking again."

"Fawn stay long time," her sister-in-law replied as she studied her brother's unsmiling features.

Two Feathers followed Pixie from their home. Clasping her arm when she turned toward him, he directed her away from the village.

When they reached a distance with privacy guaranteed, he demanded, "What Pix need tell husband."

He crossed his arms his stance wide.

"Blue Jay loves another."

Two Feathers stared at her.

"Two Feathers not care," he finally drawled.

Pixie grabbed hold of his arm. His response at Blue Jay's confession confounded her. She had thought that he would be happy. It solved their problem of his second marriage. "But don't you see? If we go to her father when he arrives, we can go back as we were."

"No."

Now it was Pixie's turn to stare and her anger rose. "What do you mean no? Didn't you hear me? She loves another."

Two Feathers pushed her back from him. "Marriage done. Tribes united and it is good."

"I want it undone!"

"Wife does not order, Two Feathers."

"I'll let everyone know she told me that you haven't *fucked* her! Her father wants children from the union. He won't be happy with that news!"

Pixie knew that Two Feathers understood what the vulgar word meant; he'd asked her one night its meaning, when she'd used it after stubbing her toe.

In a flash, his backhanded strike knocked her to the ground. Stunned, Pixie didn't move. It seemed he struggled to get his words out, his gaze violent as he bent over toward her.

"Pix disgrace to husband, ashamed Pix wife."

Jerking her back up to where she stood beside him, Two Feathers studied her. Turning, he walked away, his shoulders stiff, his stride extensive.

Pix knew deep-seated shame. She had thought she could blackmail her own husband, force him with extortion to play ball by her rules and her rules alone. If Two Feathers cared for her in even the tiniest bit, she'd just obliterated it.

Not meeting Fawn's gaze when she reentered the lodge, Pix whispered, "Thank you for watching the children."

Looking between her and her silent brother, Fawn exited the home without answering.

"I'm sorry."

Two Feathers didn't respond. Pix let the hand that she'd lifted toward him drop back to her side.

Chapter Thirty-One

"Blood Brother not seem happy."

Two Feathers didn't reply as he watched the deer cross the meadow below from where he and Crow hid. They had watched their quarry for some time as they waited for an opportunity for a clear shot.

"Two wives too much for Blood Brother?"

Raising his bow and arrow, Crow sighted in the deer. It bounded away before he could release his tautly held bowstring. Lowering his arm, he turned fully toward Two Feathers.

He seemed in high spirits.

"Deer hear Crow speak when Crow need keep silent," Two Feathers drawled.

Seven suns had rose and passed since Pix issued her ultimatum to him, and Two Feathers was still shocked at her brazen threat. He couldn't wrap his mind around her disrespect. It gnawed at him. She would willingly shame him before his people. His dishonor was her dishonor. Did she not understand that?

"We find deer again," Crow responded, his mood undaunted. Slipping his bow and arrows into his shoulder bag, he glanced Two Feathers' way again. It was obvious that he wished for Two Feathers to disclose the goings on between him and his two wives.

Two Feathers pivoted on his heel and began the long walk back to their village. He would not confide in Crow about Pix's disrespect to him or his despair over it. Blue Jay had kept her distance from him since that night also, and he was grateful for it, for now.

****

Walking up from the river bottom with the neck of a water gourd grasped in each hand, Pix paused in her step. A disturbance happened at the center of the village. She couldn't see anything. She could hear quarreling female voices though, and she recognized both. Hurrying forward, Pix squeezed through the jeering swarm. Brave Bird and Blue Jay faced off with one another. Blue Jay's cheek held the imprint left behind from Brave Bird's hand.

"What is going on here?" Pix demanded as she stepped toward the two women. She'd not let the people around her know that Brave Bird intimidated still. Blue Jay dropped her gaze, embarrassed it seemed.

Brave Bird sneered at Pix as she pointed a finger toward Blue Jay. "Woman think to scorn Brave Bird. Brave Bird not allow disrespect."

Pix's fury rose. Brave Bird was a malicious bitch who kept others intimated with her nasty temper.

Blue Jay stepped close and she spoke low in Pix's ear, "Brave Bird say Old Wife lazy. Blue Jay defend Old Wife."

Pix swiveled her gaze toward Brave Bird and then toward the gathered crowd of women. Her cheeks burned. They watched her. Did they all believe that she was lazy?

Brave Bird swaggered forward and with her face inches from Pixie's, she spoke loud insuring all could hear. "Brave Bird say Old Wife not woman enough for Chief."

Pix slammed the water gourd that she held against Brave Bird's head.

The crowd whooped.

She had had enough of this woman's malice. Either Brave

Bird would kill her this day, or she'd learn to keep her mouth shut. Managing to grasp hold of Brave Bird's hair when Brave Bird lashed out in response, Pix held tight pulling Brave Bird to the ground. Fighting for all she was worth, she and Brave Bird rolled over the ground and over each other.

The crowd followed their movement.

Brave Bird's laugher rose in triumph when with an accomplished maneuver, she sat astride Pix, her dress hiked up over her knees; Pix's arms held down with her fingers wrapped tight around each wrist. Leaning down, she spit. Pix bucked trying to jerk loose as saliva splattered across her face. Working her feet up under her hips, she managed to tilt the bigger woman forward. Brave Bird held tight even as she went frontward, and she sank her teeth deep into Pix's left wrist.

With a surge of adrenaline at the puncturing pain, Pix managed to free her unbitten arm. Brave Bird remained fastened onto her other arm and worked to stop her bid at freedom. Blindly, Pix reached upward through Brave Bird's hair and found the woman's nose. She squeezed tight her nostrils. When Brave Bird opened her mouth to breathe, teeth freed from her arm, Pix shoved her palm heel upward and luckily found her target. Blood spurted from Brave Bird's nose as she sprawled sideways.

Quickly straddling the prone woman, their positions now reversed, Pix held on for dear life. Locking her legs around Brave Bird's rising hips, Pix clung even when their foreheads connected. For a moment, Pix believed she was to pass out. Flashes of white light danced. Blue Jay stomped on Brave Bird's hair holding the woman's head down preventing her from smacking her forehead again.

Brave Bird screamed her fury.

Pix held tight. Finally, the woman under her quieted, her breathing heaving. Pix heaved also and she shook all over. She continued to keep a tight hold of Brave Bird even as she straightened her elbows so that she could look down at the woman. Blood dripped from Pix's wrist to the ground. She wasn't finished with Brave Bird, although Brave Bird had stopped struggling and sullenly stared upward at her.

The quieted crowd drew in close.

"Tell Blue Jay that you're sorry for slapping her and I'll let you go," Pix rasped.

Brave Bird didn't respond. She pressed her lips together, her gaze narrow.

"Tell her!" Pix yelled.

Slanting her gaze upward toward Blue Jay, Brave Bird rasped, "Brave Bird sorry for hitting Blue Jay."

Blue Jay leaned down her hands on her hips. "Tell all Brave Bird lie about Old Wife."

Brave Bird didn't respond.

"Tell people!" Blue Jay yelled, imitating Pix, and with surprise, Pix looked up at her.

Brave Bird looked around at the women and now a few men. "Brave Bird lie. Pixie not lazy."

At her admission, tears slipped from the corners of Brave Bird's eyes. Pix knew her humiliation was complete.

Rising, Pix gathered up the now empty water gourds. She continued to shake. If she didn't leave soon, she'd be weeping and not quietly like Brave Bird, but loud like a wailing baby. She motioned for Blue Jay to follow her as she weaved through the crowd and headed home.

Once inside their lodge, Blue Jay helped to wash and doctor her wrist, all the while murmuring her support. Her gaze centered on Pixie's forehead. "Old Wife have large bruise on forehead."

"I do?" Pix reached to touch the spot where her head still ached.

Blue Jay laughed. "Brave Bird new name now Rock Head."

Pix's laughter burst out and she grabbed at her ribs. "Ouch.

That hurts! I hope Rock Head didn't break any of my ribs."

Reaching to touch the top of her hand, Blue Jay met her gaze. "Ribs? Blue Jay not know word?"

The rest of that day, many of the village women stopped by to visit with Pix and Blue Jay and it surprised Pix. All were friendly and none brought up the quarrel.

That evening when Two Feathers entered their home, he looked from her to Blue Jay. He didn't say anything as he put away his hunting gear. His expression didn't invite comment, and Pix knew he was aware of the fight. Her ribs still hurt although she'd surmised none was broken. Thank goodness. If it hadn't been for Blue Jay stepping on Brave Bird's hair, pinning the woman in place, Brave Bird would've won the battle. And she would probably be hurting a lot worse too as a result. If Two Feathers faulted her for the quarrel, she'd be unable to keep from wailing. It'd just be too much. She had never participated in a brawl before, and that was what it had been, an outright brawl. Two women fighting to see who'd come out on top. By sheer luck, she'd won.

Two Feathers motioned that he wished to eat, and Blue Jay jumped to prepare him his platter of food. She looked at Pix in question as she handed the meal over to him.

Pix didn't move.

Still silent, his expression ominous, Two Feathers settled before the evening fire, and positioning his legs, he placed the platter of food on top of his lap. He began to eat. His gaze went past Pix and Blue Jay to where the children lay asleep. Finishing his meal, he laid his platter aside. He looked at Pix.

"Where children when wives quarrel?" he demanded.

Before Pix could respond, Blue Jay jumped to her feet. "Old Wife and Blue Jay not quarrel!"

"Blue Jay, please, I can explain to him," Pix responded although her throat was tight from suppressed tears. He blamed her. Why did it not surprise? Blue Jay, her ire high, didn't listen.

She continued her support for Pixie.

"Rock Head cause fight. Old Wife defend Blue Jay! Blue Jay glad Old Wife help Blue Jay."

Pix saw that Blue Jay surprised Two Feathers. She usually had nothing to say when he was around. His frown slashed deeper—she babbled still. The baby whimpered and Pix rose to go to her. He watched as she sat and gentled their child back to sleep. Pix couldn't keep her gaze from locking with his. She missed him. Missed their nights together.

He looked back at Blue Jay then jerked his hand up into the air his irritation apparent. "Quiet," he snapped.

Blue Jay locked her lips together.

Pix spoke up. "She just defends me, Two Feathers. Don't be angry with her. She's trying to let you know that she and I are friends. The children were with Fawn."

Standing, Two Feathers looked between them. Abruptly turning, he left the lodge.

"Blue Jay not like husband."

"Blue Jay, don't say that," Pix admonished, and then grabbed at her side when her laughter bubbled forth and she couldn't stop the response. Here she was scolding his second wife because the younger woman didn't like their husband, and yet, at the same time, she didn't want them to have a relationship, hated the thought of it.

"Why Old Wife laugh?"

Waving her hand at Blue Jay, Pix drew a shallow breath. She sobered. *Why indeed*? she thought as she stood. The situation was not funny. It was sad.

"Blue Jay, keep an eye on the children. I'm going to go find Two Feathers and explain to him what happened today." At Blue Jay's nod, Pix turned. She trusted Blue Jay with the children. She hadn't yesterday. She did this night.

"Old Wife keep husband happy for both. Blue Jay not desire

husband. Husband scare Blue Jay." Blue Jay gave a shudder.

Feeling almost indignant on Two Feathers' behalf, Pix shook her head in confusion. She didn't want Blue Jay or Two Feathers to look at each other with a hankering, so why a feeling of insult for him?

Emerging from the lodge, Pix looked around. Not many in the village were out at this late hour. Fawn was strolling up from the river so Pix started toward her. Too late, she noticed that Crow also came from the river behind Fawn. His wife walked by his side. Halting before the group, Pix ignored Crow or she tried to. He spoke.

"Crow hear Brave Bird and Pixie roll in dirt. Wife say Pixie strong woman. Crow wonder why fight?"

Crow's wife didn't look at Pix. She stared at the ground. Her support surprised Pix. Crow's wife hadn't spoken to her since the night she'd threatened for her to stay away from him. The woman confused Pix. She seemed almost afraid to meet her gaze.

Pix didn't understand where her distress came from. Did his wife worry that Crow might care for her or she for him since they were to marry? If so, Pix would be glad to clear up that misconception.

"Just a misunderstanding that needed resolved," Pix replied to Crow's question before she turned toward Fawn. She hated to question Fawn in front of Crow, but she was anxious to be on her way.

"Fawn, have you seen Two Feathers?"

"Brother at bathing place."

"Thanks," Pix murmured before taking off. She could feel Crow's stare between her shoulder blades.

Hurrying to where she knew Two Feathers bathed, Pix rounded several bushes, and then halted. Two Feathers stood waist deep in the river. He looked up at her as the water swirled past his hips.

Wading toward her, he demanded, "Why wife here?"

Pix stepped to the water's edge.

"I wanted to explain that Brave Bird and I fought. Not Blue Jay and me."

At reaching her, he grasped her arm and yanked her toward him. Before Pix could protest, he encircled her waist with his arms and bending toward her, clamped his mouth over hers. His hands moved over her. She clung to him. Abruptly, she pushed him away.

"No, Two Feathers. I love you but I can't." Pix couldn't control her tears that rose. Did he understand what she didn't say, that although she loved him, she couldn't accept sharing him with another woman and would never willingly lay with him again as long as he might desire another?

Two Feathers looked down at her. He reached to touch his chest then spread his fingers over his heart area. "Two Feathers suffers with Pix's words."

Pix leaned forward and wrapped her arms back around his waist. He drew her close. He sighed deep from above her.

"Only Pix Two Feathers love."

In surprise, Pix lifted her head to gaze upward at the man who towered over her. "You've never expressed affection for me before."

Her heart raced. Did he say the words only to ease her hurt?

"Two Feathers not lay with new wife. Two Feathers would. Two Feathers not able. Stay soft."

Anger felt, Pix started to remove her arms from around Two Feathers' waist. How noble. So he would've consummated his new marriage except for not able to keep an erection.

Two Feathers held tight and refused to let her go.

Pix stopped her struggle. "I won't say anything to the tribe about you and Blue Jay. My heart hurts and I say hateful things. I promise I'll stay silent."

"Two Feathers reveal weakness. Show Pix he care." Two Feathers took her hand to shove it between them and against him. He held it there.

Pix looked up at him. "I see you've no problem now," she drawled.

"Even with cold," he replied.

Pix's laughter erupted. Her anger evaporated. Her sadness lingered though. "What are we to do, Two Feathers?"

Stepping fully from the water, Two Feathers dressed. Then lifting her upward and onto dry ground, he sat and levered her onto his lap. Pix gladly went. They were hidden from anyone who happened to come to the river.

"I have missed you, Wife."

Pix snuggled closer against Two Feathers at his subdued words. He was warmth, and strength, and everything that she wanted.

"And I you, Husband."

Two Feathers lowered his mouth to hers. Pix could feel his heartbeat beneath her hand and its rhythm echoed hers. This was where she belonged, but would she regret her weakness?

Chapter Thirty-Two

Laughing quietly, Pix hid deeper behind the expanse of the tree when Two Feathers turned. He hadn't spotted her. She frowned when he settled down on a fallen log just a few feet from her. He didn't look her way. It seemed his hunt for her was over. Watching him a few minutes longer, Pix stepped from her hiding place. Two Feathers turned to meet her gaze.

Fawn had bestowed the alone day upon them. She'd taken the children and Blue Jay with her to gather berries. The baby fed right before their leave-taking, gave Pix and Two Feathers several hours of free time before their return home.

Pix knew Two Feathers suspected why Fawn had arranged their free day away from the children and from Blue Jay. His sister knew how unhappy she was with their situation. Even though she and Blue Jay were a unified front since the day of the fight with Brave Bird, Pix yearned for the private life she and Two Feathers had given up. Blue Jay had no wish for a relationship with Two Feathers, and he and Pix wanted each other, wanted their home to themselves and their children.

"Well, you're no fun. You gave up too easy to find me," Pix taunted.

Two Feathers stretched out his legs before him, his back straight. "Wife run, hide from husband. Wife approach husband make amends or husband leave wife behind, go to lodge alone."

Walking to him, Pix stepped between his spread legs.

"Husband see wife sorry for behavior," Two Feathers drawled. Pix leaned forward.

"Husband be sorry for his threat," she drawled into his ear copying his exact tone of voice. She then drew back as if to walk away.

Two Feathers grasped hold of her wrist pulling her back between his legs. He looked around. He smiled.

His hands cupped her derriere.

With a return smile, Pix gave a nod.

****

Walking back into the village their alone time departed, Pix and Two Feathers loosened their fingers from each other letting their hands drop to their respective sides.

"It seems that Blue Jay's tribe has arrived," Two Feathers stated his tone flat. Pix looked to where he directed his gaze and her heart dropped. Blue Jay's mother, father, and brother all seemed to be waiting for their return. Fawn stood beside the group also, as did Blue Jay.

Blue Jay's brother looked from her and Two Feathers and then to his sister, and he frowned. Blue Jay's father seemed weak, ill, and very old. Blue Jay stepped from his side to address Two Feathers.

"Husband, Blue Jay's father, and mother," she stated as she indicated the older couple.

Two Feathers greeted his in-laws. Pix felt like an interloper. She and Two Feathers had just made love and now she stood before his second wife's family. As of that day, Two Feathers may not have taken Blue Jay to his pallet, but one day he would. When that day came, would she find herself as Brave Bird was now? Would she become second choice for her husband?

Stepping away unnoticed, Pix took her child from Fawn's arms and then gathered Three Feathers to her side. Had she made a mistake in taking Two Feathers back as a lover?

Fawn watched her as she turned and walked away.

****

Pix heard the drums begin that evening, and walking to stand within the open door of her home, she looked in the direction to where the people were gathering. Puzzled, she stood and watched.

Two Feathers hadn't come home and neither had Blue Jay.

Crow walked toward her, and Pix turned to go back into the lodge. He called out to her, and with reluctance, she halted and rotated to face him.

"Pixie not curious?" he asked when he stopped before her.

His gaze moved over her. It was a degrading look. One day, she'd have the nerve to make Two Feathers listen to her experience with his blood brother.

"My children sleep and would be alone if I went to watch the activity," Pix responded, although she wanted to ignore him.

Of course, she was inquisitive. Turning, Pix started to escape into her home. Crow stepped up to block her entrance. Pix inched away from him. Where was his wife?

"Blue Jay receive Two Feathers' mark. Second wife father demand it. Two Feathers happy when inform Crow, Crow needed."

Pix's gaze darted to Crow's hands. She hadn't paid attention to what it was that he held. Trying to keep her face free from her hurt felt, Pix turned from him. She must have failed. He laughed as he walked away. Escaping into the interior of the lodge, Pix wandered around within its enclosure. She picked up this or that item of Two Feathers' only to lay each back onto its resting place. Why had he not informed her as to what was planned? Abruptly turning at a sound heard, Pix stilled. Her husband stood before her.

With long strides, he approached and gathered her within his arms. Pix didn't resist. She encircled his waist with her arms.

"Two Feathers love only Pix," he reassured her.

Laying her head against Two Feathers' chest, Pix held tight to him. She would never have this emotional closeness with him again. She had already mentally begun to distance herself. If she didn't, her hurt would be too much to bear. Before long though with that emotional distance, she would become frozen inside, no longer able to feel anything for the man before her. Pix didn't know what had occurred from the time she'd left Two Feathers' side to now, but it seemed he and Blue Jay would begin as true husband and wife this day. Pulling back, she directed a sad smile at Two Feathers. "You need to go. Blue Jay and her family will be waiting."

Laying his palms against each side of her face, Two Feathers studied her as if he memorized her features.

Abruptly, he left.

Pix went to stand beside their children, and as she gazed down at their sleeping forms, she forced her thoughts to center on them, so sweet and innocent. She loved them both with all her heart. Pix's emotions tore through her the same as they had the night Two Feathers married Blue Jay, only this night she wasn't angry with him. This night her agony defeated. She had no more fight left in her. She would do what was right for the tribe; yet in doing so, she and Two Feathers would be no more.

Fawn called out for admittance, and Pix lifted her head. Wiping away her tears, she responded, "Sister welcome to come in."

Fawn entered the lodge, and coming forward toward Pix, she stated firmly, "Sister attend ceremony of second wife."

"I can't." Pix motioned toward the children.

Fawn pushed her toward the door of the lodge.

"Sister go. Support husband and second wife. Fawn stay, care for children. It best."

"I have no wish to watch Blue Jay take Two Feathers' mark of ownership," Pix argued.

Fawn didn't relent until Pix finally surrendered to her demand. With measured steps, Pix walked through the gathered crowd until she stood before Blue Jay. Crying out her welcome, Blue Jay lifted a hand for her to take. Kneeling beside her, Pix grasped it. As Blue Jay's fingers laced around hers, Pix's gaze connected with Two Feathers'. He showed no emotion. Pix straightened her shoulders. She would try to make him proud of her for once.

Pix wondered where Blue Jay's father and mother were. Both were absent from the surrounding crowd. Blue Jay's brother, his shoulders straight and legs spread wide, stood along beside Two Feathers.

As Crow laid out his tattoo equipment, Blue Jay's fingers tightened on Pix's and Pix glanced toward her. Blue Jay's gaze wasn't on Crow as Pix expected but on something past his shoulders. Maybe the parents Blue Jay had expressed anger over for her arranged marriage. Shifting her gaze, Pix recognized the young man Blue Jay so intently focused on. He seemed not to be able to take his gaze from Blue Jay either. Blue Jay had described him exactly. With sympathy, Pix realized that Blue Jay and the young man suffered that day also.

Two Feathers seemed preoccupied. His gaze searched the crowd.

Lifting his hand, Crow, with lowered head bent toward Blue Jay, ready to begin. Two Feathers stepped forward as if to stop his action.

"Husband dead!"

Blue Jay's mother ran up to her son. "Father lay unmoving!"

Blue Jay abruptly stood and her wail of anguish sounded. Pix rose and started to follow her as Blue Jay hurried after her mother and brother. Two Feathers reached out to halt her move forward. He shook his head. Watching Blue Jay and her family and their tribe members' as they rushed away, Pix felt their sorrow. *Always death*, she thought.

Turning, she looked up at Two Feathers. "Are you not going to go with Blue Jay? Show your support for her?"

"Blood Brother let family grieve then go to wife." When Crow spoke, Pix jumped. She'd forgotten him. It seemed his presence surprised Two Feathers also. He scowled at Crow's assertion.

Crow gathered his items from the skin he'd laid out. He then whipped the blanket up and walked away.

Two Feathers turned. He looked at Pix as if cautious of her response. "Blood Brother correct, Two Feathers go to Blue Jay and family later."

"I understand, Two Feathers. I don't want Blue Jay to experience any embarrassment because of my hurt over your marriage. She suffers also."

As Two Feathers gazed at her, his eyes softened. "We go home to children. Wait for proper time."

Pix nodded.

Fawn rose from where she sat at their entrance into their lodge. She looked at her brother. "Fawn hear commotion? Not good sound."

"Blue Jay's father passed away," Pix informed at Two Feathers' continued silence. The children slept behind Fawn on their pallets. The noise hadn't woke them. Fawn looked at her brother as if to say something and he shook his head back at her.

"What?" Pix inquired seeing what he did.

"If not this night then after time of mourning?" Fawn responded.

Two Feathers frowned. "Say no more, Sister."

"What is going on?" Pix walked to where Two Feathers now sat.

"Tell wife what was planned, Brother," Fawn stated.

In confusion, Pix looked from brother to sister. Taking her hand within his, Two Feathers urged Pix to sit beside him and when she did, he turned toward her.

"Husband send Rock with message to Blue Jay's father."

Pix watched Two Feathers. "And?" she responded when he didn't continue.

"Rock relay to father union with daughter unconsummated and Two Feathers wish for one wife only. Inform father daughter love another. Also, inform father, Two Feathers give blood promise tribes still be as one without marriage with daughter. Father-in-law send return message, ill and have belief dying. Say not know daughter's feelings and wish for daughter's happiness and agree to divorce. Old Chief send message also, have concern no smooth merging of tribes without marriage."

Pix waited for Two Feathers to continue.

"Two Feathers instruct Rock, inform old Chief Two Feathers wait for arrival before make public announcement. Old Chief and Two Feathers face tribes as one. Give promise together of solidarity between tribes."

"Why was Blue Jay about to receive your mark if that is so?" Pix felt confused.

"Father angry at daughter and punish for not telling father of feelings. Father know daughter's fear of ink. Father was to stop before receive mark. Two Feathers wonder about father when father not appear."

Reaching out, Two Feathers touched Pix's cheek. "Two Feathers discuss wish for divorce with Strong Hand now."

"Why didn't you tell me all of this?" Pix couldn't understand Two Feathers remaining quiet. Especially since, he knew how his having a second wife upset her so.

"Two Feathers afraid when send message, father not agree without fight, Two Feathers stay married if so. Not want Pix hurt more knowing had chance of only Two Feathers and Pix and children as family."

Fawn left without saying goodbye when Pix leaned forward at Two Feathers' response.

****

Two Feathers decided not to inform Blue Jay of what her

father had been prepared to do on her behalf. It could harm the harmonious relationship between them all he stated when Pix wanted to argue. If Blue Jay's brother didn't agree with the dissolution of their marriage, he and Pix must accept Blue Jay as his wife and Blue Jay none the wiser as to what could have been. It was best, he stated.

Pix accepted his decision although it was a bittersweet discussion.

****

Three weeks following the old man's death only Rock, Fawn, Two Feathers, and Pix knew of that pre-arranged agreement. *Would I want to know if it were me?* Pix wondered as the days and nights passed with Blue Jay none the wiser as to the different life that she could have had. The funeral for the old Chief gave way to Strong Hand's ceremony into leadership for the other tribe. Two Feathers never approached Strong Hand with the disbandment of his and Blue Jay's marriage and still hadn't and Pix wondered why, although she didn't ask.

Her steps heavy as she carried the water she'd collected from the river, Pix glanced around at the village that bustled with activity. The day was bright and clear, with no sign of the gloom that she felt. The baby on her back whimpered, hungry.

"I know, I know," she cajoled. Crow appeared up from behind her and Pix inwardly flinched. She kept her walking pace and ignored his presence. He seemed to appear by her side at a regular rate these days and always with something to say that was inappropriate for a supposed friend. His wife straightened to stand fully erect from her chores by the side of their lodge, and she frowned. Her gaze caught Pix's.

Pix had tried to make friends with the woman, smiling when passing, and trying to make small talk. She remained aloof.

"Crow worry about Blood Brother," Crow stated from beside

Pix. Pix shifted her gaze from Crow's wife to the man who now kept pace alongside her.

"Why?" she snapped.

"Blood Brother distant, troubled, Crow believe."

Crow, it appeared, fished for information. Pix clamped her lips together. She had never gotten around to telling Two Feathers everything that Crow had said and done to her, and continued to do. He had enough worries on his shoulders without her adding her complaint against his blood brother.

"I don't know anything," she responded.

"Wife not realize husband burdened?" Crow sneered.

Pix's anger spiked. "You're supposed to be his friend. Why don't you ask him if he's troubled?"

Crow stalked away.

It surprised Pix that Two Feathers hadn't confided in Crow. She was happy that he hadn't. She had no wish for Crow to know anything about their home life.

Blue Jay looked up from her cooking when Pix entered their lodge. Lowering her gaze, Blue Jay flipped the fish that she cooked.

Three Feathers ran up to Pix to wrap his arms around her legs. His bottom lip quivered.

"Hey there, little fella. What's wrong?" Pix patted the top of his head as she put the heavy container that she carried down to the hard packed floor.

Untying the wrap from around her waist, Pix eased the baby from her back. The infant was in full whimper mode now and not at all happy. Hurrying with her preparations, Pix put the baby to her breast. The quiet within the home was immediate.

Three Feathers still hung onto her leg and Pix looked at Blue Jay in question.

"Blue Jay had to scold," Blue Jay informed.

Pix frowned. Blue Jay was stricter than she was.

Holding Three Feathers' hand, Pix walked forward to sit down.

Three Feathers sat with her and hugged up to her.

"You have to mind Blue Jay," Pix told him her tone soft. He nodded and moved to lie across her lap. Pix patted at his back.

Blue Jay watched them. She pointed to the noon meal she'd been working on. "Blue Jay not hungry go for walk. Leave Old Wife with her children."

At Blue Jay's departure, Pix's brows knitted. Blue Jay had emphasized *her children*.

By nature, Blue Jay was a happy, go-lucky girl. Since her father's death though, she'd withdrawn into herself. She no longer talked non-stop driving Pix crazy with her ceaseless babble, and recently, she'd begun to avoid Two Feathers more than ever. She never looked up when he was home. For that, Pix was thankful.

She would've been jealous as hell if Blue Jay found Two Feathers attractive and vied for his attention.

Still patting at Three Feathers' back, Pix sighed. The situation between the three of them wasn't right. Two Feathers at night went to his own bed, as did she, and as did Blue Jay. There was no marriage for any of them, all were unsettled, and all were unhappy.

Walking into the lodge, Two Feathers went and set aside his hunting tools. He looked across the room toward Pix and the children. Picking up his meal, he sat, and without a word said began to eat.

Pix couldn't remain quiet.

"Something has to be done. We can't go on like this. It has been twenty-one days, Two Feathers."

Setting his meal aside, Two Feathers looked at her. Pix could tell she'd angered him.

"Woman think Two Feathers not know this?"

Pix swallowed and lowered her gaze.

Was Two Feathers changing his mind? Did he after all want his marriage with Blue Jay? Did Blue Jay want the marriage, too?

At night when Blue Jay wouldn't look at Two Feathers or meet his gaze, was it a guilty conscious and not as she believed, that Blue Jay didn't like him. Did they meet somewhere during the day behind her back?

Pix felt her suspicion rise.

Two Feathers hadn't looked at her sexually since the old man's death. She had believed it was because he was busy with all that had happened and that he couldn't find the time for them to sneak away. Did he not, because Blue Jay now satisfied his needs?

"Did Pix and Blue Jay argue?"

Pix looked up. So now, he worried over Blue Jay?

"No. Why?"

"Blue Jay pass Two Feathers. Look upset. Two Feathers watch and Blue Jay go to Brother's lodge. Blue Jay not visit Brother since father's death. Two Feathers wonder why this day, Blue Jay visit family."

"Maybe she's unhappy and tired of living in limbo just as I am. Or maybe, she just wanted to visit with her brother and mother and there's no reason at all for you to be worried about her," Pix retorted her jealousy sharp.

Abruptly standing, Two Feathers looked down at her and he retorted, "Wife not think husband unhappy? Husband wish for first wife only and no other!"

Pix felt a jolt to the pit of her stomach. He wished for Pretty Flower? When Two Feathers stalked toward her, she strained backward not wanting his touch. Reaching down, his frown heavy, he took their child from her arms to lay the infant onto her sleeping pallet, and then he reached for Three Feathers and lay his slumbering form aside. He pulled her upward.

When Pix attempted to step away, he jerked her against him.

"Two Feathers wish for Pix. Only Pix," he rasped.

"I—I—thought—"

"Two Feathers know what wife believe."

Laying her head against his chest, Pix shuddered.

Two Feathers didn't leave their home the rest of that evening, he and she talking. Something they had needed to do.

Blue Jay failed to return and Two Feathers commented on it as the evening spanned into darkness. "Maybe Two Feathers go to Brother-in-law and speak this night. Two Feathers suspicious Blue Jay spew unhappiness and Brother-in-law easily angered. Friendship between Two Feathers and Strong Hand not built."

Pix met Two Feathers' gaze.

He worried what it might mean for the tribe, his request for an annulment. Which was why he'd waited before approaching the subject of divorce to Blue Jay's brother, he had wanted to build a friendship with Strong Hand.

"I don't believe that Blue Jay would complain to her brother of her unconsummated marriage. She would ask me to talk to you first if she were thinking of divorce," Pix comforted.

Two Feathers studied Pix at her words.

Crow called out for admittance and Pix frowned. She hated the sound of that man's voice.

"Wife still no care for Blood Brother?"

At Two Feathers' matter-of-fact question put to her, Pix shrugged. Now was not the time to inform him of Crow's behavior toward her.

Standing, Two Feathers called out a welcome for his blood brother to enter the lodge. Pix stood to step away. She paused in her step when Crow didn't enter the lodge alone. Blue Jay's brother entered also, and his expression didn't invite ease. Blue Jay entered the lodge behind him. She wouldn't meet Pix's or Two Feathers' gaze, and Pix's shoulders slumped. It seemed that Two Feathers was correct. Blue Jay had gone to her brother with a complaint.

Crow walked forward and Pix thought that he looked smug. Glancing toward Two Feathers, she wondered if Two Feathers noticed his expression.

Crow touted, "Blue Jay bring complaint against husband before Council, say unhappy in marriage. As blood brother to Chief, Council direct Crow meet with Chief. Council say keep problem with new wife quiet from tribes. Council demand trouble resolved between husband and wife."

Two Feathers winced, his anger obvious. "Two Feathers wonder why wife not come to husband before taking complaint against husband to Council?"

Pix wondered the same thing. Had she been wrong in her assumption that she and Blue Jay were friends? Why hadn't Blue Jay at least come to her before going to the Council?

Blue Jay didn't raise her gaze, keeping it steadfast to the floor.

"All come, sit before our fire," Pix invited welcoming their visitors forward, the moment awkward.

Two Feathers sat after the others did. He made a motion for Pix to settle down along beside him, and reached out a hand to her when she stepped forward. Blue Jay's brother frowned as if Two Feathers' assistance was something that he shouldn't offer.

"It is true as Sister report, Chief deprived of manhood by Old Wife."

Shocked, Pix stared at Blue Jay. How could she have been so wrong in her thinking concerning the younger woman? Where was the sweet girl with no guile in her?

Two Feathers responded and Pix felt his fury vibrate through him at the insult. "Two Feathers desire one wife only. Two Feathers make mistake in taking another."

"No strong words. No fight," Crow interjected.

"Sister say insult too big to remain second wife to Chief. If Chief unable to perform duty, Sister request divorce."

Pix glanced at Blue Jay at her brother's sliced words. Blue Jay didn't look offended. It seemed her older brother was more the one upset at Two Feathers' failed husband duty.

"Two Feathers give word to Strong Hand, alliance stay strong between tribes without children," Two Feathers responded.

Without marriage, too, don't forget to mention that, Pix thought.

Blue Jay interjected, "Blue Jay not wish for children or marriage with Two Feathers. Blue Jay love another."

Strong Hand twisted toward his sister. His surprise reflected. His features grew taut as he studied her, and Blue Jay looked down flustered. He raised a hand as if to strike her.

Two Feathers quickly reached out and his fingers curled around Strong Hand's wrist.

"Two Feathers have knowledge of Blue Jay's care for another," he growled.

Surging to his feet, Strong Hand demanded, "Men meet without women."

Two Feathers stood as did Crow.

Chapter Thirty-Three

Pix informed Fawn the next morning as to what had transpired, and quietly, Fawn listened as she flipped the small animal that she labored over to finish skinning it. Pix helped her even as she looked to where Blue Jay played with the children some distance away. It still shocked Pix that the younger woman had gone to her brother with her complaint.

Turning, Pix acknowledged her feelings in the matter to Fawn. "I am so unhappy. Strong Hand says that he's afraid the tribes won't settle together if Blue Jay and Two Feathers separate. He refuses to agree to any divorce."

Fawn looked up, and stopped her work as she studied Pix. "Fawn and Strong Hand marry. Solve problem for all. Marriage keep tribes united, allow Brother and Blue Jay separate. Fawn talk to Strong Hand."

"No," Pix retorted. She wouldn't have Fawn sacrifice her life for her.

Fawn nodded firmly. "Inform Brother, Fawn wish speak this night to him and others."

Even though Pix argued, Fawn shook her head with determination at her. There was no changing her mind.

****

That evening as Fawn, Pix, Two Feathers, Strong Hand, Blue Jay, and Crow sat around the lodge's evening fire, Fawn's expressed solution to everyone's unhappy situation hung in the air between them.

Pix noticed that Strong Hand looked at Fawn with a considering gaze. He wasn't a bad looking man. Although not quite as tall as Two Feathers, he was as broad-shouldered. The evening discussion had ended and everyone sat silent. The burning firewood popped within the fire pit and sparks shot up into the air. Fawn was a beautiful woman not only on the outside but on the inside as well, and it seemed that Strong Hand realized the jewel before him.

"It is good plan," Crow stated within the silence of the group. Pix thought that Crow looked anything but pleased.

"All wait outside Two Feathers' lodge, except wife and Sister," Two Feathers ordered. Blue Jay continued to sit as her brother and Crow stood, and Two Feathers drawled out, "Except Old Wife."

Blue Jay jumped up to follow her brother and Pix scolded, "Husband, you embarrassed her."

Two Feathers snorted. "Blue Jay disrespect husband going to Brother and Council with complaint. New wife should have come to husband to discuss wishes."

Considering him, Pix realized that Two Feathers felt his manliness was in question by Blue Jay and the others. She was glad that he'd been unable to perform with Blue Jay on their wedding night. Turning to Fawn, Pix focused on her, and pushed away the sudden image of Two Feathers and Blue Jay in a loving embrace. Blue Jay and her husband together was something she didn't want to visualize.

"Fawn, don't do this for me or Two Feathers. We will work out some other solution," she stated.

"It is what Fawn want. Strong Hand look at Fawn with awareness now, and Fawn maybe learn to love Strong Hand. Marriage good for all, solve all problem."

Keeping her gaze on Fawn, Pix frowned as Fawn wiped away

a tear. Realization dawned on Pix. Fawn wished to move on, to try to forget.

"What if the hurt of losing TJ never goes away?" Pix asked. Her tears rose in response at Fawn's continued grief.

"At least Fawn have children to love," Fawn replied her voice low.

Pix didn't know what else to say.

Two Feathers studied the walls of the lodge as if there were something on them that fascinated him. Pix knew he felt overwhelmed. Her emotion choked her too. He stood and went to the entrance of the lodge.

With words said, he came to sit back down.

Crow, Strong Hand, and Blue Jay all gathered back around the fire. Pix noticed that Strong Hand couldn't keep his gaze from sliding toward Fawn.

Two Feathers' shoulders were straight and rigid.

Pix knew he didn't like or want what was transpiring between his sister and Strong Hand, but it did solve all their problems.

"If Strong Hand agree, with rising sun, Two Feathers announce Blue Jay no longer wife. Tell all Sister and Strong Hand to marry and Fawn to live with Strong Hand among tribe members of Strong Hand. Alliance remain strong, people stay happy."

Pix sat still and silent after Two Feathers' statement, as did Blue Jay. Everyone else stood, all in agreement to the plan. Two Feathers walked out of the home behind his sister. Blue Jay, he informed, would stay another night as a married woman.

Blue Jay cleared her throat upon everyone's departure and Pix glanced toward her.

"Brother seek out Crow when Blue Jay inform not happy in marriage. Brother aware of friendship between husband and Crow, and say want to keep problem quiet. Worry about alliance. Crow inform Council members, not Brother."

"I see," Pix, answered.

Blue Jay continued, "Blue Jay not know if husband agree to separation, so Blue Jay not approach husband. Old Wife stay away from Blue Jay since father's death. Blue Jay believe Old Wife mad at Blue Jay so Blue Jay not speak to Old Wife. Blue Jay unhappy, not want be problem for friend, go to Brother with unhappiness."

"I wasn't upset with you, Blue Jay, just with our circumstances," Pix responded.

Blue Jay became closed-mouth to whatever it was she was going to reply when Two Feathers reentered the home, his presence powerful and felt. Pix watched as the younger woman quickly went to her sleeping pallet and turned so that her back was to the room. Blue Jay really was afraid of their husband, Pix realized. She hadn't known the depth of the younger woman's fear.

Gazing at Two Feathers when he came forward to sit down beside her, their sleeping children on her other side, Pix understood Blue Jay's sentiment. Two Feathers was a solemn man not prone to allowing his emotions shown to the outside world. He had frightened her, too, upon their first meeting. Reaching for her hand, he signaled for her to lie down beside the children. Pix obeyed and he stretched out alongside her.

"With rising sun Two Feathers glad to announce want only one wife."

At his low words in her ear, Pix smiled and snuggled closer to this man she'd come to love with all her heart.

Blue Jay's voice interrupted from across the lodge. "Blue Jay not want trouble on husband and Old Wife. Brother demand Brother know truth when tell Brother, Blue Jay unhappy in marriage."

Pix almost laughed aloud when Two Feathers threw his arm over his eyes.

"Humph," he responded for her ears alone.

****

It was done.

Pix watched Blue Jay and Two Feathers receive sanction for their separation as wife and husband, and then afterward, Fawn and Strong Hand declared their union. Two Feathers brought Strong Hand multiple wedding gifts to which he displayed before the crowd. With his back to the people and bringing forth yet another gift, Two Feathers' gaze caught Pix's. It shocked, Pix, when Two Feathers winked at her. She had taught him that.

The rest of the evening became a celebration for all, and Pix participated in the activities. She danced, swayed and stomped with the beat of the drums, the people laughing, and playing games. Bets were won and lost as the night wore on. The two tribes united as one.

That evening from where she sat resting, Pix noticed that Blue Jay and the young man who reclined beside her saw only each other. Turning, Pix observed Fawn and her new husband as they stood together laughing. It seemed that for Strong Hand, once he noticed Fawn, he had become infatuated. Pix hoped it was so.

Crow stood beside his wife a distance away and watched with a narrowed gaze as Two Feathers and Strong Hand conversed together.

Pix sat up straighter.

Did she just see Crow pinch the underside of his wife's arm? The woman had jumped then went completely still as if terrified to move. Crow whispered something in her ear, and when he walked away, she turned toward their lodge and hurried to it. Pix shook her head. No. She must have imagined what she thought she saw. Why would the woman have returned to Crow if he treated her cruelly? She thought she saw something that wasn't since she had no care for Crow.

Two Feathers' mother walked up and Pix gave her a smile.

Mother spoke soft, "Mother take children home with grandmother."

"If you want," Pix responded. Reaching down, her mother-in-law took the sleeping baby from her arms. Three Feathers sleepily took the hand that his grandmother then stretched out to him.

"I just fed the baby. She should sleep most of the night," Pix informed.

Her mother-in-law inclined her head in understanding before she walked away.

Pix didn't move from her comfortable spot and continued to sit and watch the people around her as they celebrated. As her gaze moved across the village and its populace, she couldn't believe that she'd ever lived another life, a life of modern times. Her previous life seemed unreal. It was as if she had dreamed that other life, that other family, and other friends.

"You were real though," Pix whispered and she looked up into the darkening sky. "And I miss you all. I miss you all so much."

Two Feathers approached her. "Wife ready to go home?" Quickly rising, Pix stood beside him.

"Your mother took the children with her," she informed.

"Two Feathers ask Mother to take."

Staring up at her husband, Pix smiled at him. She truly loved this man. If it wasn't for him, she wouldn't have survived this harsh world.

"We go home?" he asked. He looked at her in question when she remained unmoving.

Shaking off her melancholy, Pix responded, "Yes, let's go home."

It was time to forget that other life, time to move on and time to accept the change.

Upon entering their lodge, Two Feathers gathered her within his arms. He didn't say anything as he gazed down at her, and Pix raised her eyebrows at him in question.

"Two Feathers look forward to this time all day. Only Pix and Two Feathers now," he murmured.

Pix sighed when Two Feathers lowered his mouth to hers. She knew this night would be unlike their last lovemaking. This night, safe and alone and within the confines of their home, his lovemaking would be slow and easy, with murmured words of love. This night would be as the time following their wedding. They would have privacy, no sneaking around, no hiding, and no worry if someone might stumble upon them. The evening wore on as she and Two Feathers knew each other again as husband and wife. Pix heard the laughter of the people in the village, and someone shouted, another sang, and it made no difference, it was only her and Two Feathers, alone.

****

Lazily, Pix rose to sit up, and she glanced down at Two Feathers who lay sprawled by her side. There was no more outside village noise. Just the nighttime singing of crickets and the howl of coyotes heard. Pix smiled down at Two Feathers as he looked back up at her. They had washed and lay talking with hours passed she knew.

"Where Pix go?" he asked. With his eyes half closed, he grasped her hand when she reached to pick up her dress dropped along beside the bedding in their earlier haste.

"I need to gather the children from your mother's. It's time for the baby's feeding."

Sitting up, Two Feathers stood to his full height. Reaching for his clothes, he motioned for Pix to stay put.

"It is night and Two Feathers know Pix not like walk in dark. Two Feathers gather children."

The fire pit embers cast a velvety glow within the lodge, and it enfolded her and Two Feathers in an intimate world. Standing, Pix wrapped her arms around Two Feathers' waist.

"I love you, you know, with all my heart."

"Two Feathers love Pix in return," he responded as he cupped her chin. His fingers curled gently as he leaned down to kiss her mouth.

Slipping her night garment down over her shoulders, Pix waited for Two Feathers' return. The extra soft deerskin was a small comfort she enjoyed, she thought in absentminded contentment, the garment hem falling just above her knees. Fawn had shown her the method used to make the garment so supple. Pix hummed happily, as she waited.

Jumping to her feet, she gathered the baby from Two Feathers' arms when he reentered the lodge. With tender feeling washing over her, Pix ran her fingers through her child's thick, black head of hair. The infant slept contently. Pix looked in question at Two Feathers.

"Three Feathers wish to stay with Grandmother," he responded.

Going to their sleeping pallet, Pix laid the baby down. Turning, she sat beside the child.

Two Feathers squatted beside the fire pit. He seemed in quiet reflection.

"Is everything okay at your mother's lodge?" Pix softly inquired.

Two Feathers picked up the smooth wooden stick used to nudge the fire. He stoked the coals. After a moment, he looked over at Pix.

"Mother is well. She is looking forward to living with Fawn and Strong Hand."

Pix waited.

"Does Crow's wife seem strange to Pix?" Two Feathers studied the end of the stick that he held.

"I think that Crow may mistreat her," Pix responded. Two Feathers' gaze rose and Pix continued.

"She doesn't have much to say and keeps to herself."

"That doesn't mean Crow mistreats his woman," he replied.

Pix chewed at the inside of her cheek. She took a breath. "Crow is not what he seems, Husband. Today, I thought I saw him pinch her and she was just standing beside him doing nothing.

She seems terrified of him."

Frowning, Two Feathers laid aside the stick that he held. "She approach when Two Feathers go to gather children. She whisper *danger, danger* before hurry past to her own lodge. Two Feathers no time ask what woman mean. Two Feathers curious why woman out and about when all others asleep."

"Maybe she went outside for personal care and was talking to herself?"

Two Feathers stood and walked to where Pix sat.

He squatted before her.

"Two Feathers glad Pix wife and only wife."

Pix leaned toward him. "You and me both, mister," she drawled.

Two Feathers laughed.

Chapter Thirty-Four

Pix laughed aloud at Fawn's silly antics. Several weeks had passed since Fawn's marriage to Strong Hand and she seemed happy. Fawn had settled into her new marriage with ease.

Two Feathers had begun to talk about leaving to search for buffalo within the next several days. Pix knew the hunt was necessary, but she dreaded his leaving anyway. She was happy, and deliriously so. Her life had settled into a daily routine with comfortable, regular days, with quiet mornings and delicious evenings, just her, Two Feathers, and their children, a family unit.

Flopping down beside Pix at where she sat under the shade of the large tree, Fawn giggled, her face flushed and sweaty. Leaning down she kissed the cheek of the slumbering baby lying beside Pix.

Three Feathers continued with his frolic, giving no attention to Pix or the playmate that'd just left his side.

"You'll make a great mother one day, Fawn," Pix stated, as she watched her sister-in-law.

Fawn smiled wide and rose up from the baby. Her eyes sparkled. "Strong Hand make *sure* Fawn has family soon."

Pix raised her eyebrows. "Are you blushing?" she teased.

Raising her hands, Fawn cupped apparently hot cheeks. Then dropping her hands from her face, she giggled as she gazed back at Pix. "Fawn happy."

Sighing, Pix lay back onto the animal pelt that she'd spread out earlier before placing the baby down upon it. "I'm glad, Fawn. Everything worked out for the best for all, didn't it?"

"Fawn believe so," Fawn stated as she lay back also. She bent her arms to fold them behind her head and closed her eyes. Her smile lingered.

Three Feathers toddled up to crawl onto Pix's stomach. His eyelids drooped and he pouted. He had played hard. Pix patted at his back and instantly he was asleep. Strong Hand walked up to their small group causing Fawn to stir at his arrival. She smiled up at him when he lowered his hand to grasp hers that she lifted to him. He pulled her upward so that she stood alongside him. She turned to look down at Pix.

"Fawn carry Three Feathers home for Pix?"

"I think that I'll lie here a while longer, Fawn. Three Feathers will wake cranky if we move him. You two go on. I'll be along shortly. If you see Two Feathers, let him know where we are."

Fawn agreed she would and turning, she, and Strong Hand walked away.

Strong Hand seems a fine man, Pix thought as she watched the two. He couldn't seem to keep from touching Fawn. Closing her eyes, Pix let herself relax. She was sleepy herself. She and the children weren't far from home, and before long, Three Feathers would stir his rest over.

Pix didn't go to sleep completely, and later when she felt someone sit down beside her, she smiled.

"It didn't take you long to find me," she teased. Two Feathers didn't respond and she opened her eyes. Jerking upward to a sitting position, Pix woke Three Feathers. He began to whine.

His eyes widened in fear at his leg swatted.

"Don't you dare touch this child!"

The same hand used on Three Feathers slapped over Pix's mouth, suffocating her words. Dragged upward and away from the children, Pix fought in earnest.

She kicked.

She punched.

She grabbed at braided hair.

Planning to scream when the hand lifted from her mouth, she took a breath.

A fist connected against the side of her face.

Jesus, Jesus, keep my children safe! Pix's thought flashed, Three Feathers' huge and frightened gaze the last thing she saw, as darkness and light swirled.

****

Two Feathers' gaze met Fawn's when she stepped from the family home at his call for permission for entrance. He wondered why Pix hadn't come out. He'd gone hunting and stayed longer than usual. Crow had given up at their not seeing anything and had left him to it.

"Why Pix and children not come out?" he questioned.

Fawn frowned.

"Brother not find Pix home with children?"

Two Feathers shook his head. "No. Wife and children not home."

Fawn's frown deepened. "Pix stay at 'large tree.' We gather nuts and then rest under shade. Fawn walk home with husband. Pix say, Pix stay, let Three Feathers sleep. Say come home when Three Feathers wake. Fawn expect home now."

Two Feathers turned to go to the tree that Fawn mentioned. He knew it well. They feasted from its acorns each year. Crow's wife stared at him when she walked past him and Fawn. The woman looked away, seeming to search for something or someone. Coming out of the lodge, Strong Hand walked up behind Fawn.

"All okay?" he questioned. He rested a hand on Fawn's hip as he looked at Two Feathers.

Two Feathers started to respond when he saw Crow walk into the village. He had the baby and Three Feathers held in his arms. In alarm, Two Feathers hurried forward.

"What has happened, Blood Brother? Where is wife?"

Crow shrugged. "Blood Brother find children under 'large tree' alone and crying, bring with Crow to Father."

Three Feathers stretched forth his arms wanting to be taken. It was obvious that he had been crying and the baby also. Two Feathers took the children from Crow's arms.

"Pix wouldn't leave children alone," he responded.

Crow's gaze narrowed. "Crow find children alone. Crow not know about mother."

Fawn and Strong Hand came forward. Fawn took the children from Two Feathers.

"Brother must hurry. Look for Fawn's friend. Something wrong," she told him.

For a moment, Two Feathers couldn't move. Fear gripped him. It was as if he were back to when he searched for Pretty Flower. Crow had found Pretty Flower's body then and brought him to her. It seemed a bad omen for him to bring his children into the settlement. It was as if, history repeated itself. Crow stepped forward to lay a hand on his arm, and for some reason Two Feathers had the urge to shake off his touch. It repulsed.

"Blood Brother help look for wife," Crow stated, empathy reflected in his gaze as he looked at Two Feathers.

Strong Hand stepped forward. "Strong Hand search also."

Pix stumbled into sight at the edge of the settlement. She staggered several steps toward them then collapsed to the ground. Two Feathers sprang into action, and when he scooped her limp form up into his arms, he wondered if she'd clawed her way home only to die before him. Blood flowed from a cut across her forehead and it streaked her face. Fingerprint marks peppered her upper arms, and Two Feathers saw what looked like bite marks on her neck and not animal, but *human*!

"Who do this thing?" Crow growled his anger tangible.

Two Feathers' own anger and horror left him shaking unable to respond. He hurried home.

"Mother, Mother," Fawn called out as she ran to the river where their mother had last been seen.

When his mother swooped into his lodge, Two Feathers looked up in grief. He could feel no breath from Pix. She was gone. His mother and the other healers hurried forward. They pushed him aside.

"Leave!" his mother ordered him.

Stumbling from the lodge, Two Feathers gazed around at the gathered crowd. Crow looked at him in question, and he shook his head knowing what his blood brother asked.

Crow turned away.

Distancing himself from the people and their echoes of sorrow and anger over what happened, Two Feathers felt empty inside. Pretty Flower and Pix both taken from him, wives that he cherished, wives that he had wanted, wives that he had loved. Why did he have this punishment? Why his wives must die? They'd done no wrong. Raising his fist upward toward the sky, Two Feathers let his anger soar.

"What has Two Feathers done to Master of Life for wives to suffer?" he demanded.

Crow walked toward him, and Two Feathers turned his back to him. He let his arm drop back to his side. He didn't want to talk. He wanted left alone.

"Go away, Blood Brother," he rasped when Crow stopped behind him.

"Crow question who do this thing?" Crow responded.

Turning, Two Feathers met Crow's gaze. "Two Feathers find and kill who do this evil. Two Feathers not rest till person found and dead."

Crow stepped in closer to him and he looked around as if someone might overhear him. He spoke in a whisper. "Crow say person in new tribe do this to wife. Crow say Two Feathers question *all*. Maybe Strong Hand even responsible."

Crow's accusation shocked him, and Two Feathers rasped, "Why Strong Hand want Two Feathers' wife hurt or dead? Strong Hand ally now."

"Crow suspect Strong Hand wish to lead all people and plan to weaken Two Feathers." Crow's gaze was direct.

"Two Feathers come!"

Abruptly turning, Two Feathers looked toward his mother.

"Come," she called again and she gave a sharp motion with her hand.

Rushing forward, Two Feathers followed her into his lodge.

"Wife lives," she stated and she motioned toward Pix.

Hurrying forward, Two Feathers bent to his knees. He stretched forth his hand. Yes, Pix breathed, he could feel her life. His tears rose. He gulped them back down. Lowering his head, Two Feathers gave thanks to the Master of Life. He asked forgiveness for his earlier anger at his creator.

His mother laid a palm on his shoulder. "Son and mother speak alone."

Giving a nod, Two Feathers watched his mother motion for all to go from the lodge leaving only her, him, and Pix who slept.

Pix whimpered in her sleep, and fresh anger, swamped Two Feathers. He curled his fingers into fists. He'd kill whoever did this. His mother sat down beside him and took his tightly curled fists into her hands. She rubbed her fingers across his as if she tried to comfort him. In his heart, Two Feathers knew what she was about to say. He didn't want to hear it.

"Wife violated," she informed her voice soft and hesitate as if she were afraid of how he was to respond. She gripped his hands when he stiffened and pulled back, his shoulder muscles knotted.

Unable to stop his rising rage, Two Feathers tightened his fingers around hers. His mother gave a wince, and yet she held tight to his hands and refused to let them loose when he pulled back planning to stand to his feet. He needed to pace.

She held his gaze. "Mother not let any other examine. Only mother know what occur. Mother hope son no blame wife."

Two Feathers shook loose her grip. Standing, he stared at Pix's bruised and swollen face, and the bite marks left behind by her attacker. How could he be angry with her? How could his mother even question it?

"Son not blame wife, Mother. Son blame evil one who do this to wife."

His mother exhaled as if she'd held her breath, and Two Feathers met her gaze.

"Son good man," she told him rising from where she sat. Lifting a hand to his cheek, she continued her voice firm, and her gaze direct, "Mother and Two Feathers no need inform others what done to wife. Wife recover from visible wounds. Maybe, long-time heal here, though." She touched her chest.

Gazing at his mother, her face lined with age and her eyes cloudy and sad, Two Feathers wondered what she'd kept hidden in her lifetime. She turned to leave and then she hesitated as if she wished to speak to him again; however, she only laid a hand on his shoulder. When she was almost to the door of the lodge, she turned once more. "Mother care for children until Pixie well. Find Nurture Mother for baby also."

Two Feathers gave a nod. Pix would hate the thought of another nursing their child.

Chapter Thirty-Five

Entering his lodge, Two Feathers looked across its interior space to where Pix lay. She had turned over onto her side during his absence with her back now to the open area. He'd had to go to the river to get water for the evening. He had accidently knocked over the water container left by his mother. Setting down what he held, beside the fire pit, Two Feathers walked across the lodge floor to where Pix slept and had for the past twelve days. She only woke for sips of broth, bathing, and a changing of sleep covers, yet she never spoke and she never looked up. Fawn and his mother helped with her care, coming and going quietly while taking their turn, both at home now with the sun's disappearance for the day. He cared for Pix during the night hours.

It surprised Two Feathers how much concern Crow had expressed as the days continued to pass with no change in Pix's awareness to others. Each morning, Crow inquired about her welfare and worried over who'd done this terrible thing. Two Feathers had begun to study the men from the new peoples. Someone had done this, and if not one of the new peoples, then who? Had a stranger passed and done the deed, and thinking, he'd left her to die? His jawline fixed, Two Feathers squatted beside Pix. He reached out to smooth her unbraided and recently combed hair back from her face. It was long now, no longer short as when he'd first met her.

"No, no," she murmured at his touch. Her hand lifted and she attempted to push his away from her. "Don't touch me," she demurred. "Don't, please."

Her hand dropped back by her side as if her strength suddenly drained away.

Two Feathers removed his fingers from her hair to sit quietly beside her. Did she think that he was her attacker? The thought sickened. He would find the culprit who did this thing, and when he did, the man would wish, even beg for death.

Pix slept on.

The next morning, Two Feathers stretched as he stood. He was tired. He'd slept fitfully, and woke each time that Pix moved. Unexpectedly, she turned toward him, and Two Feathers heard a soft moan of pain issued as she did so. Her eyelids fluttered open and she stared upward at him.

Quickly, Two Feathers squatted beside her. He hesitated when she scooted backward her eyes wide.

"Pix, it is Two Feathers," he stated softly.

"Two Feathers?" She reached out toward him. Tears ran down her cheeks as she grasped hold of his hand. Her eyes held his. "The children, where are the children?"

Two Feathers turned to stretch back out alongside her, and she didn't resist when he gathered her into his arms. "Shhh, they are with mother and okay," he appeased.

"He dragged me from them. I couldn't stop him. I fought. I did," her voice was weak, a whisper.

"Who?" Two Feathers demanded.

When Pix didn't respond, Two Feathers leaned backward. She was asleep again. He wondered if she slept to escape from what had happened. Easing away from her, he stood once again. She was unaware of his leaving. Emerging from the lodge, to step out into the day's sunshine, Two Feathers' anger made him shake. He felt helpless.

"Mother," he greeted as she walked up to where he stood.

"Has wife woke this morning?" she asked.

"She woke. She went right back to sleep."

"Did wife speak?"

Two Feathers watched Crow stride toward him. "Yes," he stated before he turned and walked away. He had no desire to listen to Crow speculate whether Pix would know who'd assaulted her. Crow had even begun to point out some of the men in their own tribe as suspects, urging Two Feathers to question them. Accuse. Demand answers.

Two Feathers wanted to question all, suspected all, and it drove him crazy his thoughts of revenge. He'd not let emotion rule no matter his anger. Pix would heal, and when she did, she'd inform him who did this evil act.

Strong Hand crossed his path later that evening as having hunted and caught an evening meal Two Feathers strode toward the settlement and his lodge. Strong Hand held an evening meal within his hands also, he noted. Two Feathers gave a nod toward his brother-in-law when they met, and Strong Hand stopped before him.

"Fawn tell wife spoke this morning," Strong Hand commented.

Stiffening, Two Feathers stared at the man. Did his sister's husband seem apprehensive? In his heart, Two Feathers knew that Strong Hand wasn't involved in Pix's attack; yet Crow's constant whisperings made him look at all with suspicion.

"Aye, wife spoke." Two Feathers didn't expand on his statement as he watched the man before him. Strong Hand frowned. He didn't act guilty as he met Two Feathers' gaze direct with his.

"Strong Hand wonder if wife identify attacker? Strong Hand not like this waiting, Strong Hand worry. Tell Fawn not allowed outside village without husband."

Two Feathers felt his shoulders slump. He straightened them. His muscles were tight. He suspected all and it wore on him. It made him jumpy, and irritable.

"Wife not identify attacker. Go back into deep sleep. Ask only after children," he expanded.

"When wife able to inform husband, Strong Hand help Brother-In-Law find who do this evil," Strong Hand stated.

Strong Hand's obvious concern for Fawn over Pix's attack made Two Feathers feel guilty at his suspicion of Strong Hand's involvement. He was confident that if the man wasn't what he seemed, Fawn would know and speak on it. She seemed content though, smiling often.

"Strong Hand and Two Feathers confront together," Two Feathers affirmed. Strong Hand wasn't the first man in the village to offer his help.

Parting their ways, Two Feathers strode on toward his lodge. He winced at noting that Crow walked through the settlement toward him. He seemed in a hurry, his steps wide. Crow had begun to irritate, and Two Feathers hated the impatience he felt with his life-long friend. He was relieved when Crow didn't come his way but turned toward his own lodge.

Entering his home it surprised Two Feathers that Pix was alert and sitting up. Crow's wife sat with ankles crossed beside her. He wished he'd been present when Pix woke fully.

Frowning, Two Feathers stepped forward, and he wondered why his mother or Fawn wasn't present in the lodge. Each usually stayed until he returned. He didn't want Crow's woman to know anything about Pix's attack. She always seemed resentful of Pix. The woman stood at his approach.

"Husband," Pix stated her voice low. Her gaze met his.

"Wife," Two Feathers responded. He didn't know what to say and felt uncomfortable. Both women seemed to look at him in disapproval. He was glad to see that Pix seemed alert. He'd agonized at the passing days and her continued sleep.

"Crow attack wife."

The statement blunt, sharp, and exact stunned Two Feathers. He thought for a moment that he had staggered backward from Crow's wife before he realized that he hadn't moved.

Pix stared at him. Her tears welled, and they spilled down her cheeks in a silent stream. She looked away from him.

"This is truth?" he asked Crow's woman. He choked on the words. She nodded. It couldn't be true. His blood brother would not do this thing accused. Rage began to rise.

The woman spoke again, and as if from a distance, her words floated to him. "Husband have wicked mind, not think clear. Wife realize long time past, and leave husband. Husband threaten hurt wife and child if wife not return to husband."

Pix didn't speak. She watched him though.

Two Feathers squatted before her. He reached to take her hands within his. He had to know if the woman lied. "Does woman speak truth?"

Pix ducked her head and Two Feathers leaned in to hear what it was that she said.

"It was Crow."

Jumping to his feet, Two Feathers went to his weapons. He palmed his skinning knife and then tightened his fingers around its handle. His blood brother would not see another sun.

"Don't go after him, Two Feathers. Let others deal with Crow's punishment," Pix begged behind him from where she sat. Whirling, Two Feathers saw Pix quickly draw back toward the wall of their lodge. Realizing her fear, he forced his jerking muscles to calm. Breathing deep, he compelled his rage to settle.

He turned toward Crow's wife. "Leave Two Feathers' lodge."

The woman quietly and quickly exited the home.

Pix warily watched him. "Is it me that you're angry at? Me you blame?"

With shock, Two Feathers put the knife that he held away. Walking to Pix, he kept his stride slow so as not to alarm. Bending to his knees before her and with his fingers firm on her chin, he forced her to meet his gaze. His voice was low.

"Two Feathers not blame Pix. Crow own evil deed done."

At her rising sob, Two Feathers drew Pix into his arms and onto his lap.

"He not only beat me, he raped me also."

At Pix's confession, Two Feathers tightened his arms around her.

"Two Feathers has knowledge," he rasped back. Pix didn't respond and Two Feathers continued to sit with her. He was anxious to confront Crow, but he would wait for her signal.

"Take Strong Hand with you," she stated into the silence a while later and she looked up at him her gaze direct.

Two Feathers leaned down to touch his mouth with hers. She didn't flinch only raised her arms to encircle them around his neck. His relief felt at her acceptance of his touch made him pull her closer.

"Two Feathers love Pix," he comforted.

She tightened her arms around him and remained silent.

She spoke a moment later. "It was you and our children that kept me alive, made me fight for survival when he thought I was dead."

Two Feathers drew a finger across her cheeks as her tears flowed once again. His anger ripped through him at her abuse suffered by Crow's hands.

His mother called out for admittance.

"Enter," he appealed.

He turned back to Pix.

"Crow will pay for evil done."

Pix nodded and her gaze locked with his. "I love you, Two Feathers."

Chapter Thirty-Six

It was all Two Feathers could do not to reach out and shake the woman before him. To him it seemed that she stalled. The night sky had settled over the village.

"Where is Crow?" he demanded. He'd reach out and curl his fingers around the woman's skinny throat if she so much as stuttered again. Why had she told her tale and now to seem not to wish to cooperate?

"Wife believe husband run from Two Feathers. Watch husband gather hunting weapons and sleeping blanket before leave lodge. Wife not ask husband where go," she blurted out.

"Why woman shake so? Two Feathers not punish for husband's deeds." The woman before Two Feathers clutched her hands together. She didn't answer.

"Which way Crow go?" Two Feathers demanded punitively. She pointed a shaky finger north of the village.

Whirling, Two Feathers took off. He didn't take anyone with him. It was personal this thing between him and Crow, a puzzle that he didn't understand.

****

Pausing early the next morning after a night of no sleep and tracking well into the night, Two Feathers stared at the ground around his feet. His frustration was high. He'd had to backtrack twice that morning to re-pickup Crow's trail after losing it. Sweat rolled down his forehead and into his eyes. Raising his forearm, he wiped the stinging dampness away. Summer was in full swing, and the heat of it shimmered across the terrain.

Crow's direction was erratic, going one way and then another and often it seemed he disappeared as if into thin air before his tracks suddenly reappeared again. Crow always esteemed at staying hidden when on a hunt, had been the one sent ahead when checking out enemy tribes; Two Feathers never dreamed though that he'd be on the other end tracking him. Two Feathers frowned as he scanned the vista about him. The hills where it seemed that Crow now headed were full of snake dens. The people avoided the area at all costs. If Crow thought that he wouldn't follow him into the land of the serpent, he was wrong. By his calculation, Crow wasn't that far ahead, the gap between them closing fast.

The next day, Two Feathers carefully skirted multiple gray colored snakes that sunned themselves upon the boulders he walked over. Raised tails let him know that the snakes were aware of him. The ominous sound of their rattles sent shivers down his spine. Buzzards circled up ahead, as he cautiously stepped past two snakes that lay away from the large cluster, their lengths, as long as he was tall. He had a respite afterward. No other snakes around that he noticed.

Two Feathers breathed and glanced upward toward the circling buzzards. Something held their interest. Stepping forward once again, he scanned the rocks around him as he steadily, worked his way toward the birds' interest.

Glancing up, his breath caught.

Crow stood directly ahead of him and watched his approach. Snatching his knife from its pouch at his side, Two Feathers stalked forward. Crow swiftly crouched, and took a step sideways ready to fight, his eyes locked with Two Feathers. Suddenly Crow's arms flailed and he fell backward and disappeared from sight.

Coming upon the bowl-shaped crater Crow had fallen into,

Two Feathers gazed downward at him. Crow lay upon his back, and he looked upward back at him. Around him slithered the same manner of snakes that Two Feathers had just worked his way past. Crow had fallen into the vipers breeding pit. Hundreds of them writhed alongside and over him, angry with their intruder.

"Blood Brother," Crow croaked upward at him. His eyelids sagged, almost to the point of closed, his breathing shallow, his face, and body swelled in an instant. He didn't move paralyzed from the massive and instantaneous venom injected into his body.

One snake, even as Two Feathers stared down in disbelief, withdrew its fangs from Crow's testicle sack. *A fitting tribute*, Two Feathers thought even as he felt unwanted compassion rise. He fought the emotion. The man before him didn't deserve his sympathy. He didn't know this man and must have never known him. If he had been asked not too long past, he'd have sworn that he knew Crow as he knew himself. Two Feathers had to strain to hear what it was that Crow uttered.

"Crow would have fought Blood Brother if not for misstep. Crow rush when Crow need remain cautious."

"Why, Crow?" Two Feathers responded. He knew Crow understood his question. Two Feathers couldn't comprehend Crow's evil act. It mystified him.

"Pretty Flower Crow's. Two Feathers steal from Crow," Crow responded.

"No Pix was always mine. Marked as mine when found," Two Feathers asserted back. Crow must hallucinate, forgetting whom it was he had raped and beat.

Crow grunted in response and when he did, two snakes simultaneously struck, their fangs sinking deep into his forearm. He didn't flinch, their bites no longer felt. He stared upward at Two Feathers and a grotesque, lopsided, expression of scorn appeared. In that moment, Two Feathers saw his childhood friend, as he truly was, a man full of hatred. Hatred directed at him. The sight shocked. This was not the boy he'd grown up with, played with, and hunted with together. This person he didn't know.

Crow panted and his breathing rasped becoming labored. Whatever he had to say it would be his last. Two Feathers could tell that Crow wanted him to hear his dying words, and he bent forward, mindful not to topple into the pit with Crow.

"Pretty Flower... love... Crow. Two Feathers... steal from Crow. Crow hope... Blood Brother... writhe in agony... with knowledge... Crow know... both wives."

Two Feathers stared down at the contorted bulk of the man below him. Was Crow saying that he had also raped Pretty Flower?

With dawning horror, Two Feathers now understood his mother's behavior with Pix's assault. Pretty Flower, from a different tribe and with both parent's dead, must've confessed to his mother what had occurred, and his mother and she remained quiet, too, afraid of how he would respond.

Pretty Flower had never loved Crow had never wanted anything to do with him. Two Feathers knew this as truth. Now he knew why.

Crow's eyes became blank, a fixed stare, no longer seeing. Two Feathers backed away from the lifeless creature. His mother had not been told the name of Pretty Flower's attacker. If so, she would have demanded punishment. Pretty Flower must've informed it was a passing stranger, someone never to be seen again.

Once away from the snakes' domain, Two Feathers let loose his howl of rage. Hatred for the man he'd known since his childhood rose within his soul and curled around his heart, tightening, seizing, and taking hold. Two Feathers slashed at his chest, his hunting knife laying open his skin. His fury consumed him. He deserved punishment. Two wives he'd allowed Crow to dishonor.

Stumbling forward, Two Feathers let his wounds bleed freely. Through blurry eyes, he saw Strong Hand coming toward him.

Chapter Thirty-Seven

When Pix realized the evening of Two Feathers' departure that he went alone, she, with Fawn's support, demanded for Strong Hand to follow. It was eight days now that both men were absent from the village.

Rocking the sleeping infant that lay within her arms, Pix stared down at her child. She didn't need to hold her. She only did so to draw comfort from her presence. Three Feathers was with his grandmother. Absently, Pix smoothed the baby's thick head of hair back away from her face, the infant's cheeks round and fat. Her tiny mouth worked as if she still nursed.

Her mother-in-law and Fawn had assured her that Two Feathers would be okay, but Pix worried with each passing day the two men were gone. In her heart, Pix knew that Two Feathers' sister and mother worried also.

"Let's pray that your daddy and Strong Hand are okay," Pix addressed the slumbering infant. Silently, Pix sent a prayer up to a God that most times she forgot. She had been up and active since Two Feathers' leaving, and her hatred for Crow consumed her, sometimes so much that it physically hurt her. Crow's action and words that day were something she would never forget.

TJ, it seemed, shadowed her everywhere that she went these last few days. His words echoed in her head, words that he had spoken the evening she'd pushed Two Feathers into anger, and he had slashed her tattoo from her leg. *There's no going back. You can't recapture what is gone,* TJ had told her that long-ago evening.

Pix knew that he was informing her to move on and not to let Crow win in his evil, to forgive. *The man doesn't deserve forgiveness*, she thought, her anger vibrating through her.

****

"Come in," Pix called out when into the lateness of the night Fawn asked for admittance to the lodge. Coming fully into the home and to where Pix had risen from her pallet, her sister-in-law smiled at her.

"They come. Too Little and Rock met them and returned ahead with the news."

"Do they bring Crow?" Pix's muscles tightened. She didn't know if she could stand coming face-to-face with Crow again.

Fawn dropped her gaze.

"What is it?" Pix demanded.

"Too Little say not bring Crow with them. Too Little not know why."

Unease spread through Pix. Had they not been able to catch up to him? Jumping at a loud thump heard outside the lodge, Pix almost cried out with fright. Was Crow out there? Did he come back for her as his wife had told her he would do?

Strong Hand entered the lodge and for a second, Pix didn't recognize Two Feathers when he stepped up behind him and entered the lodge also. His features had changed, had become brutal, hard. His gaze sliced hers before he turned away.

"Where's Crow?" Pix couldn't stop her rapid and hostile inquiry.

Two Feathers whirled. "Crow? Crow is no more!"

Stumbling backward at the violent response, Pix shot her gaze toward Strong Hand. Strong Hand shook his head at her.

Wounds on Two Feathers' chest were visible.

He hadn't blamed her for Crow's assault before he left, but did he now after Crow's death? Pix stared at Two Feathers, and she willed him to meet her gaze. She saw from the corner of her eye that Strong Hand motioned for Fawn to leave the home. Pix remained silent when Fawn picked up the baby and took the child with her. She and Two Feathers needed this time alone.

"I'm glad Crow is no more. His wife said that he'd come back for her and for me if you didn't kill him."

"Two Feathers not kill Crow."

At Two Feathers' icy statement, Pix became still. She didn't understand? He had just stated that Crow was no more. She waited for his explanation. Two Feathers paced instead. He kept his back to her. Pix couldn't help it. She began to weep. Did he now blame her for Crow's evil?

Two Feathers whirled and in two strides, he stood before her.

Pix stiffened. His censure in this was something that she hadn't expected.

"Pix not cry," he ordered.

"Do you now blame me for Crow's assault?" Pix had to know.

With a step back, Two Feathers looked down at her. His astonishment obvious at her question, and reaching out, he shook her, his action jarring.

"Don't ever ask Two Feathers such question." Turning on his heel, he exited the lodge.

Pix straightened her shoulders. Her weeping was over. She didn't know what had happened out there but she'd find out.

At her call for permission to enter Fawn's home, Pix heard an immediate response given back. Entering the lodge, Pix paused. It was late. She had been rude to ask for admittance when others in the home slept. Fawn would have brought the baby to her if she had given her the time to do so.

Walking forward, Fawn smiled at her. "It is okay friend come late in night." She spoke low.

Strong Hand sat beside the fire pit, and he stood when Pix walked toward him.

"Is Crow alive?" Pix couldn't help her question, and may God forgive her, but she wanted the man dead.

"Crow dead," Strong Hand responded.

He looked confused as he glanced toward Fawn. Pix knew he wondered why she questioned him when Two Feathers should have informed her as to what had occurred.

"I am sorry but I needed to know. Two Feathers said that he didn't kill him."

Strong Hand didn't respond and Fawn walked toward her.

"Why does Brother not inform wife about Crow's death?"

Pix shook her head. "I don't know. He's upset with me and left the lodge. I don't know what's happening."

Fawn encircled her fingers around Pix's upper arm. "Go home. Fawn confident Brother not upset with wife. Let Brother inform in own time. Strong Hand say Brother not talk to him either. Only tell Strong Hand, Crow dead."

Reentering her home, Pix paused. Two Feathers sat beside their fire pit. He glanced up at her entrance, and when she came forward and into the lodge, he made a motion for her to hand him the baby. Doing as he wished, Pix watched him as he gazed down at their child.

"Where is Three Feathers?" he asked.

"With your mother."

Two Feathers kept his gaze on their child. "Two Feathers not angry with wife, Two Feathers angry at self for Crow's evil. Crow assault Pix and brag he assault Pretty Flower and husband never know. Pretty Flower never tell husband."

Two Feathers' anguish-filled words circled Pix, their low, rumbling, timbre impassioned with self-guilt. Gently, she removed the baby from Two Feathers' arms. Placing the sleeping infant down upon her pallet, Pix walked back to Two Feathers to kneel before him. His obvious mental pain was more than she could bear. It hurt her that he suffered with his knowledge.

"I love you, Two Feathers," she comforted.

Two Feathers stilled at her words, his moan gut wrenching. He pulled her to him and settled her onto his crossed legs, his arms around her.

Pix looked at his covered wounds. His mother must have treated them. "These he caused?"

"No," he rasped as he took hold of her hands and brought the back of her knuckles to his cheek. It was as if he couldn't touch her enough. "Two Feathers does to self in punishment."

"Why?" Pix whispered.

"Two Feathers allow Crow assault both wives."

"Don't you ever say that again. Crow hid his evil from you!" Pix cried as she pulled away from Two Feathers' embrace to look up at him.

He drew her back to him, his expression bleak. He wouldn't meet her gaze. "Husband not listen to Pix when Pix say not care for Crow. Husband deserve self-punishment."

Pix wrapped her fingers over his forearms, and she remained silent until Two Feathers looked at her.

"I love you, Two Feathers, and so did Pretty Flower. Don't you dare punish yourself for what that man did. I hate him too, but heaven help us, we must forgive him. We must forgive, not because he deserves it, and not that we'll ever forget, but because we can't live with our hatred. It will eat us alive and eventually it will destroy us both. Crow was evil and he and he alone owns that evil. You told me so yourself."

Disentangling herself from Two Feathers' arms, Pix went to their sleeping pallet and when she lay down, he followed her. She remained silent as he told his story. He needed to talk. Leaning up on her elbow when he grew quiet, Pix gazed at Two Feathers in disbelief. Crow's death was fitting for a man like him. She sighed. It was going to take her a long time not to have that twist of hate and fear in her gut when she thought of Crow. Scooting closer against Two Feathers, Pix clasped her fingers with his. She was grateful that he'd come back to her.

"I'm glad you didn't have to kill Crow, glad that the deed was taken out of your hands."

Two Feathers didn't respond.

Chapter Thirty-Eight

Pix smiled from where she sat in front of her home as she worked on weaving a much-needed basket. The sun was high overhead. The day was crisp and cool. She watched the young boy who strutted forward and who walked along beside Two Feathers. He had gone hunting with his father that morning. At the age of eight winters, it was time for Three Feathers to start providing for the family, Two Feathers had stated that morning. They had left early, the village asleep at the time. It now bustled with activity. Her other three children were with their aunt Fawn, playing with their cousins.

"Mother, look!" Three Feathers held up the four rabbits that he carried. He beamed from ear to ear.

"So you give me work," Pix stated, giving a laugh as father and son approached her.

"Yes," Three Feathers replied. His chest thrust out.

Two Feathers looked at Pix. He didn't smile but Pix knew that he was proud of Three Feathers. His eyes shone with his approval.

"Three Feathers will clean his own meal," he drawled.

"Why? It is woman's work," Three Feathers cried out.

"So that Three Feathers gain knowledge," Two Feathers dryly replied.

Pix looked at Two Feathers, and she knew that he was remembering the first time he'd taught her how to clean and cook her own meal.

She dearly loved this man. Some days she felt guilty for what she kept to herself. On days like this where father and son were so close, she knew that she'd made the right decision.

Pix watched father and son stride away, Three Feathers chattering nonstop. He showed a playmate what he held. The playmate turned to skip along beside him.

It looks as if Two Feathers will teach another child, too, Pix thought, giving a smile as she turned back to her basket weaving.

The years had been good to her and Two Feathers, and to Fawn and Strong Hand. Fawn now had two children of her own with another on the way. Two Feathers and Fawn's mother had passed away two winters ago. She had died in her sleep. Pix believed she'd gone peaceful and content. All who knew her missed her.

Looking up from her work, Pix let her hands rest on her lap as she gazed out over the village. The village thrived, its people happy. Seeing Brave Bird some distance away, Pix gave a grimace. That woman had never been content, and most of her trouble, she brought upon herself. Little Bird was as she had always been: happy, thoughtful, and sweet. Pix didn't know how she put up with Brave Bird, though. Pix lifted a hand as Too Little and Rock passed by her. They nodded in response and then stopped to talk to Two Feathers when he approached them.

"Where is Three Feathers?" Pix asked when Two Feathers walked up to where she sat. Too Little and Rock had gone on about their business. She rose ready to go help Three Feathers with his chore.

"Oh no, Pix don't," Two Feathers growled, and he grabbed her hand and halted her movement. He knew what she was about to do. "Three Feathers will obey father and clean and cook what he has hunted with no help from others. It is time Pix stop favoring the boy."

"I don't." Pix couldn't look at Two Feathers at her denial. Without response, he led her into their lodge.

"What are you doing? I need to go gather our children," she demanded. Pulling her into his arms, Two Feathers covered her mouth with his. Pix instinctively wrapped her arms around his waist and leaned into him. She breathed deep when he finally straightened. Even after all these years, he could still make her forget everything but him. Two Feathers smiled and reached to loosen her braids from their bindings.

"The children," Pix voiced, although she didn't move.

"Children stay with Aunt Fawn this night. Strong Hand say help Three Feathers finish duties then take Three Feathers home with him," Two Feathers countered.

"It is still daylight. What if someone calls out?"

Two Feathers gave a slow smile and his eyebrows rose.

"We won't answer."

"Fawn and Strong Hand do love a houseful, don't they," Pix responded. Her enthusiasm for Two Feathers' wanted pastime gained ground as she realized the evening was theirs and theirs alone. With a laugh, Pix wrapped her arms around her husband's neck. He swung her up into his arms and strode toward their bed. Pix admired Two Feathers' strong jaw line. He was all male and she loved that maleness. The birds chirped, the crickets sang, the frogs croaked, and the evening wore on. It was an evening of endless loving Pix didn't believe she'd ever forget. Lying back, Two Feathers propped an arm over his eyes, and his breathing rasped. His other arm Pix now rested upon. Pix smiled from where she lay beside Two Feathers. She had seen that enduring arm gesture numerous times and it usually meant that something was on her husband's mind. He didn't speak, so she rolled toward him and placed the palm of her hand over his heart. She could feel its strong, steady beat. His skin radiated warmth from their recent lovemaking. Silently, she waited for Two Feathers to say what it was that was on his mind.

He finally spoke, his voice low. "His smile is his. His laughter the same as Two Feathers remembers."

Pix stilled. Her heart thundered. He must hear it.

"What...what...are you saying?"

Two Feathers lifted his arm and he looked at her. He took her chin within his hand and forced her to meet his gaze when she dropped hers.

"Wife must stop being afraid. Pix frightened husband will hate son if husband know truth. It is why Pix quick to defend boy, why Pix favors. Two Feathers wonder when wife has knowledge and keep knowledge to self?"

Pix fully sat up and took Two Feathers' hand within her own trembling ones. "How long have you known?"

Two Feathers didn't respond and Pix sighed. It was time to admit what she'd known since her attack.

"When Crow beat and raped me, he bragged about what he'd done to Pretty Flower and that he knew that Three Feathers was his. Pretty Flower never admitted it to him though, he said. It seemed that it confused him, her hostility toward him. He said he'd been gentle with her." Pix snorted. "Rape is gentle, really?"

She looked directly at Two Feathers. "I...I...I've wanted to tell you so many times, what he told me, only each and every time I thought to, I was terrified of how you might react. I didn't want more heartbreak for you and especially not for Three Feathers. Crow's crime is not his to bear. And I...I...guess I'm more lenient toward him than our other children, because, in truth, I've been terrified that I might resent him because of what Crow did to me."

Sitting up, Two Feathers drew her to him. "Three Feathers is and will always be Two Feathers' and Pix's first son. Two Feathers and Pix must forget Crow ever have life."

Pix could tell that Pretty Flower's death still haunted Two Feathers and her next words were soft, "What is it that still disquiets you about Pretty Flower?"

Two Feathers didn't immediately respond. When he did, his

words were slow. "Two Feathers show anger at wife day wife took own life. Pretty Flower not want to nurse or hold Three Feathers and Two Feathers not understand behavior.

"When learn from Pix what some women experience after having child, Two Feathers believe Pretty Flower suffer from—what Pix say?"

"Postpartum Depression."

Two Feathers nodded. "After Crow reveal evil deed, Two Feathers realize truth. Pretty Flower blame self and take life. If only had trusted and told husband, wife might be alive now."

Pix knew that Two Feathers wasn't saying that he didn't love her. If Pretty Flower were alive, Pix didn't believe she would have lived through the tornado, or if she had, that she would be in this time and place. She had cried out for mercy that day and her prayer was answered, answered for her and for Two Feathers, because Two Feathers had needed her as much as she had needed him.

"I love you," Pix whispered turning fully into Two Feathers' arms. Cradling her against his chest, he returned from his memories.

"Two Feathers love Pix when Pix land at Two Feathers' feet," he responded.

****

The next morning Pix stepped from her home, and she watched as her children returned from their sleepover. Three Feathers, always the big brother, herded his brothers and sister before him. Some days, as that morning, Pix wondered the exact year that she lived in, and on those days, TJ always came to her mind. He had loved the past, had loved learning about history, about things and people before his time. Why she survived and he hadn't, Pix didn't understand. She still missed him, her link to that other world, and other memories. No peoples besides known tribes had ever visited the village so Pix guessed she lived in a time before the discovery of the New World.

Knowing how the indigenous people faired with that finding, she hoped and prayed that her descendants survived the upheaval and that they adapted to their world changing, their survival instinct strong. With a sigh and a shake of her head, Pix went back to her work.

Sensing movement from the corner of her eye, Pix lifted her head again, and she watched Two Feathers walk toward her his gaze meeting hers. She smiled at him, happy.

He was her world now, and as long as she had him, she was content.

The End

Two Feathers and his tribe

When I began the process of writing the story of Pixie and Two Feathers, I didn't know what Indian tribe my fictional male character—Two Feathers—originated from, and so began my search.

As I went through my hunt for a people that Two Feathers could belong to, none that I found spoke to me, until, by sheer accident, I came across the website for the Kanza (Kaw, Kansa) tribe.

I know it sounds strange, but when I read that Tribal name, and without my having any knowledge of the tribe, my character (Two Feathers) who lived so many years ago, and in my make-believe world, whispered to me, *That is my people*.

The modern day Kanza tribe consists of 3,559 members (as of the writing of this page) with some as far away as Canada and the United Kingdom. Other members live near Kansas, Missouri, and Texas. The Kaw nation almost died out; however, they are making a comeback. In the year of 1905, the Kanza population had only 90 full blood's still alive. The last full-blooded Kaw Indian passed away at the age of 82 on April 23, 2000.

~The information in the above paragraph
cited from the Kawnation.com website~

I want to thank Justin T. McBride (Language Director for the Kaw Nation in Kaw City, Oklahoma (year 2015)) for his gracious response to me upon receiving my email and my asking him for more information on the Kaw people. He directed me to read the book *The Kansa Indians (A History of The Wind People, 1673-1873 written by William E. Unrau)* which I did. It is a fascinating read and helped me to understand Two Feathers.

To learn more on the Kanza (Kaw, Kansa) people visit the Kanza Museum in Kaw City, OK or visit their website at Kawnation. com

****

** The characters in the story *Across All Boundaries* originated from the author's imagination and any resemblance to actual persons living or deceased is by chance only. All tribal life and activity within the work *Across All Boundaries* is fictional and may not be a true historical representation of the Kanza (Kaw, Kansa) daily life. **

About The Author

L. J. Vant and her husband make their home in the great state of Oklahoma. Blessed with a vivid imagination, L. J. is never short of a story brewing and it wanting to be written down. Besides writing, she loves working in her yard and flowerbeds. With a Masters in Applied Psychology, she is always people watching and wondering what is going on inside of them.

CPSIA information can be obtained
at www.ICGtesting.com
Printed in the USA
LVHW091548180321
681863LV00001B/230